THE SPRING HOUSE

He grimaced. "DCI Smith's been making Madame Thingy's life hell. He's positive she's the mole."

"Makes [illegible] person, wouldn't she? What I mean? Why the wretch Smith pretends to be [illegible] and won't spell things out . . . Presumably you've tried to ask him what he meant?"

Dave nodded.

She thought again of the comparative lightness of the damage Madame Christianne had suffered compared with that inflicted on [illegible].

"And I've been stood down — back to normal duties."

She shook her head. "Why? I thought there was something odd about your bringing the flowers . . . I'm just so dim. Ideas come and go without giving me time to make sense of them."

"That'll be the shock and the anaesthetic," he said kindly. "They say it's at least a week before it's clear of the system. No, we're so short at Sexton House that Oxnard said Zayn and I ought to be released to normal duties if Smith was so sure everything was sorted."

"Sorted? Like hell it's sorted! They're supposed to be investigating Phil Bates's death, and I haven't heard anything that ties it in with the Albanians, nothing that's not circumstantial at best." She took a breath. "Anything else I should know about?"

"Neil Drew's got his knickers in a twist over his Christmas childcare. Seems he'd done some sort of a deal with Phil about swapping shifts, and now there's no Phil . . ."

THE SPRING HOUSE

A Day in the Country II

RUTH TOMALIN

LARGE PRINT
Oxford

First published in Great Britain 1968
by Faber and Faber Ltd.

Published in Large Print 2004 by ISIS Publishing Ltd,
7 Centremead, Osney Mead, Oxford OX2 0ES
by arrangement with Ruth Tomalin

British Library Cataloguing in Publication Data
Tomalin, Ruth
The spring house. – Large print ed.
1. Large Type books
I. Title
823.9'14 [F]

ISBN 0–7531–7019–1 (hb)
ISBN 0–7531–7020–5 (pb)

Printed and bound by Antony Rowe, Chippenham

Everything is only for a day: that which remembers and that which is remembered.

Marcus Aurelius

Hoc erat in votis: modus agri non ita magnus,
Hortus ubi et tecto vicinus iugis aquae fons
Et paulum silvae super his foret.

This used to be among my prayers: a portion of land, not so very large, but which should contain a garden, and near the homestead a spring of ever-flowing water, and a bit of forest to complete it.

HORACE

"X = O: a Night of the Trojan War."

JOHN DRINKWATER
1917

Sussex Flora

REV. F. H. ARNOLD
1887

Contents

CHAPTER ONE

A Lure for Magpies

A magpie chattered from a hawthorn clump as the two boys came silently along the path. Ralph stood still at the sound. Flip halted for six seconds, poised on one foot, then scurried ahead to an oak tree by the path. Swinging up into the boughs, he called, "They've found it! They've found it!"

"Do shush. You'll scare them."

"It's all gone! Come and see."

"I can't *see* what's *gone*." But Ralph climbed eagerly, using knobs and warts like steps on the craggy trunk, and crouched beside Flip in a nook where five branches met. Here they had scattered bait the day before — chopped apple, cheese and bacon rind, worms and slugs patiently collected. All had disappeared.

Ralph said slowly, "We don't know it was magpies."

"I bet it was though. Listen." Again came that low chattering sound, like companionable laughter, from the hawthorn patch near by.

"Yes. Only there's no evidence."

Something fluttered from a twig above their heads: a feather. Flip pounced on it. "There is! Look here. They've left a swop."

"A tip," Ralph agreed happily, running his fingers along the feather. It was white, edged in brownish-black like old marking-ink. A magpie's for certain.

"But the ring's still here." Ralph pointed to a crevice where a small bright object gleamed.

"I expect they'll find it next time."

They began to empty their pockets. Out came more crumbs and kitchen scraps, with beads, pearl buttons and safety pins.

"Look what I found, while you were at the dentist." Flip showed a card of Christmas pudding charms, a little ring, a cat-bell, a thimble, a button, a horseshoe. Ralph said with respect, "Not bad."

"Twopence. In that doll's-eyes shop near the river." Flip cut the threads with his penknife and jingled the trinkets in his palm.

Ralph was planting gilt beads in the oak bark. Like mistletoe seeds, he thought to himself. He pictured a magpie spotting them with its sharp eye, nipping them out, flying off to hide them — where? That would be the next part of the experiment: finding the magpie's hoard.

Yesterday they had marked the big domed nest in the hawthorns; an old nest, to which the birds had returned. Ralph and Flip had found it last year. Perhaps the magpies would hide their treasures among its thorny twigs? Later on, when the young had flown, he and Flip could come back to see. At half-term, perhaps . . . Ralph looked thoughtfully at the last thing he had brought: his French ten-centime piece. Must he sacrifice that too? He might never see it again. He polished it on his shorts and once more read the inscription, Liberté, Egalité, Fraternité — a good motto for magpies. Yes, he must let it go. Wedging it into the bark, where it shone faintly from a drift of earth like fine black soot, he thought how the bird would chuckle with pleasure, turning it over with that strong clever beak.

Ralph had first thought of his experiment on Christmas Day, when he found the diamond ring in his cracker at dinner. The crackers, pre-war and damp, refused to crack; but their contents made up for this. All the rest of the day, tin whistles shrill as parrakeets, small clackers and other atrocious instruments were swopped among the boys and tolerated by the staff: because of air raids, London boys were spending Christmas at school. Ralph kept the ring — being mute, it fetched no bids — and at bedtime he put it on his locker under the open window. Lying awake, watching its glimmer, he dreamed that a magpie came in by moonlight and took it. He had often heard that they stole bright things and hoarded them for fun. People would tell how great-aunt Jane's diamond brooch disappeared, or old Mr. Gadget's gold sovereign, and then years later a tree would be blown down and the hoard would come to light. He slept at last, and did not hear the matron's firm soft tread from locker to locker as she commandeered the whistles. Matron felt she had earned a little peace. But she was no magpie; the ring was still there when Ralph woke. He told his friend Flip Humphreys about the magpie stories.

"You see — they always are stories. You never meet the one it happened to."

"Like ghosts."

"Yes. Look, Flip. Let's make it happen to *us*."

"The thing is," objected Flip, "where do we get a diamond brooch?"

"My ring . . . no, the thing is, there aren't any magpies hereabouts. We'll have to get home. Remember that pair on the heath?"

But home was in Chelsea, and this was December 1940. Ralph and Flip, sent back to their school in the country in the summer holidays — after the London blitz began in earnest — had not been allowed home since. Nor were they now, despite skilful pleadings over the telephone. Flip, more ingenious than Ralph, did manage by the fourth day to wring from his mother a faint relenting, "We'll see." But that night, stealing out of the shelter for a moment to watch a great glow in the south as London burned, they knew they had lost their chance. After a raid like this, they wouldn't be allowed home, except perhaps for a day, and what use was that? The experiment they had planned would take a week at least: two or three days to watch for magpies on the heath and find out their haunts; several more days to put down food and lure them to one special place; another day to plant the jewels. They might as well forget the whole thing. And for weeks Flip did forget it; but the idea lay at the back of Ralph's mind, and the ring with its rough diamond went on pricking a hole in his shorts pocket. Every time he touched it, he thought for a moment of magpies.

Easter drew near, and again he was hopeful. Spring would be the best time for his plan; nesting birds would keep for weeks to the same place, and the bait could be left close by. But again the raids flared up all over the country, and again the boarders found themselves at school for the holidays. They passed the time building a pillbox and digging a tank trap, ready for the invasion. Then, out of the blue, came a letter from Flip's mother: he might come home on Friday for his birthday, and stay the night, and go to a theatre. Ralph was invited too; his father had sent permission. At least they could visit the heath, and leave the diamond ring there.

Two nights before they left there was another heavy raid on London. The drone of planes went on until dawn, and the milkman said it had been the worst night yet. Ralph and Flip waited gloomily for a message cancelling their visit, but to their surprise none came. After such an attack, Flip's parents thought, London might well be left alone for a while. For once, they would chance it. The boys, on the contrary, thought a follow-up was certain, but they kept this hope to themselves until they were in the train.

So far as a raid went, they had been disappointed, but the experiment was well begun. In Ralph's home they consulted a bird book to see what food would lure the magpies.

" 'Small animals and birds'," Ralph read out.

Flip simmered with ideas. "You know those mice we saw at Kew? Wood mice, you said, in that ivy hedge? We could smuggle your cat in, and make him catch them, and —"

"You funny boy. 'Eggs, young birds, fruit, grain, acorns' — peanuts would do, I suppose. 'Insects, snails —' "

"Are spiders insects?"

"Just animals, I think. But we won't use spiders. Aunt Lizard likes them about the place."

"Cockroaches!" cried Flip. "Grocers' shops get swarms of them. I read about it in the local paper. They shovel them up every morning. Come on, let's go and ask."

No shopkeeper, however, would admit to cockroaches. After several haughty denials, and one threat of a clip on the ear, they fell back on what they could find in the garden or coax from Mrs. Snell, Flip's mother's daily help. Then, escaping by tube to the heath, they found the magpies' nest again and looked about for a likely spot to leave their bait. They fixed on the oak tree, often used as a perching place by the magpies. Here the food and the ring were planted, high up in the crown of branches. Wild boys were roaming the heath in gangs that spring. They hoped the magpies would find the ring before these marauders. They fixed on another tree as a look-out post, but could not linger to keep watch because of getting home to Flip's birthday tea. And tomorrow morning they had to go back to school. It might be months before they could come again.

Next morning, however, Flip complained of a slight toothache. A busy dentist agreed to see both boys after lunch. Then Flip's father suddenly said that he would snatch some time off from the office on Sunday, and perhaps the boys might stay till then; he would see them back to school himself. Ralph's aunt hesitated at first. Though the school was only thirty miles away, it was obviously safer than Chelsea; but in the end she agreed.

These new plans were made by telephone. When the two met, they did not allude to their good luck, but grinned at each other like conspirators. Now they could visit the tree again. Flip's toothache did not seem to depress him. They decided to spend the morning collecting a dazzling cache of jewels; the magpies should be tempted handsomely.

The problem was to find things gay enough to attract the birds, but no longer treasured by the owners. This did not apply, they found, to odd ear-rings in Aunt Lizard's ring-box, or to a gilt star won by Flip's mother at school, or a silver brooch inscribed *Mizpah*, with which Mr. and Mrs. Snell had plighted their troth long ago.

"Mizpah! Is *that* your Christian name?" asked Ralph, much interested. To the boys Mrs. Snell was a romantic figure, for her maiden name had been Penderell, and her ancestors, she claimed, those very Penderells who had helped King Charles to escape after the battle of Worcester.

"Hilda's my name, thank you. Nothing Christian about Mizpah. It's a Hebrew word. Meaning," she added glumly, " 'The Lord help you, because I'm off'." Mr. Snell, it seemed, had disappeared soon after the wedding.

Flip's mother was out, and they stealthily rifled her work basket for buttons and snap-fasteners; but not stealthily enough. Mrs. Snell caught them fingering a thimble, and demanded, "Now what are you playing at?"

"Hunt the thimble. It won't be *lost*, you know. That's the whole point."

"Put it back at once, Philip. Your mother had that since a child, she was telling me."

"Lot of magpies," muttered Flip.

"Magpies, what sauce. 'Thimble pie'," she retorted, rapping his skull with the thimble; then put it in her pocket.

Flip sighed. Mrs. Snell was usually an ally; but this morning she was tired. Nowadays, she said, she often slept better in a raid. On quiet nights she would lie awake waiting for the siren.

"Come on," said Ralph. "Let's try someone else. Let's ask the wheelchair lady."

"No good. She got bombed."

"Not *killed*?"

"No, just windows. But she's pedalled her way out to Ealing."

"Oh. Mrs. Hopper, then. Only," Ralph added doubtfully, "she's gone off such a lot." This lady lived in the flat below Ralph's home. Her name was Mrs. Hooper, but they had renamed her; she had an engaging habit of hopping from one topic to another as she talked, so that often it was hard to follow her train of thought. She lived alone, except for a gloomy spaniel, but dearly loved a chat. In the past she had often waylaid the two boys on the stairs, holding them with chocolates and spirited tales of her girlhood. They had heard many times how she had climbed with one brother in the Alps and learned to "do a chimney", and had gone with another to the Holy Land, where they bathed in the Dead Sea and "bobbed about like corks"; and of her wedding in Bombay, and the fabulous trousseau, her godmother's gift, with its hundred nightgowns — never failing to add with her gentle smile, "You know, I'm still wearing the last of them!" Well aware of their laughter, she took it in good part. Ralph and Flip were much attached to her, delighting in her oddities. They felt betrayed when, on the outbreak of war, she seemed to emerge from her dream of the past, exchanged her fringed silk jumpers, beads and bangles for a neat sage-green uniform, and went to work in a canteen. Meeting Ralph the day before, she had greeted him briskly — "Well, young man. Why are you back in the danger zone?" — but did not wait for an answer.

"Just like a *teacher* or something. And there wasn't a bead about her," he told Flip now in disgust.

"All the more for the magpies. She'll have them squirrelled away somewhere." But there was no answer to their knock. Mrs. Hooper was at her canteen.

Woolworth's, of course, had all the trinkets they were searching for: "but," Flip pointed out, "we might just as well leave sixpences and have done with it." Still, even without this extravagance, they had a fair collection in the end.

Now the five oak boughs were studded as far as they could reach with little glittering objects. They lingered a moment, crouching in the niche, watching one of the magpies in the distance. It seemed quite at ease, cruising from thorn to elder and back again, now and then giving a chekkering call to its mate inside the nest; tasting a bud or a withered haw, vigorously wiping its beak on a branch, then sailing off once more across the heath. The flash of its wings, greenish-black and white, made Ralph think of white admiral butterflies in a Sussex wood. If only his camera hadn't got broken! Now he would have to wait until after the war for another. Flip lolled back against a bough, still twirling the feather he had found, and hoped the bird might shed some more. So intent were they that neither heard the gang racing towards them. Quite suddenly, the path below was seething with boys. Their approach had been unusually silent; they halted directly under the tree, and broke into yells and laughter. A dozen small boys seemed to be milling around one taller boy whom they had been hunting. The gang leader, an older youth, swaggered up after the rest and thrust something into the victim's face, jeering at him. The boy pushed his hand away with a yelp of protest. The pack closed round. He was being forced to hold something, and trying to resist. The two overhead held their breath, craning to see what was going on.

A gamekeeper had once told Ralph, "If I want to hide, I get up in a tree and keep still. Hardly anyone ever looks *up*." That seemed to be true. In grey shorts and jerseys, hidden among the grey branches, Ralph and Flip had not been spotted yet. As soon as they were, they knew, the gang would drop this wretch and come up after them. Yet they were too curious for caution. Now the hunted boy was standing by himself, gingerly holding the object he seemed so much afraid of. It was small and dark . . . what *was* it? A bullet? A hand grenade? The leader was organizing the rest to light a fire. They scattered to look for firewood, while the unhappy victim slouched against the oak tree. Peering down, Ralph saw the thing move in his hands, then saw him drop it with a cry. It lurched a little way and stopped. Not a hand grenade: it was a toad.

Two or three of the gang appeared from the bushes, shouting, "He's let it go! Here, Smiler, he's dropped it!" One aimed a kick at the toad. Another bent down and jabbed it with a lighted cigarette. The leader pushed them aside, picked up the toad and handed it back, snarling, "You hold that, d'you hear me?" The two overhead could not see the other's face, but they saw him shrink as he whined, "No. No." Still, he took it. The lout called Smiler yelled to his followers, "Get that fire going, can't you? We'll roast it. That'll make it holler." Then dropping his voice to an ugly note, "You let that drop again and we'll make you eat it." They heard a gasp and a whimper. Flip saw Ralph get ready to jump, to save the toad. Then the whole gang was back, dragging sticks and trails of dead bracken. The fire flared up, smoke and sparks blew about. Dry grass crackled; a dead bush caught alight. In this cold late spring the brushwood was like tinder. Suddenly flames were roaring through the bushes. A keeper appeared, shouting angrily, and began to stamp out the fire. Half-blind with smoke, Ralph and Flip had slithered to the ground. The gang fled, Smiler dragging the frightened boy with him. Ralph started after them, but Flip grabbed him. Ralph cried frantically,

"Come on — didn't you hear? The toad — they're going to torture it . . ."

Flip brought his other hand from behind his back. He was holding the toad.

"I just took it off him, when they weren't looking. Gosh, was he glad to get rid of it."

Ralph felt dizzy with admiration. For a moment he could not speak.

"Easy," Flip said modestly. "Well, you saw how he was. Quite a bit wrong in the head."

Ralph found his tongue in a hurry.

"They'll find out. They'll be after us. Quick!"

They ran the other way, Flip still clasping the toad in both hands. The keeper's threats sped them on their way. They put gorse and hawthorn thickets between themselves and their pursuers; but there was no pursuit. The wild scrub and pale tussocky grassland was left behind. They jumped a ditch where kingcups flowered, and paused for breath, listening. No sound; only a yellowhammer trilling in the gorse. They crossed open country and ran up a green hillside, resting for a minute at the top. Below, under floating silver balloons, lay the roofs and spires of London. All was peaceful in the afternoon light. They searched for the dome of St. Paul's, where in the last raid a bomb had fallen; then raced downhill towards the station, giddy with excitement and hunger. At the first shop they passed, Ralph found a packet of salted nuts.

"Any biscuits?" Flip asked.

"No, they only had dog today."

"Oh, those will do. They taste fine."

"Yes, but what of? — dried blood, ugh, and powdered horse. Now let me hold the toad."

They strolled on, Flip shaking the bag of nuts over Ralph's free hand: "I'm giving you the lion's share."

"Lions wouldn't want peanuts — here, you've only given me two."

"Yes, that's what I meant."

Suddenly, in the tube, the toad began to struggle. Ralph protested, "It's like trying to hold an old leather glove full of water." They coaxed it to squat on the seat between them. A nurse sitting opposite eyed all three with distaste and changed her place. They reeled home from Gloucester Road station, laughing, scuffling over the toad, very pleased with their day.

"Tomorrow," Flip suggested, "we'll make daddy come up to the oak tree, before we catch our train."

"Yes," Ralph agreed, in his grandmother's phrase, "if we're spared."

CHAPTER TWO

Long Night

Ralph's mother was dead, and his father at sea. He had been brought up by his aunt, Miss Letty Izard, always known to her friends as Lizard. Since the Munich crisis she had been living in Chelsea with her married sister, Aunt Emmy. Uncle Hal, like Ralph's father, had joined the navy at that time. Aunt Emmy worked in a government office, while Aunt Lizard belonged to a wardens' post near by. Just now she and Ralph had the flat to themselves. Aunt Emmy was on a visit to Nine Wells, Grandfather Izard's farm in Ireland, where her small daughter Rowan had stayed since the war began.

Flip Humphreys lived a couple of streets away. When he was sent, two years before, to join Ralph at school in Hertfordshire, their families hoped the two would make friends and amuse each other in the holidays. Unlike many hopes of this sort, the plan worked well. The boys got on happily together, in spite of their different ways. Each was an only child, but Flip in the past had always attached himself to grown-up people, while Ralph had led his own secretive outdoor life. Flip was flippant, restless and a chatterbox, but remarkably amiable. Being the younger, he was ready to fall in with Ralph's schemes, contributing ideas and devices which Ralph would never have thought of. Ralph proposed and Flip disposed. Wild creatures were Ralph's passion; the magpie research was typical of their joint enterprises. It was Ralph who discovered that one could support a dormouse at the Zoo by paying a shilling a week for its food; and Flip who arranged that their fathers should forfeit this sum as compensation for holidays spent at school. Without Flip, Ralph would never have got on chatting terms with Mrs. Hooper, or the "wheelchair lady", or various sweetshop owners who now gave them under-the-counter service. At these holiday times they ran freely in and out of one another's homes, and their elders fed them wherever they could be caught, alerting one another by telephone like two farms with straying animals.

This evening the pair went straight to Ralph's room, took down *The Book of a Naturalist* and turned to a chapter on toads. They lay on the floor, each with an arm curled round Ralph's sponge, on which the toad was resting — the nearest they could manage at present to its native bog. Tomorrow, at school, it should have every luxury: a tank to itself, pond mud, rushes, watercresses. Later it could live by the garden pond. Meanwhile, how should they feed it? It needed flies, they read; but they could not find any in the flat, Aunt Lizard was too fond of spiders. Ralph pored over the book; Flip fingered the toad's back. It was gnarled like the oak bark. The gold eyes gazed steadily about, blinking now and then. A tiny pulse beat in its throat. Once or twice it moved one long hind leg, then the other, in a sprawling movement, ready to explore. They gently nudged it back on to the sponge. Their own hunger was forgotten. The flat door had been left unlatched for them, but no sound came from the other rooms. Aunt Lizard must be out.

Soon they heard her quick step on the stairs. She clicked the door shut, switched on the kitchen light, filled the kettle, then paused and gave a little whistle. Ralph answered without moving. She came along the passage and looked round the door

"There you are. And how quiet you are. Is something wrong?"

Ralph struggled up, one finger in the book, and said with dignity, "Why should anything be wrong?"

"Well. With you two, one does expect to find a sort of bear-garden. Golden syrup tins flung in corners," she added, smiling. "Ah well. I suppose you're growing up." Then she saw the toad.

"Now, Ralph. If you kidnapped that in Kenwood, it belongs to the nation. Poor fellow, never mind" — she bent to stroke its head — "you shall go back tomorrow."

Their reaction startled her. They sprang up with cries of protest, pouring out the story of the gang, but so feverishly that it was some minutes before she could piece it together.

"They — one of them had a cigarette —" Ralph turned white at the thought of this monster. "And they said they'd roast it. How can we take it back?"

The shriek of the kettle interrupted them. Aunt Lizard ran off, calling, "Tell me at tea. And, boys" —

she sent her voice round two corners from the kitchen — "*Scrub* your hands, will you? Toads are so juicy, as bad as bluebells."

"Frogs are worse — all slimy," Ralph called back.

"Yes, but toads *exude*."

"They what?" asked Flip, carefully lifting the sponge.

"Ooze," said Ralph. "Swelter. They're wet and covered with warts," he added. They began to exchange personal remarks. Aunt Lizard called again, "Come along. Leave that creature in the bath."

Cuckoo, her tabby cat, strolled into the sitting-room, his fur smelling of lemon leaves; he had been asleep on the balcony under a lemon bush. He went purring from chair to chair, accepting sardine spines. Aunt Lizard poured him a saucer of weak tea, which he tasted doubtfully. Tea nowadays had an odd metallic tang — from extra chlorine in the water, people said, in case of typhoid. Ralph asked:

"Won't the toad be thirsty?"

"I doubt if they care for tea."

Flip said, "Let's give him a local shower," and this was done after tea, in the bath, with a good deal of hilarity.

Flip wanted to take the toad home to show his parents, and this seemed fair, since it was he who had saved it by his presence of mind; but Aunt Lizard begged him to leave it in peace. "Poor thing, remember what it's been through. I think it needs an early night. We all need one," she added for Ralph's benefit. Last night they had been at the Palladium "till all hours".

But none of them had an early night.

The sirens began to wail as Ralph came back upstairs after seeing Flip home. The sound made him gasp, then skip with excitement. In the flat, Aunt Lizard went on washing up. He dashed to the sitting-room window, drew aside the blackout curtain and stood in the dusk on the balcony. Suppose it were only a false alarm! But soon came a rumble of gunfire in the distance. The twilight was seared with flashes. He heard the beat of an engine high up, and craned his head to see. A searchlight raked the sky. He cried out, "There it is!" A little plane, like a gnat, hovered for a second in the beam. He heard a queer sound, like a canvas sheet being ripped apart by a giant. As he held his breath, Aunt Lizard gripped his arm from behind and whisked him back through the window. Bombs crashed; the building rocked. He found himself lying on the floor, where she had pushed him, with a sofa cushion over his head. They picked themselves up. Surprisingly, the french window — criss-crossed with sticky tape — was unbroken. From somewhere near by came the tinkle of broken glass; it was like the ring of icy twigs, Ralph thought, in a freak storm last year.

Far off, the guns began again. Soon, with a roar, the gun in the park half a mile away set the house rocking again. To Ralph it sounded as though it were in the square outside. He and Aunt Lizard sat in the hall, away from the windows, until there was a lull; then she stood up.

"Quick now. Let's get downstairs."

He said furiously, "I bet you and Aunt Emmy don't go to shelter. I bet you stay up on the roof and watch."

She let this pass. She was buttoning Cuckoo into a thick warm bag which made him easier to carry. Coats, torches and a hold-all, called the "fleeing-bag", lay ready by the door. Ralph ran to the bathroom, scooped up the toad, wrapped it in a face flannel and slid the damp package into his coat pocket.

"Oh, I wish Flip was here. Couldn't I ring him up?"

"He'll be in the shelter by now."

"He won't. You know they haven't got one, they just sit in their front hall. *Do* let me ring."

"Certainly not. We mustn't make frivolous calls in a raid." She was going to add, "It's nothing to gloat about. It's not fireworks, you know." But she refrained. After all their precautions, here were the two boys in London, in danger, in the middle of a raid. She blamed herself bitterly. At least let Ralph enjoy it if he could.

Another thought struck him. "I say, aren't you going to your post? You didn't yesterday either."

"Not when you're here."

"Me! But I'm twelve. I don't need a nanny."

"All the same, I get leave if you're here, till you're fourteen." She switched off the lights at the main, and opened the flat door.

The stairs were in darkness. Then, as they groped their way down the second flight, a brilliant flash lit up the fanlight above the outer door. When the park gun fired, it seemed to Ralph that the walls swayed in and out. Behind him Aunt Lizard ordered, "Scamper," and they reached the basement stairs as another bomb crashed.

Sandbagged and shored up, the basement gave a strange illusion of security; as though to be in a burrow, an underground cave, was to be out of the storm and safe. Neighbours, sitting on camp beds, greeted them with rueful smiles; thinking of the noise three nights ago, and hoping they weren't in for that all over again. Still, they were ready for anything — siren suits zipped on, emergency bags to hand, books by Jane Austen and Trollope pocketed, with the ear-plugs, the wad of india-rubber to bite on (never used yet, for suppose one swallowed it?) the patience cards and hoarded chocolate. It made Ralph think of a cabin in the Irish mailboat before a stormy crossing; everyone a little brighter than usual to show they weren't windy. Some were taking a nap while they could, in case it grew rough later. He had always preferred to be up on deck. Perhaps he could slip out presently.

Mrs. Hooper's spaniel lay drugged and snoring under her bed. Aunt Lizard and Ralph sat near by, restraining Cuckoo. The cat did not seem to notice bombs or gunfire, but would dearly have liked to scratch the unconscious spaniel while he had the chance; they were old enemies. Mrs. Hooper, Ralph was pleased to see, had recaptured her best form. Gone was the neat suit, the official manner. She wore a fluffy turban and flowered kimono over a long white robe, frilly about the hem, and a great many rings, brooches and necklaces — the safest way to carry them, she murmured, seeing his look of surprise. She was drinking coffee from a thermos, and it seemed to him that with every sip she took her manner grew more far away, her smile more gentle and dreamy.

Determined to stay awake, he propped himself against the wall and read aloud to Aunt Lizard: "Hints to Adder Seekers," from *The Book of a Naturalist*. At first he stopped when the noise outside grew louder; but for hours, it seemed, there was no lull in the thuds and crashes. He raised his voice and read on. Once they caught the roar of a plane, low, intermittent, threatening; and then he did pause and listen. The guns had not fired for some time. "Night fighters up," said a knowing voice. Was that "one of ours", or an enemy bomber? Was it circling? Was it hit, and coming down? It sounded very near. Mrs. Hooper leaned towards him. "A man in the air force told me, a squadron leader, such a charming man — when you hear a plane quite near like that, you should *count up to a hundred*, and by the time you get to forty — I think it was forty — it will be miles away. Like labour pains," she added vaguely, and began to count aloud in a rambling way. Just as she said "forty", the bomb fell.

As the tearing, rushing sound came nearer, Ralph dropped the book and burrowed into his pillow, waiting for the awful uproar. But there was no explosion: only a queer sort of thud. People sat up, a little shaken, saying "Phew! That was close."

"Dud shell," said the man who knew about night fighters. But still the guns were silent. Mrs. Hooper remarked, "The plane *has* gone, you see," put in her ear-plugs and composed herself to sleep. Aunt Lizard said sharply in Ralph's ear, "Take Cuckoo. I'm just going to look —" but before she reached the area door there came new sounds: shouts, running feet, then a heavy banging on the door. A warden looked in, switched off the lights and flashed his torch, calling, "Sorry, all. Got to leave. Bomb in the square, not gone off. Come along now, please, quick as you can. Come along. That's right, lady, Rover and all. We'll take you to shelter. No sir, sorry, no going upstairs. Very sorry. That's right, ma'am, bring baby, cover him up, he won't hurt." Trying helpfully to pull up the hood of Cuckoo's baby-bag, he caught a glimpse of whiskered face and fierce green eyes, recoiled and shone his torch again; then recognized Aunt Lizard and grinned. In the torchlight Ralph saw that his clothes and tin hat were powdered grey as though with chalk. Mopping his brow, he muttered to her, "Murder out there tonight," and like a bus conductor, which he had been, began his chant again, "Hurry along please, that's the way, that the lot? Hold tight." He beamed the torch round the empty shelter, then followed them up the steps. Ralph heard the crash of Mrs. Hooper's thermos. She and her spaniel were taken in hand by another warden. Beads dangling, she was led away, still arguing and tripping over her skirts. Amazingly, it was light as day outside. Brilliant flares hung in the sky. Ralph felt wide awake and full of triumph. What a tale he would tell at school! He thought of Flip, and urged, "Can't we go to the Humphreys?" but Aunt Lizard was following the warden. Swinging the bag in one hand, clasping her arm with the other, Ralph chattered and laughed as they hurried along the street, stumbling over broken glass. The first shelter could not hold them all. He and Aunt Lizard went on to another, a huge dim basement where someone made room for them on a mattress. Ralph looked at Aunt Lizard's watch. Only one o'clock: surely it must have stopped. No, it was ticking away. How long and slow the night was, longer than any night journey; the longest he had ever known. Excitement had suddenly ebbed away. He felt cold, he was aching a little with weariness. Then Aunt Lizard put a cup of thermos soup into his hand. He drank, and lay down under his coat. Something stirred in the pocket. He had forgotten the toad! He stroked it, and it was still. The only bombed-out toad in London, he thought, and fell asleep.

He woke to the high vibrating song of the all-clear. It was dawn. Grey light poured down the wooden steps into the shelter. People trailed away homeward, stooping under their load of rugs, bags, and sleeping children. Aunt Lizard, Ralph and Cuckoo could not go home. They found the square railed off, and a man on duty beside a placard: "No Entry. Unexploded Bomb." Aunt Lizard talked to the man, while Ralph stood shivering and yawning. All of a sudden he thought again of Flip. At once he felt lively and energetic, remembering all he had to tell — the D.A. bomb on their doorstep, the midnight trek, the spaniel, old Hopper tripping over her ninety-ninth nightgown. He called, "Aunt Liz! *Now* we can go to Flip's."

She turned, but her look was withdrawn and inattentive. He saw that she had forgotten him for the moment, thinking of her friends at the wardens' post and all they had been through. Then she said quickly, “Yes, you go, darling. I’ll come soon. I want to call at the post.” She turned back to question her colleague again.

Cutting through side streets towards Flip’s house, he was astonished to see how little difference the bombs had made. In the night, listening to the din, he had thought the whole neighbourhood must be in ruins. Yet here was a whole street untouched, looking just the same as last night, when he and Flip had passed — roofs with every slate in place, even windows intact. Only a queer musty smell hung in the air, a smell of burning, like the Guy Fawkes bonfire when it comes at last to the old clothes and boots . . . the thought made him shiver. He remembered stories told at school: a human foot in the gutter, a corpse stranded five floors up in a bath, still clutching a sponge. All agog, he dawdled up one street and down another. But, if there had been horrors, they had been removed already. He saw nothing more startling than broken windows.

It was still very early. The streets were deserted, while tired people snatched a few hours’ sleep. Lucky them, Ralph thought, not homeless like Aunt Lizard and himself. Still, they were lucky too. The flat was still there, they could go back later when the bomb had gone off, or when its teeth had been drawn. He had read about bomb disposal squads. One team had survived now for nearly a year: their leader had been decorated by the king. He was a lord; and a master at school had shown the boys an admiring newspaper cartoon with the hero at work in coronation robes, holding a bomb, and wearing a tin hat instead of a coronet. Underneath was a quotation — "... *did nothing in particular, and did it very well* ..." — which the boys thought odd, till the master explained about irony, and then about *Iolanthe*.

The toad stirred in Ralph's pocket, and he took it out. It looked rather seedy, he thought, and its skin was dry. Perhaps it would like a swim in the tank at the corner of Flip's street. Last night they had noticed a hole in the fence. But, when he reached the corner, the toad was forgotten again.

The street was not deserted like the rest. Men in overalls were standing about — firemen? rescue workers? — and then he saw a warden, a fire engine, great hosepipes trailing everywhere. He felt a quick pang of disappointment. Here, too, there had been "an incident". Flip would have his own tale to tell. Then, half-way along the street, he saw a ruined house, a pile of rubble, smoke still hanging about in wisps. Nearer, he saw window-frames hanging loose. The bomb must have fallen very near Flip's house. Could it actually be next door? He began to count as he ran. Then a car came up from behind and stopped beside him at the kerb. Aunt Lizard's voice called him. Turning, he saw her in the driving seat. It was not her own car — she must have borrowed it from the post. She had been quick about it, he thought. The nearside door swung open and he scrambled in, saying excitedly, "Look. They've had a bomb —" But, instead of going on, she backed and turned the car, unskilfully for her, bumping the far pavement, and drove back the way she had come. The car was going more and more slowly. She drew into the side and stopped. He asked impatiently, "Aren't we going to Flip's?" and then, as she said nothing, "What's the matter?" Still she did not answer, but sat still, her head turned away, looking at a church where a clergyman in a long black robe was sweeping up broken glass. Ralph remembered that this was Sunday — Low Sunday, it was called in his diary. The name depressed him. And what was wrong with Aunt Lizard? She said at last, "He's not there." Her voice sounded strange.

All at once Ralph felt the raw chill of the morning begin to creep through him, down his spine, over his knees, along his fingers. The burnt smell was stronger now. It caught at his throat. He felt sick. What was wrong? — she was bending down, her head on her lap, her hands groping as though she had dropped something. He caught his breath. The attitude was somehow familiar, and ominous. He had seen it before: a boy turning green in prayers, and matron pressing his head down between his knees . . . because he was fainting.

"Aunt Liz!"

His voice had an edge of panic that roused her instantly. She sat up, and her hands went to the gear and the steering-wheel. Then she realized — *I can't start the car. I don't remember how*. She waited quietly for the shock to pass. It was only a few minutes since she had learned that Flip and his parents were in the mortuary. Then her one thought was for Ralph: to go after him, to save him from coming unawares on that smoking heap of rubble. Now they stared at one another, and she saw him beginning to understand. He stammered,

"They're not — ?"

She nodded.

After a moment she managed to say, "They got them out. But they were dead."

"Oh. Oh, I see," he whispered. "I see."

There was nothing more to do or say. They sat stunned, as though the car had stopped on the edge of a cliff from which they were afraid to move.

Cuckoo stirred them at last. He had been sitting on the back seat. Now, disturbed by this queer silence, he sprang on to Ralph's knee. Two churchgoers, arriving for the early service, glanced in, smiled and spoke to the cat. Ralph sat with bent head, stroking Cuckoo with both hands, silently willing Aunt Lizard to get them away. After a long time, the car jerked and began to move.

CHAPTER THREE

The Spinney

This moment of waking was the worst so far. Ralph shut his eyes at once; but he could not sleep again, and could not bear to lie still with his thoughts. He got up and went to the window.

All night, in his sleep, he had heard the roar of the sea wind in a clump of trees across the road. Listlessly, leaning out, he took in his surroundings; this old house with its orange brick-work and broad low window-sills; a brown mill stream running beyond the front lawn; the village street, edged with cottage gardens, lilacs and green hedges. Over the way was another big old house, standing back from the road, sheltered by horse chestnut trees. Clumps of daffodils were tossing in the wind. The sea, he knew, was just round the corner, at the end of the street.

He and Aunt Lizard had driven here yesterday, because he had begged her not to take him back to school. She had said, "There's a place Merren told me about. The Race, at Beaumarsh. We might go there for a day or two."

"Is it an inn?"

"A sort of inn. Shall I ring them up?"

"Oh yes. Yes." Anywhere but school, he thought, with Flip's half-dug tank trap in the playing field.

"We might see Merren, at her cottage."

"Yes." Their friend Merren McKay had taught him in his first year at prep school. Now she was an air-raid warden at Portsmouth.

"Can we start now?" he urged.

Aunt Lizard had things to see to first. Her little sports car was parked near by in a garage. She thought there might be enough petrol for the journey. She left him in the café where they had taken refuge, sitting over coffee and toast which he could not swallow, hugging Cuckoo. The place was empty, and once or twice the waitress hovered, looking at him thoughtfully. At length she took away the cold greenish coffee and brought a fresh cup, and a saucer of milk for Cuckoo, and stood there while they drank. One glance at Aunt Lizard and Ralph must have told her that something had happened to them; but, with rare mercy, she never mentioned the raid, but spoke only of the coffee and the cat; and, because Ralph could not stop shivering, remarked now and then how cold the morning was. He steadied the cup between icy hands, unable to think of answers, yet glad of her company. At last Aunt Lizard came back.

The long day went on, after the long night. It was better, he found, to be in the car, going somewhere. He did not want to arrive, and Aunt Lizard felt the same; the journey to Sussex took many hours. Aunt Lizard kept him busy reading a map, which he spread out over the sleeping cat; Cuckoo, who liked motoring, lay curled on his knees like a fur rug. Soon he remembered the toad, still stifling in his coat pocket. They stopped to pick leaves and grasses, and made it more comfortable in the glove-hole. It sat there staring out; Cuckoo lifted his head to watch it. Green eyes and gold, mile after mile, cat and toad gazed steadily at one another. They stopped again by a stream, to collect gnats and pick damp cresses for it; and again to drink tea at a wayside café; then on the edge of a wide heathery valley, to look at the view, while Aunt Lizard smoked a cigarette; and later on a grassy verge at the edge of a pine wood, where they sat so quietly that a hunting stoat ran to and fro in a ditch beside them, making Cuckoo twitch and growl like a dog. Aunt Lizard referred only once to what was in their minds. She broke a long silence to say,

"They weren't touched, I heard. It was blast. They can't have felt anything." Ralph nodded.

Dusk had fallen when they reached The Race, and all at once he was too tired to go and look at the harbour, or eat supper, or do anything but go to bed.

That was yesterday. Now they were here. There was nothing left to do.

Aunt Lizard at once dispelled that notion, coming in with the toad in a borrowed shoe-box.

"It's alive, so far," she said pointedly, "but I think it's done enough travelling. We'd better find a pond and be quick about it. Why aren't you dressed?"

They set out after breakfast, Ralph with the box, and Aunt Lizard carrying Cuckoo, in case he should stray if left alone. Going seawards down the street, they found a high tide rippling in to meet them. The end of the street was flooded, and swans bobbed between the last two houses. Water covered the shore road under the harbour wall. They took a path along the top of the wall. Waves, driven by a keen wind, slapped about below, drenching them with spray. Here, away from the cottage gardens, spring seemed to have vanished. The morning was grey and bleak, more like November than April. A curlew called from down the creek, a desolate note. At the head of the bay, where salt water lapped among weeds and reeds, they turned inland along a narrow lonely road. Soon they came to a pond, but it was dark and stagnant, fringed with rotting willows: a suicide pond. Ralph, after one glance, walked on ahead. They passed wet ditches, then another dismal-looking pond, where trees knelt in black slime. Aunt Lizard called, "What about here?" but Ralph trudged on, hunching his shoulders. A willow wren was singing somewhere; he did not stop to listen.

Suddenly the dreary stretch of road was left behind. The lane curved round, and they were walking north, with the downs on the skyline. Larks sang overhead. Clumps of white primroses, with long pink stalks, appeared along the ditches. To their left, behind a high thorn hedge, was a wide field planted with rows of slim trees and bushes, stretching away into the distance, towards the spire of the village church. Pink buds showed between small green leaves. They were young apple trees, Aunt Lizard said.

Ralph had come out without socks; now he began to regret this. Both heels were rubbed, and would soon show a notable pair of blisters. They came to a yellow gate in the hedge, where a farm road seemed to offer a short cut back to the village. A notice on the gate read, Seaforth Farm Nurseries. They passed through, Aunt Lizard saying, "If we meet the farmer, we can ask permission."

They did not meet a farmer, but near the gate they found a land girl pruning small gooseberry bushes. Aunt Lizard stopped to ask, "Do you think we might get to the village this way?"

The girl paused, and seemed glad to stand upright.

"I should think you might. I'm not sure." She pulled off a glove and looked at her right hand, flexing it and wincing a little. She said wistfully, "Is it twelve yet, I wonder?"

It was not yet eleven by Aunt Lizard's watch. The girl sighed and went back to her pruning. There must be acres of bushes; it would take her days and days to prune them all. They walked on into the cold wind. Ralph wondered how she would know when it was dinner-time, or time to go home. She might stay there all night. He worried for a minute or two, then forgot her. Soon the road ended in a barnyard. Following a track round the walls, they saw a grey pony standing alone with a cart; inside the barn, pigs were squealing. Ralph clicked his tongue at the pony, which laid its ears back and turned away with a vicious clash of yellow teeth. The track gave way to a grassy footpath along the headland between two fields. On one side, again, there were endless rows of young fruit trees; on the other, a wide plain of winter wheat. Ralph pulled off his shoes, slung them round his neck and ran along the path. He came to a tangled hedge. Over a wicket gate he saw a small round cottage. It was grey, like a tree trunk, built of Sussex flint, with a mossy roof and one chimney-pot. A little old man was drawing water from a well. Ralph dawdled, letting Aunt Lizard catch him up. He asked,

"Is that the smallest house you ever saw?"

"I'm sure it is. And," she dropped her voice, "I see a gnome lives there."

"Not a gnome," he said, as they walked on. "They live underground, I think. A dwarf, perhaps." Afraid that this might sound "wet", he added quickly, "Merren told us, when we did *Pook's Hill*." He broke off — "Look! Here's just the place for a toad."

Beside the path, the hedgerow merged into a spinney of small oak saplings, crab trees, ash and hazels. Through the trees he saw a patch of yellowish clay, the colour of yellow ochre in his paintbox; watered as though by an underground spring, and overgrown with rushes and wild periwinkles. Ralph dodged under the branches and put down the toad. At once it hopped out of sight among the periwinkle vines. He jigged on a bent hazel sapling, cooled his blistered heels on the moss and dabbled his toes in the pleasant ooze. He let one foot sink in deeply, then thought of leeches and pulled it out again. Looking about, he thought this seemed a peaceful spot. He hoped the toad would be satisfied. Beyond the patch of bog the spinney sloped down to a dell, scattered with wind-flowers and slippery with bluebell leaves.

Aunt Lizard was waiting on a stump beside the path, watching Cuckoo stalk an orange tip butterfly on a clump of mauve cuckoo flowers. It flew. The cat stood on hind feet, with boxing paws, but it fluttered out of his reach. Ralph blew at a dab of cuckoo-spit to find the green mite in the centre. Now, he thought, we ought to *hear* a cuckoo. The sun came out for a moment, and cloud shadows blew across the downs. The grey wheat turned vivid green in the sunlight. Through the hedge they could see the little man busy again with bucket and windlass.

They walked on. Ralph swiped at last year's thistles with a hazel twig and scanned the wheatfield, hoping to see a hare. He seemed to have forgotten the blisters. For the first time, Aunt Lizard was glad they had come to Beaumarsh.

But the gladness did not last. They set out that afternoon to find Merren McKay's cottage on the downs; she might be away, but they could leave a note. Then, as they reached the first slopes, cold rain came down. They climbed on, skirting a valley full of dark yew trees, while the clouds hung lower and the wind veered east, chilling them through and through. A vixen wailed from the thicket; they started at the eerie sound. The flurry of rain became a downpour. Admitting defeat, they turned round to plod the long three miles back to The Race.

In the night, Ralph dreamed of a voice calling outside in the darkness, *The house is burning down*. This was an old dream. Even in his sleep, he knew that the voice belonged to another war, over before he was born; the time of the troubles in Ireland, when Grandfather Izard was farming in Kilkenny. One night, while the owners were away, men had burned down a mansion near by, locking the servants in an outside laundry so that they could not give the alarm. One brave girl, Nellie someone, climbed out of a window and ran bare-foot to the farm to call grandfather. It was her voice that Ralph heard in his dream. Grandmother had often told him how they had woken and jumped up and looked out of the window, to see the girl's small white face below, as she stood on the gravel, calling for help. Before, Ralph had always woken at that point. Now he did not wake. The dream went on. He knew the voice; he knew the face down there in the dark. Flip was calling him: but Flip was *dead*. Instead of going to help, he hid under the blankets, pressed them against his ears, fought in terror and woke screaming. Aunt Lizard ran from her room next door. With shame he saw other faces on the landing, before she closed the door. He could not explain. He could only shudder and cry, protesting over and over, "But I liked him. I *liked* him." That Flip should become a thing in a nightmare seemed unspeakable. For a few moments, while the imprint lasted, he was wild with grief and remorse. Soon he was quiet; but he did not want to sleep again, or to be left alone. Throwing pride to the winds, he asked Aunt Lizard, "Could you stay and read for a bit?"

"All right. The *Naturalist? Three Men in a Boat*?"

He did not want either. "Read me what you're reading."

She hesitated. "It's not a boy's book."

"You mean it's bawdy? I don't mind."

"I do *not*. I mean it would bore you."

"I don't mind," he repeated. She fetched the book and a rug and switched on the electric fire.

"I'll start again, shall I?"

He had not meant to listen, only to keep her there. Yet, as the hours passed and the pages turned, and her low steady voice grew husky, he found himself attending with a sort of heartfelt sympathy. It was not a boy's book. It was about a poor country clergyman, Mr. Crawley, who was accused of stealing a cheque, and could not remember how he had come by it. His case was to be tried later at the Assizes; and meanwhile the bishop's wife, Mrs. Proudie, thought he should not be allowed to take the services in his own church. The clergyman thought this unjust, and said so. Then the bishop sent for him, and on a bitter winter day Mr. Crawley set out to face the Proudies in their palace fifteen miles away . . .

Years later, in *The Last Chronicle of Barset*, Ralph would come on the chapters Aunt Lizard read that night. Grateful to the writer for his tale and the reader for her nimble skipping, he would find he remembered every detail of that absurd triumphant pilgrimage, the rout of Mrs. Proudie — ("Peace, woman!") — and then the long agony of Mr. Crawley's homeward trudge, stumbling over mud and stones, tottering with weakness — for he was an old man, past forty — ending at last with the exultant whisper, as Mrs. Crawley tucked him into bed, "I do not think the bishop will send for me again."

A knock: someone had brought a tray of tea. Aunt Lizard drew back the curtains. Incredibly, it was morning. A blackbird sang from the chestnut trees. Soon a doctor came and gave Ralph some tablets to swallow. Daylight and the blackbird faded out. He slept for hours like the drugged spaniel, waking now and then to drink something, but too drowsy even to hold the cup for himself. His sleep was too deep for dreams. Once, in the middle of the next night, he asked Aunt Lizard sharply, "They haven't sent him to prison, have they?"

"Who? Oh, Mr. Crawley! No, no, he never stole the cheque. It was all a mistake." He slept again.

Waking in the morning, he felt empty and languid. The doctor came, called him "old chap" and suggested a walk after lunch. What for? thought Ralph; but there seemed no point in saying it aloud. Lunch was brought upstairs. He did not want any. Aunt Lizard said, "You might go and see the toad." Again he thought, What for? But it wasn't worth arguing. He found the stile where the field path joined the village street, beside the blacksmith's forge. He jogged along the path towards the spinney. Out in the open, the pale white light made his eyes ache a little. It was warmer today, but there was still a teasing wind. He came to the spinney and poked about for a while without finding the toad. He had not really expected to. Most likely, perverse like all wild creatures, it had left this pleasant spot and toiled across the fields, painfully as Mr. Crawley, to one of those miserable ponds.

A brown bird slipped out of a scrubby juniper bush. From habit he looked into the bush at once, gently drawing a branch aside. There was the nest; a thrush's, with four eggs, pale blue and speckled, smooth and hot to his touching finger. He put the branch back and moved away, so that the bird could return to her nest. For some reason the moment was comforting; the nest, the eggs, the sunlight, the feeling of being alone in this little wooded dell.

Years ago, when he was eight, he had fallen out of a tree and bumped his head badly. For several days he had lain in a darkened room, afraid to move or even to blink, because of the pain that was lying in wait. Then one morning he moved his head an inch, and the pain was still there, but not so sharp; and he knew he would get better, though not yet. He remembered that moment vividly. Now he felt much the same.

He went and sat on an ash root at the edge of the spinney, near the cottage garden. No one was at home there, today, it seemed. No smoke came from the chimney. Aunt Lizard's gnome would be at work, of course. His wife too, perhaps; or out walking with an infant gnome? Had there been chimney smoke when they passed before? He could not remember. Perhaps the man lived here alone, and let his fire out in the daytime. It would be a good place to live, with the wide fields and the open sky. Miles from anywhere, he thought, but not lonely. He could hear voices and laughter from the field beyond the cottage. Two girls in green jerseys were working there in a thicket of almond blossom. One was the girl they had seen in the gooseberry field. She seemed more cheerful now, he thought, as he prowled along the hedge to watch them. They were cutting off the tops of the young trees. The sun shone, and bees hummed in the pink blossom, against the pale blue sky. Ladybirds rose from beds of speedwell under the trees. "Ladybird, ladybird, fly away home —" He could not remember how the rhyme ended. He went back to sit on the ash root.

The wild hedge enclosed the cottage, making it snug and private; a ring of briars and blossoming crabs, and among them one tree he did not know, with long gold leafbuds. At this end there was no hedge; the cottage garden ran straight into the spinney. The ground was scattered with pennyroyal, moss, empty nutshells, small sorrel flowers with delicate shamrock leaves. He popped a few lady's-smock pods, nibbled a sorrel leaf and picked up several nutshells. Each had a round hole bitten at the end. Fieldmice, he thought. He knew from Gilbert White that mice opened nuts that way, while squirrels sliced them in half. Pocketing the shells, he thought this might become one of his own places. He had been collecting places all his life, as he collected nutshells, feathers and bird bones. Before the war, when he and Aunt Lizard lived in Sussex, he had had a dozen; a harness room, a derelict rock garden, a woodland hut. Earlier still, at Nine Wells in Ireland, there had been the wilderness behind the orchard wall; a place no one could visit but himself, because the door in the wall was locked and the key lost, exactly like *The Secret Garden*. He had thought of the wilderness at once, directly he saw this spinney. Each had the same low-growing hazels, the same kind of moss, green herbs, small flowers; and mice. Long ago at Nine Wells, being very young and impressed by grandmother's tales, he had looked in the wilderness for "little men". Instead he found mice. Afterwards, mice and magic were so linked in his imagination that he could never quite separate them. It had been on the tip of his tongue, the other day, to tell Aunt Lizard about all this; but he had thought better of it. He realized now that he couldn't have told her. It was too late; or perhaps too soon. Still, it amused him to think of it. And he felt at home here, as he had felt in the wilderness. He would come here again.

The sun was slanting low over the fields. He had better go. Running along the headland, nutshells clicking in his pocket, he was overtaken by the two girls, on bicycles, with bunches of almond prunings tied to their handlebars. He might have brought some for Aunt Lizard to paint. Before the war, she had had a commission from an American publisher, to paint all the flowers in Shakespeare. Alas, the first batch had gone down in the *Athenia*; but she had started again. The ones she had done were mostly wild flowers. He did not know if she would need almond or not. At the flat, she had long lists of them. He stood still for a moment, ready to turn back. It struck him that he might come out later, when that old man would be at home in his cottage, and ask if he might take some prunings. It would be a good chance; he wanted to go through the wicket gate, to see the well and the windlass properly, to knock at the door of the round house. He might even be asked inside. He hurried back to The Race.

Tea was laid by the fire in a small sitting-room, and no one was there but Aunt Lizard. He said doubtfully, "I'm still not hungry."

"You needn't be hungry, to eat this sort of tea."

He found she was right. There were brown eggs, homemade shrimp paste, little hot scones and watercress. Lost in thoughts of the wilderness, the round house, the spinney, he ate whatever was put before him. He made a childish model on his plate: a scone for the cottage, a watercress hedge. Afterwards they began to play chess. When she was called to the telephone he sat looking into the fire; then suddenly remembered his errand.

The room had been already in twilight. Outside it was still day, not yet blackout time, and lights shone from windows in the village; but none from the round house. Coming nearer, he saw that the windows were unscreened. There was no smoke from the chimney. Surely someone would come soon? The girls had left piles of pink-flowered sprays at the edge of the field. He was sure they were thrown away; but it might be best to wait and ask. He sat down near the wicket gate, under a Spanish chestnut tree; a good tree for climbing, he noticed, with low strong branches. The evening was still and windless, the sky pale, streaked with brightness in the west, behind the steeple of the village church. Miles away to the east, he could see an ancient abbey tower. Birds flew over, high in the air. Another bird piped from the marsh, "terwit, terwit".

Then the sirens began. The first was so faint that he took it for a bird call. As he listened, another took up the sound, then another, until he was ringed with warnings. They died away, and the evening was still. Even the birds seemed to be listening.

Ralph had sprung up. Now he sat back against the tree. These sirens were the first he had heard since *that* night. He felt numb, but not frightened, yet. He waited, and heard a drone of aircraft flying low over the harbour. Enemy bombers? Soon three planes came in sight, and he laughed to himself, then jumped up to watch them. They were Harvard training planes. They made a wide circle, round and round. He thought they must belong to the airfield on the west side of the harbour. But soon the bombers would be crossing to the coast, and the guns would begin. Over there, just across the water, the naval gunners would be waiting. He sat still, feeling excited now, and glad to be out in the open, as he used to be on the Irish boat; not shut away in a cabin — or in a shelter, under a tall house. The sea bird piped again. The white sky darkened. The three planes circled. Stars came out, very faint, then growing brighter. Frosty air began to nip his fingers. A high-pitched sound made him jump and catch his breath — a screaming bomb? Then he laughed again. It was the all-clear.

He stood up, shaking the dead leaves from his jersey. It was too dark now to see the almond twigs clearly, but tomorrow the blossom would be spoilt. He wouldn't wait any longer. The cottager might be away all night —

in the home guard, very probably. He collected an armful of the prunings and ran towards the village. The path now seemed familiar, even in the dark.

Aunt Lizard was standing at the gate. She followed him into the house, humming a little under her breath; a habit of hers sometimes when she was worried. Could anything be wrong? It seemed not. Her tone, when she spoke, was casual. "Did you hear an alert?"

"Yes, of course. Look, almond —"

She was eyeing him rather oddly, he thought.

"Were you . . . where were you?"

"Oh, out in the field. I got these, look." He explained about the prunings, thrown away, unwanted. She asked absently, "By that little house?"

"Yes. Does almond come in Shakespeare?" She looked vague. He cried in exasperation, "You're not even listening!"

She smiled at that, and said with relief, "I did wonder — I thought you might be nervous."

"No. Have you brought any painting things?"

"They're in the bag, I think." She took the bunch of sprays and breathed in the light bittersweet scent.

"I can't remember if it come —"

"I can't either." After a moment she quoted at random,

> "*Rich almonds colour to the prime*
> *For Adoration; tendrils climb,*
> *And fruit-trees pledge their gems . . .*

And another verse I thought of, in that nursery:

> *. . . marshalled in the fencéd land*
> *Peaches and pomegranates stand . . .*"

"Shakespeare?" he asked patiently.

"I'm afraid not. But I'd like to paint this all the same. Thank you, Ralph."

She took a book of poems from the fleeing-bag and found *Song to David* for him. Two verses caught his attention; he read over several times:

> *. . . Ivis with her gorgeous vest*
> *Builds for her eggs her cunning nest,*
> *And bell-flowers bow their stems.*
> *The spotted ounce and playsome cubs*
> *Run rustling 'mongst the flowering shrubs,*
> *And lizards feed the moss.*

"What's Ivis? A thrush?"

"A humming bird, I think."

Still, he thought it was a thrush, and for "spotted ounce" read "vixen". He saw all this happening in the spinney, and fell asleep repeating it.

CHAPTER FOUR

The Spring House

It was queer to lie awake because one was afraid of dreaming. A wretched business altogether.

Ralph had gone to bed tired but peaceful, his thoughts in the spinney. He slept for some time without stirring. Then a dream began — quite a harmless one, gone as soon as he woke — but at once, like a diver surfacing in panic, he made himself wake properly. Then he lay gazing out at the sky, listening to a brown owl in the chestnut trees. He thought he heard swans flying over, and got up to look. He thought of reading, but that would mean drawing the curtains and he hated to feel shut in. Instead he sat in the window-seat, looking out at the sky. Aunt Lizard glanced in on her way to bed, and asked, "Would you take one of those tablets?"

"No, I'm all right. Just looking at swans."

He went back to bed, fell asleep again, and again woke on the edge of a dream. This went on all night. At last, tired out, he slept till daylight, and woke to the song of the blackbird. Often, at school, he had cursed at the sound of the dressing-bell; now he felt relief. The night was over, and there wouldn't be another for hours.

After breakfast he went straight to the spinney. The thrush had laid a fifth egg. She would start sitting today, he thought. It was late for a thrush's first brood, but all this spring had been late.

The two girls were in the field again. They had moved on from the almonds to another batch of trees, much smaller, with green buds and white flowers. Pear trees, perhaps; or cherries? On white wooden labels by the path he read: Doyenne du Comice; Beurre Hardy; Conference; Pitmaston Duchess. He was none the wiser. The girls swished through a thick carpet of speedwell and pimpernel between the rows of bushes, dew swirling off their gumboots, secateurs snipping. Each carried a marked rod. They seemed to be measuring the small trees with it, then nipping off the top shoots. He found his ash-tree chair again and sat in the sun, watching a lark get up, twirling higher and higher, until his eyes were too dazzled to follow. Then he watched two starlings in the cottage chimney. Their shimmering colours, green and purple and white, reminded him of wild fritillaries in a field near Oxford. One perched for a moment, piping a double note, and that too was a reminder — "terwit, terwit", like the marsh bird; and then the starling "sizzle". The other appeared with a twig; it hopped down inside the chimney pot, came out again and flew off, just as its mate alighted with a straw. This too went into the chimney. Ralph bent down to watch a bumble bee. A sudden idea made him jerk upright and stare again at the chimney. He got up and walked to a rhubarb patch on the edge of the cottage garden, and stood there, watching intently. The starlings came and went. They brought more twigs; they hopped busily in and out. They were building a nest in the chimney.

Starlings, Ralph thought, should have more sense than that. But again no smoke was coming out. There had been none yesterday. The chimney would be cool. Perhaps no one had lit a fire for days. Perhaps the old man used an oil stove, and lit his fire only on Sundays, to cook his meat ration. Or — it struck Ralph for the first time — perhaps he didn't live there at all. Perhaps the cottage was empty. He felt a throb of excitement.

As though to steady himself, he thought — What about the man at the well, then?

But we didn't see him *in* the house, he remembered. We only saw him drawing water, and anyone might do that. I bet he was feeding those squealing pigs. Or he might have been getting a drink for himself.

He stepped back into the spinney, behind a hazel tree, and gazed for some minutes without moving. He saw no sign of anyone at the windows, or in the garden. And, he realized, no curtains hung by the windows. But they might have shutters instead.

He began to circle quietly outside the hedge, passing the clump of cuckoo flowers, the wicket gate, the Spanish chestnut, the crab trees, the unknown tree with golden buds unfurling into leaves. He passed three windows, east, south and west; they were shaped like arrow-slits, only wider, and diamond-paned. The chimney was on the north side. The garden looked wild, he now realized; no spring cabbages, no early beans or shallots, no flowers except a clump of white narcissi in the grass; and last year's grass had not been cut. He could see a lot of withered stalks, like Jerusalem artichokes, a stack of old bean-poles — ash poles from the spinney? — a tangle of roses, some young green mint under bushes by the door. Nearer the spinney were two old mossy apple trees, the rhubarb patch, a privy in a clump of privet. Between the apple trees, half buried in young nettles and bishop-weed, he could make out a rough square enclosed by cockleshells, with forget-me-nots and wild primroses; the sort of garden a child might have made for itself. But not this year.

He circled again and came back to the gate, and stood there making up his mind. He pushed it open, hurried up the path and knocked at the door. If anyone's at home, he thought, I can ask for a drink of water.

No one came. He knocked again, and the knock had a hollow echo, as though the house were empty. There was no other sound from inside. He had time to study the door — church-door-shaped, he thought, meaning that it was rounded at the top. The green paint was faded; there were few houses freshly painted anywhere this spring. A sort of leather bootlace hung from the latch-hole. *Pull the bobbin*, he thought, *and the latch will fly up*. He knocked a third time and waited, and now excitement stirred in him again. He looked down at the grassy brick path, and the doorstep overgrown with chickweed; then up at the starlings busy in the chimney.

He said aloud to the starlings, "Empty, but for *you*." Excitement seemed to explode in him like a firework, in a shower of brilliant sparks. He darted away to find Aunt Lizard.

She was not at The Race. She had gone out, he was told. Oh, where? She might not be back for hours. He must find her at once — his plan could not wait. He was in a ferment. After hanging about her room for a while, fuming to himself and teasing Cuckoo, he decided to return to the cottage. He might be able to get in by a window; he might find a key under a flower-pot. It might be a good idea to look round, perhaps tidy up a bit, before he took her there. With this new idea in his mind, he could not bear to stay away any longer. His irritation vanished as soon as he was over the stile and back on the field path. Already, he noticed, his feet had made the path more plain.

By the almond trees he found the old man with the grey pony, raking up heaps of faded blossom and pitching it into his cart, now and then calling "Git back there" as the pony moved to a fresh tuft of grass. Ralph approached with caution, so as not to startle it; but it was he who was startled. The pony lifted its head and eyed him insolently, yellow teeth clashing on a mouthful of grass, then laid back its ears and ran at him. The cart lurched; after a moment's fright he side-stepped easily, while the carter dropped his fork and grabbed the pony. He backed it on to the path again, scolding it in a low growl, then turned an amiable grin on Ralph. At close quarters, with his brown wrinkled face, he looked more gnome-like than ever.

"Poor old Silver. He don't like the cart." He went back to his loading.

Ralph had been going to ask a question about the cottage; but it was not so easy. Supposing he had made a mistake, and this old fellow lived there, after all? He waited until the cart was on its way to the barnyard with a load, then turned and went back to the wicket gate.

What he saw made him groan aloud. Smoke was trickling out of the chimney. It seemed too bad to be true. The door was open, and someone was inside. As he stood, cold with disappointment, a billow of smoke curled out of the doorway.

For an hour he had imagined the place might be his. He and Aunt Lizard might have gone to live there. They had often talked of a cottage of their own. Now the real owners were home, and that was that. But he went on staring over the gate.

Wisps of smoke were still coming from the chimney, then another great gust of it from the door. The cottager was having trouble. He heard coughing. Then a figure appeared on the doorstep, and he almost shouted with surprise. It was Aunt Lizard.

He bounded forward, his face alight; she looked back at him soberly, and wiped her eyes with a handkerchief. He said eagerly, "You thought of it too! How did you get in?"

"I went to see the farmer. They told me at The Race —" she took another breath of smoke and choked.

"Then it's empty! We can come here?" He began to laugh with relief. "I knew it must be, I guessed this morning —"

"I'm very sorry, Ralph . . ."

At her tone, his heart sank again. Something must be wrong with the place, after all. What could it be? He gazed at her, waiting.

Smoke engulfed them both. She said, between fits of coughing, "I thought I'd look round, and start a fire. But it's no use, I'm afraid. If you've just one room — you can't live in smoke. Of course, that's why it's empty."

"Smoke!" he cried. "Why, if that's all —" He ran to the pile of bean-poles by the far hedge, and seized one. It snapped in his grasp; it was dry and rotten. It would make good kindling. He took another and ran back, dragging it.

"What are you doing, Ralph? Don't burn that — you'll make it worse!"

He turned in the doorway, dancing with impatience. "Don't you see? You can't burn anything with a starling's nest in the chimney!"

He was sorry for the starlings. They had been working hard. Still, it was lucky they had no eggs yet. Raking the chimney vigorously, bringing down a shower of twigs and straw, he could not waste too many regrets on them. The nest crackled and flamed on the hearth. He broke the ash pole into sticks and laid them on the blaze. Aunt Lizard opened a window. The fog cleared, smoke went sweetly up the chimney. They looked at one another, and then round the room.

A hollow tree, Ralph thought; a sea-cave.

The single room was bare except for sand-coloured matting on the floor. An open brick fireplace took up most of the north wall. A black pot swung from the chimney on a chain. Aunt Lizard turned back the matting and felt the stone floor with her hand. She walked to and fro, touching the walls here and there, humming to herself. He watched her anxiously. Walls and ceiling had once been washed pink; the wash had faded, it was netted all over with veins like a primrose leaf. Under the last coat one could just see a Peter Rabbit frieze — surprising, Ralph thought, in a farm cottage. Through the window he looked in turn over wide fields to the village steeple, the abbey tower, the streak of brightness away to the south where sea and sky met. He thought of sleeping out here, waking under the skylarks, cooking meals in the black pot, drinking from the well. Just then he heard a clank from the well. A man had come through the wicket and lifted the heavy iron cover to let down the bucket. It was not the old man with the pony. He turned the handle, drew up the bucket, dipped a tin mug and drank, then looked across at Ralph, rolling a cigarette. Something in his face recalled the surly pony Silver.

"Chimney smokes, does it?" He sounded pleased.

"Not now. It was just a bird's nest." Ralph could not help adding,

"We're coming here to live."

"Tcha." He dipped the mug and drank again, grimacing as the cold water pinched his gums.

"Running away from the bombs? You won't stop here long. Damp poky little hole."

Ralph thought of Aunt Lizard's inspection. "It's not damp."

"Not another place in sight."

"No. We like that."

"Oh, you like that? Swarming with spiders and mice —"

"Is it?" cried Ralph. "Oh good."

The surly one slouched away. A voice called from behind the hedge, "Git back, Silver, darn it," and the carter appeared at the gate. He grinned when he saw Ralph. "Mind if I draw a drop of water?"

Ralph nodded permission, and turned to look in amazement at Aunt Lizard. Hardly an hour could have passed since she spoke to the owner; yet already they had had two visitors. And this old man had asked *him* for water! Now the carter asked shrewdly, "Jim Honeywood been here moaning, has he?"

Aunt Lizard heard and came to the door. "Is that his name? — he seemed upset. Does he want to live here himself?"

"Not him. That's just his way. Old Wormwood, we calls'n. Mind you," he added delicately, "this old well do come in handy, working out here all day."

"But of course you must come for water. The well belongs to the farm."

He looked satisfied. Winding up the chain, he set down the bucket and said, "Now I dare say you could do with a hand, getting moved in. Tacker Brooks, my name is. Chimney want sweeping, for a start?"

"Thank you, that's been seen to."

Only a light dusting of soot had come down with the nest. Tacker glanced in and nodded. "The boss had it all kept straight, I know. His nippers had it for years. Used to come and play here."

"Oh, did they? That accounts for the frieze, I suppose. And the well cover."

"A nursery *in* a nursery," said Ralph. He felt a twinge of disappointment. "You mean, it's just been a sort of summer-house? Not lived in properly?"

"Oh dear yes. Many a year, before my time. Always been a cottage here," said Tacker Brooks, settling comfortably by the well for a long talk. "The spring house, they call it. You ask my mate, George Doggett. His grandfather had it for one, thirty years or so. Then after he died it got a bit ramshackle, and they used it for hens and pigs till the roof fell in. An old ruin it was, when I first come here. Then our boss bought these fields, New Barn and Sallows, and Little Stint over there, and he had the little house all done up for his children. Later on their friends'd come for the sailing, and sleep out here in the summer, some of them. You can see by the windows, where they had bunks set up."

"Bunks!" said Ralph alertly.

"All shipshape and weather-proof, you'll find it. The boss was going to thatch the roof, but he reckoned it might catch fire too easy, so they put on those old tiles, off a barn that was coming down. Made a proper nice job of it. Now those bunks — I wouldn't be surprised if they're not stowed away somewhere, if I was to have a word with the boss. And you'll need a lick of paint, and a load of firewood, and there's curtain-rails up all ready —"

A commotion broke out from behind the hedge. Silver came into view by the gate, with one of the girls catching gingerly at the rein. Tacker ran, hallooing to the pony, then calling over his shoulder, "Why, you could get settled in tonight!"

"But," said Aunt Lizard helplessly, "I haven't decided yet."

Aunt Lizard was a painter, but not of the Bohemian kind. When another painter or writer told her of plans for a free untrammelled life in some caravan or remote cottage, she would listen with sympathy, but was heard afterwards to wonder how, in the daily struggle for food and warmth, he would find time for painting or writing. Invited to stay, she learned the answer: these were Spartans, prepared for hardship — living on tinned food, breathing whiffs of paraffin stove and bottled gas ("like rotting cabbage stumps") all day, and trying to bath in a toothglass. Brought up by candlelight in a lonely Irish farmhouse, she knew that a truly simple life sprang from hot water taps and electric switches; all the amenities, in fact, except the telephone, to which she grudged time and attention. Some day, even isolated cottages might have all these. Until then, she declared, the delights of country living would still depend on the many hands that make light work; on belonging to a village, a farm, or a country estate.

Certainly there was nothing Bohemian or casual about grandmother's housekeeping. Her home at Nine

Wells was run like a beehive. Out of doors, besides their work with the horses, grandfather and the farm men pumped the day's water supply, grew vegetables, milked cows, carried milk and coal, firewood and turf. Pig-killing, apple-picking, potato-digging had their seasons. Indoors, on three days a week, a great pan of bread was set to rise. In the little dairy, once a week, the butter churn creaked and somersaulted on its swivel. Later came the thud of butter-pats, as the butter was made up into neat blocks. Apart from the household meals, hens' potatoes simmered all day on the kitchen range; chick food, pig food, calves' food, dogs' and cats' food were ready at set times; horses might need hot gruel. Then there was the seasonal routine of fires and lights. Every morning in winter the fires were lighted, lamps trimmed and filled, bedroom candlesticks cleaned. There was really no end to it, Ralph could see. Yet, because of what father called "division of labour", no one appeared flurried or overworked. With all her tasks, grandmother seemed a leisured person, resting in the afternoon, sewing and reading in the evening, writing long weekly letters to relations in America. When his mother had died in China, and Aunt Lizard brought him over to live at Nine Wells, the life there enclosed them both without a ripple; grandfather found a donkey for him to ride, grandmother gave him lessons, Aunt Lizard cooked, painted a little and mended his clothes. He himself learned to clean silver, feed the hens and amuse himself for hours alone.

When he and Aunt Lizard went to stay on an estate in Sussex, they found the same kind of communal life.

Here, water and electricity were "laid on" by the estate; and so, he thought, was everything else. If you were making a cherry pie, a basket of cherries appeared at the door. If you had to go to the village, there was a pony and trap in the stable yard. If a room had to be painted, or a tree cut down, or anything mended, there was what Ralph called "a proper man" to do it.

For himself, all the same, he felt secretly on the side of the Bohemians. He loved camping and caravans, longed to be a gipsy, and approved every line of Stevenson's *Vagabond*, except for the bread dipped in the river, which seemed a mistake.

Now, with misgivings, he tried to see the spring house with Aunt Lizard's practical experienced eye; no taps to turn, no lights to switch on, no sink or stove even; a little bare room alone in the fields. It would be like camping out. They would have to do everything for themselves; yet he could not see that as a drawback. At Nine Wells and Hurst Castle, and in Chelsea, they had shared other people's homes. At last, this would be a home of their own.

Watching her, he ventured, "It's handy, isn't it, with a well at the door? And so light and airy, three windows —"

"Three lots of blackout. And draughty. Wait till they're all open."

He ran to open them. The windows swung outward on sliding metal bars. "They run easily — look, someone's oiled the hinges."

"Yes. It's all been well looked after."

"We can look after it now. I can draw the water. Look, we can heat it over the fire — that pot holds gallons, I should think."

She said in musing tone, "We might have baths at The Race, I suppose."

"Oh, we can bathe in the sea! Just for the holidays."

She laughed. "You sound like the Oxford don in the story. 'What do they want baths for? They're only up eight weeks!' "

He saw nothing to laugh at. Again, he was in torment. If only she would hurry and agree! Looking out of the window, he said without thinking, "Oh, I do hope we're here for the invasion!"

At once he regretted this. She sat down on a window-sill and looked at him without speaking.

Every day last summer they had expected the invasion. One night in September it seemed to have come; but that was a false alarm. As autumn turned to winter the night raids had grown fiercer, but people no longer talked of invasion. But soon now — this month, next week, tomorrow? — it was bound to come. Here on the coast they must be in the thick of it; these fields would be battlefields, the skies black with planes like rooks, parachutists floating down, thick as dandelion seeds; tanks and mobile guns mowing down the almonds, like last year's tulip fields in Holland. Ralph saw himself lying in the ditch by the spinney, hurling home-made petrol bombs at the foe, if only Aunt Lizard didn't whisk him away inland . . . if only he had kept quiet.

But she said slowly, "I don't think we can *plan* for the invasion. No one knows where it will come. We'll just take one day at a time. Seven more days of the holidays. We're here, now . . ."

He held his tongue, waiting.

". . . So let's get the place straight, for a start."

He said swiftly, making sure of his ground, "And come back, won't we? For the summer holidays?"

"If we can. I'm paying a year's rent. Don't worry," she added, "Rollo — father put some money in the bank for us, in case of something like this."

How did she know he worried? He had told no one. For a long time now — since the *Athenia* sank, right at the start of the war — he had wondered what would happen to him if his father were lost. Perhaps he could stay at school without paying, till he was fourteen; the headmaster was also his Uncle Alfred. But what then? He couldn't expect Aunt Lizard to support him. For a moment, when she spoke of money, he had a familiar pang of dread. He asked, "How much did Rollo put in?"

"I said you weren't to worry. Well, a hundred pounds, to start with."

"Oh! That's all right then." It sounded a fortune. And the spring house was theirs. He cried, "Oh, we must sleep here tonight!"

Lizard was going to say, Nonsense; but she knew that last night, at The Race, he had been afraid to sleep for fear of calling out again in a nightmare. A bad habit, and each night could make it worse. Besides, he needed something to do. Out here he would be busy all day and tired at night; and if he dreamed or shouted, no one would know but themselves.

She said, “Then I don’t see why we’re idling here. We’ve a lot to do before dark.”

He thought of kettles, food, matches, knives and forks, blankets, mattresses. Where to begin? She took pencil and pad from her handbag and began to make lists.

“Blackout,” she said, and wrote it down.

“Curtains? Can we? Tonight?”

“Coats and rugs will do — tucked in the rails. Just for one night. And they’ll lend us two camp beds from The Race.”

“And a lamp, don’t forget.”

“Not tonight. Firelight and candlelight.”

At that, all the morning’s hopes and fears flared up and drove him wild. He began a whirling dance from one window to the next, touching each sill as he passed it, round and round till he was dizzy, chanting, “*This ae night, this ae night, every night and all — Fire and sleet and candlelight* —” He stopped then with a painful gasp; but it was too late to stop. Aunt Lizard finished quietly, “*And Christ receive his soul.*”

The words seemed to echo in the silence. They were like a benediction. Grief and shock would haunt him all his life, but the cruel horror was gone. In that moment, Ralph knew for certain that Flip would never come here in a nightmare; and he never did.

CHAPTER FIVE

May Day

Ralph lay in his bunk gazing round at the walls and ceiling. All the veins and lines were gone. He and Tacker Brooks had spent Sunday with buckets of distemper and brushes, after Ralph had covered the floor with newspapers and brushed off all the loose flakes. Now it looked fresh and clean. He sniffed the delicious pungent smell and admired the colour once again. He and Aunt Lizard had chosen a pinkish gold tint — "like a kingfisher's egg before it's blown," he had said as they walked to the village shop.

"Ralph, you haven't blown a kingfisher's egg? What a waste."

"No," he admitted, "I read it somewhere. I've never found a kingfisher's nest, if you want to know."

"I'm told they're disgusting, all fishy. You might find one here, with all these ponds."

"Yes. And a little stint. And a butcher bird's larder." He had read how this shrike impaled beetles, grubs, bees, even small birds on thorns before eating them. "The books make out you can find them all over the place," he explained. "But I've looked and looked, and I never have."

"I know. The way they write about harvest mice. Dear little nests in the corn — did *you* ever see one?"

Ralph had his eye on the high thorn hedge enclosing the fields called Sallows and Little Stint. But so far there had been no time for bird-watching. They had been so busy settling into the spring house. Today would be busier still. He was on his own.

He had been up already, hours before, to see Aunt Lizard off. For two years now she had spent one day a week giving art lessons at a London girls' school. The school had moved to Surrey, and she still went there on her day off from the wardens' post. Now term had started again, and she did not want to miss her classes. They found that by catching a train soon after five at New Beaumarsh station, and taking her bicycle along in the van, she could reach the school in good time, with only one change and a bicycle ride at each end. Tacker, on duty at the home guard post, came by arrangement to rap on the door before dawn; but Aunt Lizard was already up, cooking breakfast — boiled eggs for speed, and cocoa for staying power. She began to tell Ralph what meals she had left in the larder, but he stopped her. "Don't. I like to be surprised."

"Promise you won't light the primus?"

"No, no, I *have* promised."

"Or open the well? You've plenty of water in the churn."

"Not unless there's a prairie fire."

"Or stand at the windows, if there's a raid?"

"No!"

"And you'll remember to get bread? And keep Cuckoo in? And the fireguard, when you're out? Oh, and the blackout, if I'm not back?" Buttoning her coat, she added, "You're sure you won't come? Do!" This time he only laughed. She pulled on an old pair of knitted gloves for bicycling, and tucked a neat suède pair in her bag.

"Careful Annie," he mocked at this, quoting a family legend.

Watching her bicycle lamp flicker away across the path, he felt a moment's regret. Still, he couldn't waste a day in a girls' school — not, above all, the last day of the holidays. At home he had so many things to do. It was not yet light, and bitterly cold. He shut the door and lay down again to enjoy the warmth of the little house.

Aunt Lizard's bicycle had passed a useful week. Bought from a friend of Tacker's, and fitted front and back with baskets, it had gone to and fro across the field path from the gate, ferrying kettle, primus, paraffin, candles, curtains and groceries. Two wooden bunks had come out of store, and Tacker had screwed them into place when the walls were dry: Aunt Lizard's by the west window, Ralph's by the east. On Tacker's advice, too, they went to the town on market day and found mixed bargains in a sale; two kitchen tables, one for work, the other for meals; garden tools; a washbasin wreathed in purple irises; cups and saucers; two old hand-painted dinner plates, one with a missel thrush, the other with a cuckoo, going at twopence each. At a hardware shop, Aunt Lizard bought a white wooden store-cupboard, a small churn for water, a kettle and pan and cooking pot, cheap knives, forks and spoons, a basin for washing-up, a zinc-wired larder like a ferret cage, a crock to hold preserved eggs. Ralph carried them over the fields from the gate, singing to himself: the more things they bought, he knew, the less likely they were to leave. Their seats at the moment were sugar boxes, a present from the village grocer. Another box held shoe brushes and dusters. A new birch broom stood by the door; coats hung from a row of pegs behind it. Later, Aunt Lizard said, she would bring down a trunk to hold their clothes.

Ralph had done some shopping of his own, in the narrow back streets between the cattle market and the abbey. He found one street called Little London, named, he was told, by Queen Elizabeth. "Quite a little London!" she had said graciously as she rode through. Queen Elizabeth, he had noticed before, was a great one for leaving names behind her. As he had foraged in Chelsea for magpie bait, now he searched here for small shops that would sell him something for the new store-cupboard; peanut butter, pickled shallots and capers, anchovy sauce, a bottle of orange squash — swede juice and saccharine, Aunt Lizard called this. Her plans for stores were more independent: eggs bought from cottage henruns and "put down", vegetables from the garden, perhaps a beehive later. These plans, too, seemed to anchor them here more firmly. Already, under Tacker's eye, Ralph had dug a plot of ground and sown five rows of haricot beans in shallow drills — "so they can see the gardener leaving the plot", Tacker said, meaning that you mustn't put them in too deeply.

From the start, Tacker Brooks had adopted them. That first evening, he had brought over a sack of coal, and then a barrow load of apple twigs from the barnyard — last year's prunings, baked white through last year's hot summer. The next evening he had bicycled to a public house behind the downs, near an estate called Wild Hill, and there met the head forester over his evening pint. Now a pile of seasoned logs, beech, birch and chestnut, was stacked between wattle hurdles on the south side of the cottage.

Already there was comfort and routine. Overnight, the water churn was filled, and sticks and wood left ready on the hearth. They lit the primus and drank tea in their bunks while the fire crackled and the great pot of water heated; it was too chilly yet, Aunt Lizard said, for baths in the creek. Ralph fetched the milk from the gate in the lane, left there by a girl who drove a milk-float and pony round the neighbourhood at dawn. Then came breakfast, washing-up and a quick "do round" with broom and duster by Aunt Lizard, while Ralph drew water and chopped sticks; then a walk to the village to buy food, ride-and-tie with the bicycle; coffee at The Race, and home to the day's "make and mend" — curtain-making, gardening, window-cleaning — while the vegetable stew simmered over the fire. After tea they walked round the harbour, then strolled home to fry sausages or dig baked potatoes from the ashes, and play two-handed demon by candlelight.

Today would be quite different. He had to do everything himself. Besides, he meant to astonish her in various ways — for instance, by cleaning and weeding the brick path to the door. She had said yesterday, "We must leave that for half-term." So she meant to come here at half-term! He would finish the path today, and start clearing a place to grow tomatoes, and mend a loose tile on the roof. When he had offered to do this, she had said, No, he might fall down the chimney into the pot, like the wolf in the story. But the dry weather wouldn't last for ever. He remembered a bitter complaint by an old lady in the lodge at Nine Wells: "All through the drought there wasn't a sign of a crack, and then as soon as the rain came, didn't the roof start leaking." He saw her point; that mustn't happen to this house. A window-pane needed sealing, too, or the rain might seep in on to Aunt Lizard's bunk.

He raised himself on one elbow and drew aside the curtain. No sign of rain yet. A round red sun, at eye level, was breaking through white mist. The sky was pale and clear. As he watched, the mist seemed to roll itself into a cloud and float away like smoke, high over the fields.

Something flopped on to his feet. Cuckoo, sensing that they were alone, had woken and crossed the floor, seeking company. He curled on the end of Ralph's bunk. There was no sound indoors but the cat's purr and the flicker of the fire. Outside he could hear a thrush's song, a double phrase, "I've found it, I've found it" — then the starling's whistle. Ralph grinned to himself. A medley of imitations followed: yaffle of green woodpecker, Cuckoo's mew at the door, a clicking sound that might be secateurs; at other times he had heard the starling do a duck quacking, Tacker's "Werp!" to the pony, the distant *tink, tink, donk* from the blacksmith's shop by the stile. Flushed from the chimney, the starlings were building again in the eaves.

He realized with a start that the sun was high in the east. He must get on; there was a lot to do. He dressed quickly in front of the fire and set off for the milk. How cold it was! He was not surprised to see white frost on the grass, as though it were December, although the crabs and the little bush apples and pears were covered with pink and white blossom, all flowering together after a bleak windy April. He walked slowly home again past Little Stint and New Barn fields, enjoying the sun on his back and the crackle of frost at every step. No one as yet was out in the fields. He was alone in glittering light and space. The sky made a perfect dome, horizon to horizon; as though I were out on the prairies, he thought. He left the milk can beside the well, under a shady clump of ivy and small flowers like violets. They would keep it cool even when the frost was gone. Aunt Lizard kept bottles of beer there for Tacker.

The flint coping of the well was full of small holes. As he put down the can, his eye caught a twinkle in one of them. It was gone at once, but he thought he had seen a small brown head and bright eye. A mouse, perhaps. In spite of Jim Honeywood's promise, he had not seen one yet.

Now for the housework; but first he thought he would go and look at the chaffinch's nest in the spinney. Yesterday it had been empty, ready for laying. Now he was puzzled to find two eggs. Could she lay two at once? Or had she laid the first yesterday, after his visit, and the second early today? Or could one be a cuckoo's? No — they were both the same, grey-green with dark red scrawls. He admired the little nest, then took a quick look at the thrush "sitting tight" in the juniper bush, and at the rabbit burrow in the garden hedge, and a bigger hole that might be a fox earth; then ran back again to the spinney, to look once more for the toad, but without success. The first bluebells were out in the dell, with cuckoo flowers and early purple orchises. He picked a bunch for the spring house. Coming out on to the field path, he heard a small lisping note and stood still. Two long-tailed tits were fluttering from bush to bush; one alighted on a barbed wire fence running along a deep ditch between the spinney and Old Park field. It stayed a moment, then flew to a tangle of blackthorns. He saw that the tits were building there, gathering flat lichen from the sloe trees, whiskered lichen from an ash, perhaps a wisp of fur from the rabbit burrow — but what could they find on barbed wire? There they were now, back on the fence: he walked quietly towards it, and saw horse-hairs caught on the barbs, grey, brown and black — grey from the pony Silver, chestnut from old Captain, black from the mare Violet. The nest, he knew, would be beautiful; even better than the chaffinch's. If they didn't hurry too much, he would see their brood at half-term. If only he needn't go away!

He heard a shout from farther along the ditch, where Tacker was clearing out dead leaves and sludge, and cutting back brambles with a long-handled slasher. It was late for hedging and ditching, Tacker said, but all the winter they had been short-handed, with orders piling in for fruit trees. Now the work was all upside down; they had even been pruning in April, trying to catch up. And look at this lot, all filthy with weeds . . . Tacker was working knee-deep in ragged robin, yellow deadnettle and lady's-smock; now he sat down to eat his nine o'clock sandwich on a bank thick with speedwell and pink crane's-bill. He had called Ralph over to warn him that he had put two or three things in the woodpile as he passed — a tin of paint for the gate and the front door, a piece of putty for the window. He would be along on Sunday to do them. And while Ralph was here, he might like to look at a robin sitting on her nest in the bank — "only don't start her".

Ralph looked at the sitting robin, and then at a bumble bee going in and out of a burrow that might have been made by a fieldmouse, and then at a tuft of thin dry grasses in the hedge; a whitethroat's nest, perhaps, but last year's. Tacker stood up again to his job. Ralph thought of his own day's work, and ran round the spinney into New Barn field.

Here he had a surprise. In an hour, the blossom had changed. Pink and white apple, snow-white pear and crab were now flushed with a delicate biscuit colour in the sunlight. Frost had burned their petals, as though someone had walked up and down the field waving a lighted torch. Ralph went to look at their own two apple trees in the garden. Yes, some of the blossom was turning brown; they would be short of apples. But the damson fruit had set already. As he examined the trees, Cuckoo padded out to meet him, mewing plaintively. Ralph picked him up and carried him indoors, feeling guilty at his neglect. While he was away in the spinney, the cat might easily have strayed off to the lane in search of Aunt Lizard. Whatever happened, he must take care of Cuckoo.

He had heard of buttering a cat's paws to make it settle. This seemed extravagant in wartime, but perhaps he should try it? He held the cat firmly on his knee and treated all four paws with strict fairness; the back ones being larger than the front, he plastered one of each from his own butter dish, the other two from Aunt Lizard's. It seemed to work. Cuckoo sat down at once and began to lick the butter off. Ralph followed it up with a boiled fish head from the ferretcage larder, which was nailed to the damson tree. Feeling hungry himself, he inspected the store-cupboard: a whole bacon pudding in a basin — that would do for supper, when Aunt Liz came home; apple cake; a salad in a damp cloth, chicory, watercress, spring onions, mint; cold sausages — he would not starve. He decided to leave all this for later, and made himself a three-decker sandwich with a little of everything else: a slice of bread with bacon dripping, grated cheese, mustard; then bread, butter, marmite, capers; then bread spread thickly with peanut butter and anchovy sauce, topped with pickled shallot. He carried the sandwich out of doors and sat down on the well to enjoy it slowly, in small delicate mouthfuls. A faint rustle by his foot made him look down, in time to see something flick into a hole between the stones. Cuckoo, who had followed him out, crouched and stared intently into the hole. A small brown head reappeared for a moment. Not a mouse; a lizard.

Her familiar, he thought. It was a reminder. He *must* get down to all those jobs. At this rate, she would be home before he had started. Which first: housework or weeding? The morning was too fine to be wasted indoors. He fetched Aunt Lizard's potato knife and began without enthusiasm on the path, hacking away at dock roots and couchgrass. Sitting back for a rest, he caught sight of the woodpile. Better make sure that Tacker's things were safe. He found them, tucked between two logs; a tin of paint, apple green, the label said; a paintbrush, a bottle of turpentine, a broken knife, a slab of wood, a lump of putty. The putty smelled agreeable, like cricket-bat oil. He rolled the lump between his palms and tossed it from hand to hand. It struck him that the weather might change before nightfall. He might as well do the window himself.

He passed an interesting half-hour, slapping the putty on, then patting and smoothing it with the knife; it was like icing a cake. Having finished, and put back the knife and board, he thought he would just open the tin of paint and see what the colour really was. But you couldn't tell by looking at it; he would try it on the gate. While he was about it, he might as well finish the first coat. Aunt Lizard would be pleased. He could do the weeding later. Why not paint the door too? It wouldn't take long. Painting away, he had another good idea. What about a name-plate for the gate: a white one, like the fruit tree labels, with The Spring House in neat black lettering?

While the first coat dried on the gate, he took a stroll along the path to study the labels again. The lettering was neat as print. An artist must have done it, or a printer. He had a vision of Aunt Lizard coming home to find both gate and door painted apple green, spruce and shining, the name-plate already in place. He must get it done today. He scanned the fields. No one was in sight. He went back to the ditch, but Tacker was gone. The two girls were nowhere about. Who else would help? Where could he find them? He could see buildings across the wheatfield, at the other end of the nursery; a greenhouse, stables, a great barn. They might be working there. He would go and find them. He had to get bread from the village anyway.

Cuckoo was curled on Aunt Lizard's bunk. He locked the door, put the key in its slot in the well head and set off along the nursery road, passing fields called Bullrush and Foc's'les on his right hand, and the wheatfield, Chequers, on his left; he knew the names from Tacker. The road curved round Chequers; now another big field, Hammers, lay on his right, planted with fruit tree stocks. Tacker had told him about these too: hundreds, thousands of sturdy shoots, crab, quince, wild plum and cherry, stood there in rows, awaiting this year's grafting and budding. In other years, skilled men had come from Holland and

Denmark every spring to help. Now only five knifehands were left: Joe Lock the foreman and his brother Ted, tall gipsy-looking Larry, and another pair of brothers, Jack and Arthur. Soon three of these would be gone, six-foot Larry into the Grenadier Guards, Jack and Arthur into the air force. The Locks were older; they had a young brother in the navy. Just as Ralph came to Hammers gate, he met the whole troop on bicycles, back early from dinner — they were all on piece work, Tacker had said, picking up their six pound a week from what he heard. Ordinary farmhands got forty-eight shillings. They started in at once, each with a bundle of cherry twigs slung under one arm, and a sash of white bast round his middle. They moved with swift concentration from stock to stock, knives flashing in the sun, faces intent and serious — all but Ted, who was quick and deft as the rest, but kept up a flow of quips and chat to make the other men laugh. A boy ambled along behind the knifehands with a pot of grafting wax. The boy's nickname was Sally, no one remembered why.

Ralph leaned on the gate, forgetting his errand. With lightning speed a man's sharp knife would pare down a twig into a six-inch shoot, trim the stock and cut it off cleanly, make a neat sloping cut in each and fit twig to stock, then bind them together with raffia and seal the join with wax. Sally, under the foreman's eye, was learning to tie and seal. Ted came to the end of his row and stopped for a smoke, saying amiably to Ralph, "Like to try?" Ralph was over the gate at once, grasping the twig in his left hand and Ted's knife in his right. He spoiled several twigs before Ted approved of the cut he made. There must be two good buds on the graft, he learned, ready to grow, and another on the stock, to "draw up the sap" while the cut parts grew together to make a tree. Ted showed him how to tie the graft. "Now, do one on your own." Trying to make a quick bold cut like Ted's, he lost control of his knife. The blade slipped, slicing off the top of his thumb knuckle. Blood streamed down. "There," said Ted, without surprise, "that'll put you off knifework." Ralph pressed the skin back, like a graft, bound it tightly with dock leaves and finished it off with bast. Then, to "show" Ted, he tried again. This time the cut was firm and neat, and the twig fitted to the stock; but he spoilt it by fiddling with the tie. "Make a half-hitch, see? No, that won't do. You've torn it. Once more." At last it seemed right, and he looked with pride at the waxed and bandaged stem that might be a cherry tree next year. They were Early Rivers cherries, on mazzard or wild cherry stock — but the names meant nothing to him. It was the cutting and joinery he liked, and the fresh smell of the sappy green twigs. He would have stayed for the rest of the day, but suddenly he remembered the name-plate. He left the field and ran on to the nursery buildings. First came a frameyard, with rows of garden frames full of small trees and shrubs. He approached the greenhouse door; going more slowly now, hoping to meet someone, but not sure how to explain what he wanted. Then, as he reached the greenhouse, a bicycle shot out from behind it, careered down the steep slope to the road beyond, missed the turn, shot across the road and landed with a sensational crash in the ditch. As Ralph tore down the slope, the victim was already on her feet, looking peevishly at a great tear in her khaki drill trousers and a bloody gash on her shin. He recognized Jill, the second land girl; the novice they had seen that first day was called Tess.

"Blast. I can't go like this. Is the bike bust too?"

"Only the chain off," he told her. "I'll put it back in a sec. What happened? Did your brakes pack up?" Untwisting the bicycle wheels, he tried the brakes. "They're all right now."

"I just missed the turn," said Jill, "I usually do. You go so fast down that steep bit, you can't help it." She was mopping her shin with a knotted handkerchief.

"But," said Ralph, "if your brakes work — what's wrong?"

"Wrong? I told you. It's so steep."

They looked at one another, bewildered.

"If your brakes were on," said Ralph, "you wouldn't be going fast, would you? However steep it was?"

"Do you mean," Jill said, "the brake's for slowing down, too? No one ever told me that. I thought it was for *stopping*."

"Well then," said Ralph, astounded, "it's a marvel you haven't gone slap into a car before now. Whizzing out on the road like that — !"

"Oh, I have. Last year. I was in hospital a week. I've only just taken to the bike again. Everyone," she added, "was witty about "Jill fell down" etcetera. In case you were getting ready to say it."

He was too staggered to reply.

Working the chain into place, he took the bicycle back up the slope and showed her how to crawl safely down, both brakes gently applied, and turn into the road.

Later, when he knew Jill better, he realized that she was not only quite sane: for a girl, she was also remarkably handy. She could set a rat-trap and drive a tractor. She simply had a blind spot for bicycles.

He was going to hand over the bike, but she said with tactful hesitation, "I suppose you wouldn't have time for another good deed?"

"As a matter of fact, I was coming to ask *you* something." It was easy now. He explained about the labels and the nameplate.

"Yes, you've come to the right place. I'll soon show you how we do them. Only — the baker has doughcakes today, about three o'clock. We get so hungry. Could you possibly — ?" She unknotted a shilling from her handkerchief.

He was back in a few minutes with the doughcakes steaming in newspaper. He had bought three for himself, and had even remembered Aunt Lizard's loaf. The two girls were planting tomato seedlings in the greenhouse, and before eating they went to wash their hands at a tap in the yard. Jim Honeywood, passing with a barrow, laughed heartily at this refinement. With the doughcakes they ate Bramley apples, given to Jill by Arthur, her admirer.

"You can make the most of *them*," Jim told them. "Won't be no apples this year, not after this frost." The apples were wrinkled and shrunken, but full of juice;

the doughcakes fresh from the oven, crisp outside and soft within, laced with spice and a few currants. Jim refused a share, and asked Jill gleefully, "Heard the latest? Eighteen acres o'sprouts in Flint Walls next winter." Jill groaned. Sprout-picking, she said, was the coldest job of all, like picking icicles. Beet-trimming was nothing to it. Tess and Ralph listened with respect. Jill had already survived two winters on the land.

Ralph asked Tess, "You know that day you were pruning gooseberries?"

"My first day. Hell, yes."

"You were all alone, and you hadn't a watch. I did wonder how you'd know when it was time to go home?"

"I can tell you that," Tess said calmly. "When I got to crawling along the rows on my hands and knees, then I thought it was about time, and I went."

Jim Honeywood took himself off, with a glance into the greenhouse and another dose of cold comfort: "Tomatoes! Those won't never come to nothing."

A potting shed next door held pots, canes and labels of all sizes. Jill had washed the labels and painted them white on wet days in the winter, when sprout-picking was over. She showed Ralph a set of lettering blocks and an ink pad, like a child's printing set. He practised on a piece of paper, then chose a slim white label for The Spring House. His first effort wobbled a little. He tried another label. This time the lettering stood out, clear and even, in glossy black on the smooth white surface. As he waited for it to dry, there was a clop of hooves outside, and the horses were led past to the stables. The horses coming in already — it must be after four, he realized, and the weeding hardly begun yet . . . but the nameplate could blow dry on the way home. Jill gave him two screws from a box, and he sped away along the nursery road, the loaf tucked under his arm. The fields here were lined with poplar wind-breaks, the young leaves golden in the sunlight. They swayed and rustled with a sound like running water. He passed more autumn-coloured trees, tall cherries with sticky dark red leaves, a row of walnuts, their young shoots glowing bronze, then a row of honey-tinted saplings like the one in the hedge at home. He went back to read the label. It said, *Cydonia: Portugal*. He had never heard of a tree called that. He passed Fo'c's'les, a small sheltered field with fruit trees growing on wire fences, and Bullrush, a jungle of roses and briars beginning to run wild: no one had time for roses this year. Now he was on the narrow white road leading to the New Barn — new, perhaps, fifty years ago. He skirted the barnyard, reached the footpath and sprinted like a racer to the spring house gate.

The label had dried as he ran; the gate too was dry. No time for a second coat — he must see how the name-plate looked. Using Tacker's putty-knife for a screwdriver, he fixed it and gazed contentedly at his handiwork.

It must be teatime now. Doughcakes and apples had made him thirsty. Cuckoo too was awake and ready for tea. He realized how shamefully he had neglected the house — fire out, kettles cold, even the beds still unmade, as in the ballad of *Lord Randal*. He must have it all tidy for Aunt Lizard. He had a feeling that she wasn't yet reconciled to living here. She might still say that it wouldn't do, that he must stay at school again in the holidays. Coming home to this squalor, she might say so at once, tonight. In panic at the thought, he poured milk for the cat, relit the fire, filled the kettle, and slung the pot on its chain to heat up the bacon pudding. Aunt Liz would be late; she had an extra class after tea, he remembered. But there was still that weeding to do. Beds next: Aunt Lizard was a quiet sleeper, but his own was what father would call a Hurrah's-nest. He began to bundle the clothes together, but habit was too strong. At school, bedmaking was a ritual. In the end he stripped both bunks and remade them properly, turning the mattresses, even remembering "hospital corners". Cuckoo returned to Aunt Lizard's bunk. Ralph swept the floor, brought in wood and water, laid the table, put candles and matches ready. In the firelight and warm sunset glow, the room looked its best; but clouds were rolling up from the south. It might rain tonight. What about that tile? He climbed a drainpipe, disturbing the starlings, crawled up the roof and examined the tile. It hung awry, and wagged like a loose tooth under his finger. He set it straight, as well as he could, and jammed it there with putty. That would do for the moment. Going back in at the door, he thought the new paint looked rather streaky; better give it another quick coat. There was just time before dusk.

Now the sun had gone down behind the marshes. The cottage was full of shadows, shifting with the firelight. Time to draw the curtains, in case an enemy plane sneaked in. He had heard that a pilot could see a lighted match *half a mile away*. Going out to check the blackout, he tripped over something on the path: the potato knife. Ah well: too late for weeding now. He took it into the house.

The pot was bubbling; time to put in the pudding. He managed this, slightly scalding one finger, and covered it with a saucer. He set out bread, sausages and apple-cake, and looked the table over critically. There should be something more; he was not sure what. Putting the bird plates to warm by the hearth, he jogged the potato bin. At once he had a good idea. He would make chips. He scrubbed the earth and dock juice from the knife, chose six large potatoes and set to work. The cutting fascinated him, as the grafting and printing had done. Kneeling by the hearth, he melted bacon dripping in the pan and threw in a handful of wet chips. They spat over his fingers, nearly making him drop the pan; then he remembered that they should be dried in a clean teacloth. The room began to fill with blue smoke and a luscious smell of frying. Dishing up the first batch, he realized that he was ravenous. He might as well eat these; there would be plenty more. He set a tin plate to warm; but, although he went on steadily frying, the pile on the plate did not grow fast. He was too hungry to leave them alone. How late Aunt Lizard was; she should be back by now. The last batch of chips went into the pan.

He was half-dozing by the hearth when the latch clicked. Aunt Lizard cried, “Good gracious!” He could hardly see her through the haze. He jumped up quickly, the tin plate in his hand. "Look, have one!" She took a chip and nibbled it, then stared in surprise at her gloves. They were sticky with green paint. He saw with relief that they were the old pair: hurrah for Careful Annie.

"Look, I've painted the door, and the gate — come and see!" He blew out the candle. By the light of her bicycle lamp she examined the name-plate. Indoors again, she sat down, still in her coat and cap, on a box beside the fire. He offered the plate again. "Do have them. I've had masses. Are they all right?"

"They are indeed." But he saw that her face looked wan. She added after a pause, "How nice it all looks." Yet he felt something was wrong. He cried suddenly, "Oh, I know what you want. Stay there — it won't take a minute." He might have guessed she would like tea. But it was all ready, and the kettle boiling — he had never made any for himself, after all. How the day had flown! She sat still, watching him. Bringing her cup, it dawned on Ralph that she was too tired to move or speak. He had a flash of that discomforting grown-up insight that sometimes came to him now, and said slowly, with chagrin, "I suppose it was a bit grim . . . being met at the door with a plate of tepid chips."

"No. It wasn't grim, not a bit." She took a sip of tea and looked round the room. The smoke had cleared. She saw the bright fire, the purring cat, the bluebells in a beer bottle. She repeated, "Not a bit."

* * *

Lizard had passed a desolate evening. It had been one of those wartime journeys when the train, hours late, crawled and stopped and crawled again. There was a long wait at the junction; the second train was blacked-out, lit only by dim blue lights, and crowded with servicemen going back from leave, weighed down by their heavy gear, their heavy thoughts. She stood in a packed corridor. Someone said there had been an alert. After that no one spoke. Her own thoughts turned to the perils and dangers of the night; to the black war news; to Rollo — God knew where; to her sister Emmy crossing tonight from Ireland; to Ralph all alone, perhaps frightened by an air raid, or by her lateness; and then to the other boy who had run home so full of life, only thirteen nights ago. Here in the dark train, where no one could see her, she cried bitterly at last for Flip; but not for long. She thought she had not made a sound, but she felt the young men stir uneasily on either side, and dried her eyes at once, ashamed of adding to their burdens. The train crawled on as though through an endless tunnel.

After such a journey, the relief of this cheerful homecoming was almost too much for her. She felt close to tears again. Appalled at herself, she sat up, pulled off her coat and stirred her tea briskly. Glancing at the table, she cried, "But Ralph — you've eaten nothing!"

"I know. There just wasn't time."

"But all day! — what *have* you been doing?"

"Painting — I told you. And the name-plate." What else? He could not remember. "There were so many things," he said, and then, "Come on. I'm starving."

As she served out the bacon pudding, Cuckoo sprang on to her knee. Ralph said, "Oh, yes — and I buttered his paws. He'll settle now, you'll see."

"I feel," said Aunt Lizard, beginning her supper, "as though you'd buttered mine."

CHAPTER SIX

Little Stint

A white foxglove leaned out of the spinney. Hawthorn blossom lay in drifts over the hedge; moondaisies and cow parsley hid the bare gnarled roots. A cuckoo called, and the air was filled with pipings and lispings of young birds. In Chequers the wheat was a foot high. The countryside had changed in three weeks; now the house was hidden in the white and green of early summer.

Aunt Lizard unlocked the door, Ralph flung open the windows. They sat down for a minute under the damson tree, sharing a glass of ice-cold water from the well. They made plans and discoveries.

"Look at all those bees in the mint."

"Yes. Remind me to get some parsley seed."

"And let's have an artichoke, can we?"

"Why, we have some already, over there."

"Not Jerusalem, those big thistle ones. Uncle Laurie said you see them in France, in every cottage garden."

"Oh, look, the path. It's been cleared." Tacker must have done this. As usual, he had made a good job of it, rooting out every weed and relaying the bricks; and here was Tacker himself, on his way home to tea, with a bundle of lettuce seedlings and young cabbages.

"I'll plant them tonight," Ralph promised.

"Better heel them in and wait till Sunday. I'll be along with a bit of wire netting."

"Wire?"

"Rabbits. See there." When he pointed, they could make out the rabbit run quite plainly, starting at the burrow in the hedge, crossing the garden, dipping under the gate and so into the wheat.

"You've a regular warren," Tacker said, "under that old quince tree."

"Quince tree?"

Tacker nodded at the tree that had puzzled Ralph. The opening leaves had turned silvery green, and now it was starred with flowers like wild roses. A good cropper, Tacker said. They should have a lovely lot of quinces, if the grey squirrels didn't grab them first. "Bold as brass they're getting. You used to see one or two in the woods. Now they've crossed over the main road, swarms of them, and started in on the corn and apples. Same with the blessed rabbits, not enough cartridges to keep them down. Keeper over at Wild Hill says they're sitting up laughing at him."

"Oh, I'll set snares. We can eat them." Ralph turned to Aunt Lizard. "Rabbit pie from our own garden, and quince jelly, and wild potatoes, and horse radish, look — and opium," he added, laughing, snapping off a poppyhead. He watched the white juice drip; but a moment later he had forgotten it. He was staring at Tacker: he could have sworn that he had said, "When I was in China . . ." Yes, he *had* said that. He was talking about Shanghai. Tacker, in China? Ralph had been born there himself; but Tacker he had thought of as a simple farmhand, toiling all his life in the Sussex fields.

"Three voyages," said Tacker calmly. "I went as cook in the old *Osprey*, time I gave up riding."

Aunt Lizard said, "Yes. I thought perhaps you'd been a jockey."

"Fifteen years in Max Winnick's stables, and I wish I was back there now." Ralph felt in a whirl. Simple farmhand, indeed. From now on he would see Tacker in a new light. A ship's cook, a jockey — with his ancient corduroys and stubbly gnome's face and brown horsy teeth, he shared the glamour of Long John Silver and Steve Donoghue.

It was wonderful to be back. Whitsun leave had been staggered, and the younger boys packed off while the seniors took an examination. Next year it would be his turn for that. No London boys had leave, however; but for the spring house, he would still be at school. He walked round the garden in the twilight, while Aunt Lizard scrambled two eggs for supper. From Ireland, Aunt Emmy had brought them grandmother's skillet, a little three-legged saucepan for cooking by the fire.

Then it was wonderful to fall asleep to the sound of the breeze in the Spanish chestnut and the drowsy grunting of young pigs in the barnyard, and to wake at dawn and visit all the nests in the spinney. He thought he would start on the garden at once, and by breakfast time he had cleared the weeds from a good square of earth. Groundsel, with its tiger-striped caterpillars, came up easily. The rest were tougher. Now and then he stood up for a rest, listening to the chorus of birdsong, trying to pick out separate notes, while he looked across at the white late apple blossom in the field. As he bent down to grub at a clump of nettles, some lines from a play came into his head.

> *. . . I have seen*
> *White orchards brighten under a summer moon*
> *As now these tents under the stars. This hour*
> *My father's coppices are full of song*
> *While sleep is on the comfortable house . . .*

and then something about nettles:

> *Thoughts that make me older than my youth*
> *Come even from the nettles at the gate.*

He knew the lines well. The play had been acted by four sixth-formers in the Christmas term, produced by a temporary master aged eighteen, awaiting his call-up; even to Ralph, Mr. Ferris had seemed quite young. It was about four soldiers, two Greeks, two Trojans, in the Trojan war; all longing for the war to be over so that they could go home and get on with their real work. It was called *X Equals Nought*. Ralph could still remember whole pages of it, because rehearsals had gone on every evening in the art room, where he was copying pictures of spiders' webs for a lecture. He had never tired of listening; the more you hear a play, he realized, the more you can go on hearing it. He remembered the producer now, crying in anguish, "No, no, Russell, 'I was to build *a cleaner state*' — not '*a cleaner* state' — you're an idealist, not a sanitary inspector," and then Russell's voice again:

I was to bring
Princedom to every hearth, to every man
Knowledge that he was master of his fate.
The dream is dulled. Three years of Trojan dust
Have taught me but to pray at night for sleep,
An arm stronger in cunning than my foe's,
A quicker eye to parry death . . .

Now, thinking of young Ferret in the army, Ralph saw him in a Greek tunic, talking in verse. For the first time, as he tugged at a dock root, it struck him that perhaps Mr. Ferris had felt like the soldiers in the play; perhaps he didn't really want to go into the army, and thought it a waste of time. That must be why he had chosen the play, and produced it with such care. And the actors must have guessed; now he remembered one of them saying daringly, "You're a pacifist really, aren't you, sir?" and Mr. Ferris's answer, "Ah well. We were all pacifists, weren't we?" — with just the note of gentle scorn that he was trying to drum into Russell.

It was a new idea to Ralph. Thinking it over later, as he dug the patch he had cleared, he was sure that neither his father nor Uncle Hal had minded joining the navy. Before the war, father had had an adventurous life as a newspaperman in China. Now, though he never talked about it, he seemed to be enjoying himself in naval intelligence. Yet he was much older than Mr.

Ferris. Could that be something to do with it? Ralph had always taken it for granted that the younger you were, the keener you would be to get called up. Now he was not so sure. He would have to wait six years to find out for himself what it was like. Everyone said that this war, like the Trojan war, would last ten years.

His thoughts strayed away to other things. Presently his ear was caught by a soft quacking sound from the spinney, and he realized that he had heard it several times before. Perhaps a duck was nesting there. He would go and search; but first he must water-in the lettuces he had planted. He ran to and fro with slopping buckets from the well, dished out a spoonful to each seedling, then poured away the rest for the birds, in a puddle by the hedge. Soon a young bluetit came to crouch there, fluffing and preening itself and throwing up showers of drops. Its feathers, he noticed, were slate-blue and khaki, not yet sky-blue and yellow. Its antics reminded him how hot and dusty he was, and he went to call Aunt Lizard: "Let's go and see if the tide's up."

They set off for the shore, carrying lunch and swimsuits, but they did not bathe that morning.

In the barnyard young pigs were being hustled, protesting, into a lorry, to be taken to new piggeries three miles away. Close by, in Little Stint, Mr. Doggett — the head horseman — was driving a horse-hoe, led by one of the girls. Shading her eyes, Aunt Lizard asked, "Is that Jill?"

"No, Violet."

"The girl, I meant. She might know about tides."

When the hoe turned and came towards them, they saw it was Tess. At that moment one of the pigs broke loose, dodged the pig man and careered out of the yard into the field. Mr. Doggett called "Werp" and the mare stopped. Tess ran to head off the pig. She grabbed it, slipped and fell on top of it, but let it go again. Lithe as an eel, it wriggled away and galloped across the field. Ralph brought it back at last, after a long chase, its shrieks muffled in his towel. He returned it to the lorry. Tess said defensively, "I thought it might bite me."

"I knew it might," he agreed, "that's why I had to gag it." He showed a white scar on the back of his leg, where an old sow at Nine Wells had caught him. In strict fairness, he might have added that for weeks he had played a game of "dare" with her, dropping off the orchard wall beside her as she slept, then fleeing in terror for the gate while she snorted at his heels. Just once she had been ready for him.

Nor had Tess escaped without injury. In tackling the pig she had twisted her ankle. Now, trying to walk back to the horse-hoe, she found she could only hobble. The ankle was swelling rapidly. She limped off beside Aunt Lizard to try a cold bandage.

Mr. Doggett had gone on hoeing without a leader, coaxing the mare Violet down a drill between the gooseberry bushes. They came to the farm road and turned again. Mr. Doggett bent to clear the prongs of weeds. Ralph screwed up his courage and stepped forward.

"Could I lead her for you, Mr. Doggett?"

Mare and horseman both gave him a long thoughtful look, and then sighed. Ralph felt Mr. Doggett saying to himself, "Crazy girls and bits of boys" — but he did not say, "Clear off." He said, "Keep her over, then." Rightly taking this for assent, Ralph seized the rein and whispered, "Come on, Violet." The mare stood still. Ralph tugged and repeated more loudly, "Come on." Mr. Doggett chirruped to her, and muttered something Ralph could not catch. Violet plunged and set off down the drill. Before they had gone a dozen paces, Ralph saw what "Keep her over" meant. Violet was a leaner; she had a habit of veering to the nearside, bringing the hoe with her to grub up the bushes, and forcing her leader in among the thorns. Ralph had once tried to ride a wicked pony that had scraped him along a thorn hedge; but there was no malice in Violet, she was simply clumsy. He pressed his knuckles into her soft whiskered cheek, his shoulder against her near foreleg. After they had stopped twice for the hoe to be straightened, he took the initiative. Before she could begin to lean, he pressed all his weight against her. This time he overdid it, and she made for the offside row, trampling with iron-shod hooves on several small gooseberry bushes. They righted themselves. He stole a guilty look at Mr. Doggett, but the horseman only grunted, "Come up then." Again they set off, and again she was veering left, and Mr. Doggett calling, "Put her over right," and then, "Pull her left." At the end of the row he waited to be dismissed, but Mr. Doggett said, "Bring her round."

Bring her round! But how? The next drill was on his left. Violet strayed right in a wide circle, and he tugged at the rein, shouting, "Whoa!" She took no notice. It was like trying to stop an elephant. Then the horseman said, "Haw-whup!" Her ears flitched back, she stopped. Mr. Doggett muttered, "Dooce, dooce, dooce," and she came round briskly into the right row, taking Ralph by surprise and treading on both his feet in turn. He rubbed them furtively, feeling for broken bones, while Mr. Doggett cleared the blades. The horseman called "Coop, Violet," and once more they set off. Ralph suddenly remembered what he had learned about leading marks, when grandfather taught him to ride. "Never let a horse dither about," he had been told. "Look straight ahead and keep him straight." He began to aim for a definite mark, a white stone, a dandelion, a red dock leaf. This worked well. Violet covered half the row without swerving. Then something distracted Ralph, and he looked down as they passed. It was only a scrap of yellow china; but now the mare was leaning again, their steady rhythm broken. Mr. Doggett called something that sounded like, "Dirk, dirk, dirk," and she straightened. They finished the row without mishap.

By the time they had staggered through four more rows, Ralph had come to a decision. Amiable as she was, Violet could not be guided by hand; she was too big, and she had no "mouth". She would respond to commands, but they had to be the ones she knew, in Mr. Doggett's language. Words like Whoa, or Giddup, or Steady, meant nothing to her. Next time the hoe dragged, choked with weeds, Ralph shouted, "Haw-whup!" Violet stopped. Blushing to the ears, Ralph did not dare to look round. Mr Doggett chirruped and they went on. At the headland, with one finger on the rein, Ralph called, “Dirk, dirk, dirk,” and Violet circled into the right drill. Ralph stole a glance at Mr. Doggett. If he were offended, he gave no sign. Ralph went on recklessly copying his yells and crooning sounds. It was quite simple really. Violet knew that what sounded like “Dirk, dirk, dirk,” meant a wide turn to the offside, bringing the hoe clear of the trees, with room to turn; and “Dooce, dooce, dooce,” meant a bearing to the nearside, or, at the headland, a direct turn in her own length. Now they were getting on famously. Once, after bawling, “Haw-whup,” Ralph caught Mr. Doggett’s eye, and thought he saw the ghost of a grin flicker across the horseman’s face. It was gone in a second.

By the end of the morning he could spare time to notice other things without unsettling the mare; green wild strawberries in the hedge, clumps of little wild pansies, more bits of coloured china. He wondered how these fragments came to be in a field. You quite often saw them in gardens, he knew, where broken cups and plates had been buried some time. Perhaps there had been a house here once. He noticed a smooth dark red piece just by his foot, and bent swiftly to pick it up. In the same instant, something frightened the mare. She reared, snorting, jerked the rein from his hand and would have bolted, dragging the hoe with her; but Mr Doggett was at her head, holding her fast, talking gruffly and patting her while she trembled and shuddered. The horseman reached up and pulled something out of her ear.

"See that?" He held out two fingers, tips pressed together. Ralph could see nothing. "What was it? A flea?"

"Bee sting."

It was time to stop. Mr. Doggett unhitched Violet. Not venturing to ask, "Shall I come on Monday?" Ralph followed them to the barn. The horseman did not look round. They clopped away along the nursery road, and Ralph ran home. He found Tess still sitting on the doorstep, mopping her ankle with hot and cold water in basins. He said, "It's quite swollen, isn't it? Twice as big as it was."

"Three times at least," Tess said shortly. She was rather proud of her ankles.

"Do you — I wonder if it'll be better by Monday?"

Aunt Lizard tactfully intervened. "Ralph, will you fetch Tess's bicycle — are you *sure* you can get home?" Tess lived seven miles away.

"I think so, if you'll just help me start." She seemed all right; when Ralph brought the bicycle, she mounted by the wall and rode off along the path, pedalling with one foot. At the gate she turned precariously to wave. Ralph asked Aunt Lizard, "Will she be all right by Monday?"

"Very unlikely, I think."

He could hardly reply, "Oh *good*." He was silent. If Tess didn't come to work on Monday, no doubt someone else would be sent to lead Violet — Jill, perhaps, or the boy Sally. A pity, when he was getting on so well.

"Did you enjoy yourself?"

"Mm." That was true; he had enjoyed his morning thoroughly: not only the job, simple now he had mastered it, but the fact that Mr. Doggett had let him do it. That was encouraging, as though he were not just a visitor from London, "running away from the bombs", but a country boy like Sally. Of course he had lived mostly in the country, but the horseman didn't know that. Supposing he were to go and see the manager, and tell him about Tess's ankle, and offer to do her job? He was not due back at school until Tuesday night.

Aunt Lizard broke into his thoughts. "High tide this afternoon, Tess said. Do you still want to swim?"

They followed the back road to the harbour and round the bay, where a few boats bobbed at anchor. Leaving the shore road, they walked along a rough pathway among tall blue-green reeds and scrubby sweetbriar bushes. The tide rippled in to lap the marshes. In peacetime the water would have been alive with sails. Now there were only swans. They swam, and lay in the sun, watching the lapping waves, cloud shadows far away on the downs, swallows dipping over red-tiled cottages across the water, on the harbour wall. Ralph thought it must be fine to live there in stormy weather, when great waves would lash against the cottage doors and windows. On the whole, though, he was glad the spring house was safely out in the fields, where even a tidal wave could hardly reach it. Winter seemed a long way off; and so did the war.

On Sunday morning he again woke early, and thought at once of his plan to go on leading the mare.

Better get it fixed up at once. Mr. Riley, the manager, lived by the lane between Chequers and Hammers. At Ralph's knock he came to the door in observer corps uniform, after a night at the post, and raised his eyebrows at such an early visitor. He sighed, as Mr. Doggett had done, when he heard about the sprained ankle, and shook his head at Ralph's plan. Ralph pleaded, "He let me help him all the morning."

"H'm." Mr. Riley looked down at a folded newspaper in his hand. After a silence he said absently, "Good. Eightpence an hour, then."

It was Ralph's turn to be surprised. "You mean, I'd get paid?"

The manager smiled. "Well, you see — it's up to George Doggett. If he'll take you on, that's fine."

"You mean, to ask *him*?"

"I mean, you turn up tomorrow morning, if you're so keen, and see what happens." He looked back at the paper, his face grave, and said abruptly, in a different tone — "Seen this, have you?"

Black headlines leapt from the front page. *The* Hood *sunk in battle with Nazi* Bismarck *off Greenland*. And underneath: BLOWN UP BY SHELL THAT HIT MAGAZINE.

Ralph's stomach gave a lurch, before he remembered: for once, they knew that father was at Portland, and Uncle Hal was on leave.

He stared at the page. Yesterday, while they swam in the creek, this battle was being fought. Today the cold north sea was full of drowned sailors. At school, people said that in those icy waters you would pass out in a few seconds; no chance of floating about and being rescued. Yet still it all seemed a long way off. The sound of the guns had not reached quiet Beaumarsh.

Briefly, he told Aunt Lizard the news. They ate breakfast in silence. Afterwards, wandering into the garden, he stood for some time looking down at his lettuce bed, before he realized that the seedlings had vanished, each one nipped off at the root. Instead of annoyance, he felt relief. Here was something to do.

Tacker, usually so talkative, did not talk about the *Hood* either. Arriving with a roll of wire netting on a barrow, he shrugged when he saw the ruined lettuces, but made no comment. They set about fencing the patch, cutting hazel rods in the spinney and pinning down the netting with forked pegs like catapult sticks. Ralph pocketed the strongest peg and made a catapult, using one of the black elastic garters off his school socks, while Tacker went home for more lettuce seedlings. He brought a box of tomato plants as well, but he would not set them out; there might be another frost yet, he said "with the wind following the sun this way". Ralph promised to bring the box indoors when he went to bed. After Tacker had gone he tested the catapult with pebbles, and promised the rabbits a shock next time they appeared. He did not tell Aunt Lizard about this plan; time enough for her to know when he strolled in swinging a plump dead rabbit, its feet crossed through a slit tendon in the proper way. She might disapprove of the catapult; but snares would be more cruel. He watched the burrow under the quince tree, but saw no rabbits that evening. Before going to sleep he banged his head five times on the pillow, to wake at five o'clock. The charm did not always work; this time it was nearer six when he opened his eyes, but because of "double summer time" it still felt very early. He wriggled into his clothes and crept out without waking Aunt Lizard. He had left a cache of suitable stones in a cranny in the wellhead. Collecting these, he walked quietly round the hedge to the spinney, and then through the trees to the edge of the garden. Kneeling between two hazel clumps, he had a clear view across to the quince tree, with the breeze in his face, so that the rabbits wouldn't scent him. He chose a bullet, loaded the sling and waited. There was no sign of a rabbit. The morning was chilly, the sun hidden behind a low bank of cloud. He grew cramped; when he moved, his shins were painfully crisscrossed with a pattern of twigs and moss. He yawned and groaned softly, shifting from time to time, but never taking his eyes from the hole in the bank where the first rabbit would appear . . . still it did not appear. A blackbird chattered, then sang. Larks rose; starlings whistled; the mysterious duck quacked from the spinney. Fred Buckler passed along the headland on his way to work, moving lightly and rapidly, with his seaman's roll — like someone with corns, walking gingerly, Ralph thought — and his leading seaman's punctuality: whoever turned up late, it wouldn't be Fred. Next he saw Aunt Lizard's curtain twitched aside, then smoke coming from the chimney. The door latch squeaked and Cuckoo appeared. He went first to look for lizards in the wall, as Ralph always did himself, then made a bee-line across the garden for Ralph's hiding place, picking his way fastidiously through groundsel and bishop-weed, pausing now and then to shake the dew from his pads with an irritable twitch. Ralph had not stirred, and Cuckoo did not lift his eyes from the ground; he advanced unerringly to within a yard of the hazels, then sat down to stare at the boy with frank curiosity. No chance of seeing a rabbit now! Ralph barked like a fox to make him jump; Cuckoo sat unmoved, still marking him like a pointer dog. A smell of kippers drifted over the garden. Ralph pocketed the catapult, draped the cat round his neck and went in to breakfast. At least, the seedlings were still there; the fence was doing its work.

He could see the knifehands working down in Fo'c's'les, but the horses always came out later; they were not yet in sight. He swallowed his kipper, took a cup of tea in his hand to wash the bones from his throat, and began to potter about outside, waiting for Violet and Mr. Doggett. He wandered along the path to the spinney, and sat on the stump by the patch of cuckoo flowers; they were nearly over now, long and straggly, with green seedpods. He heard a faint "quack" behind him and turned his head. What he saw would not have been at all unusual in Kew Gardens; here in the spinney it made him gasp with delight. A duck was leading a line of small black ducklings through the undergrowth. Suddenly she stopped, as he told Aunt Lizard, "just as though she'd thought of something. And she turned right round and went along the line, I swear she was *counting* them, and then she quacked at them and they all got into a huddle and sat there. Then she went back the way they'd come, and stood under a tree quacking, and what do you think? Down came another duckling, sort of fluttering and sprawling, and it dropped to the ground, and she marched back, and it followed. Then they all lined up and started off again, off to one of those ponds, I expect. Well, but," he added, "here's what I can't make out — how did she get them roosting up a tree to start with? They didn't look old enough to fly an inch. D'you think she'd carried them up on her back?"

"I think —" began Aunt Lizard.

"Yes, what? It's funny, isn't it?"

"Yes. But I think, if you go back and look, you'll find her nest in the tree. I shouldn't think they'd left it before at all."

He laughed, hitting his forehead with his fist: a gesture learned from Mr. Ferris at the play rehearsals. He ought to have thought of that for himself! Wild ducks, he knew, usually nested in colonies, in reeds and rushes; but here, by herself, this one might have built in a tree, to be safe from rats and weasels. He started back to the spinney, but the sound of clopping hooves made him stop short. He had forgotten to keep watch on the road. Mr. Doggett, leading Violet, was already near the barn. The duck's nest could wait. Ralph hurried down to the field and hovered behind Mr. Doggett as he hitched the mare to the hoe. When the horseman looked up, he said breathlessly, "Hello," and went to take the rein. He was breathless from doubt as well as from running; but Mr. Doggett said only, "Coop then," and they started work as though there had been no interruption.

Finishing the gooseberries and blackcurrants in Little Stint, they moved the hoe down to Fo'c's'les. Pink bramble flowers were already thick in the hedge; Ralph thought he must come here in the autumn for early blackberries. The knifehands were at work on fruit stocks at the far end of the field. He saw Jill with them. While Mr. Doggett looked over the field, Ralph waited beside the mare. Jill came up to tell him that Tess was still away. "She's got to keep her foot up for a week at least." Then, lowering her voice, she asked, "You've heard about Sid Lock?"

"Who?"

"Joe and Ted's young brother. He was in the *Hood*."

The sound of the guns had reached here after all.

They began to hoe again, moving carefully between long wire fences that supported the "trained" trees, young apple and pear trees with horizontal branches, fan-shaped peaches and cherries.

At noon, Joe and Ted Lock cycled off alone, looking at no one. The others hung back. When the two had gone, there was an awkward pause. Larry said, "They're after her, it said on the wireless," and they all nodded. Since yesterday, "her" meant the German battleship *Bismarck*.

At four o'clock they finished Fo'c's'les. Mr. Doggett unhitched Violet and set off for the stables. Ralph found Aunt Lizard busy in the garden, clearing a potato bed. He called, "I'll help you after tea," and felt like a seasoned farm worker. His legs ached, his right arm ached where he had held the rein, his feet had new bruises; but how light and easy gardening seemed, after toiling in the fields! Aunt Lizard asked, "Are you going tomorrow morning?" and he burst out laughing: "You see, I don't *know*. Mr. Doggett never says a word, except for 'Coop' and 'Whup'."

Later, Aunt Lizard wanted a letter posted. As he went along the field path to the village, he met Mr. Doggett again by the paddock gate, turning out Captain, Violet and Silver after their evening feed. Each one, as the halter was released, broke into a snorting gallop and careered about the field. Captain, the big Suffolk Punch — Dobbin, he should be called, Ralph thought — got down and rolled clumsily. Violet pranced and whinnied. Silver cantered in a circle, kicking up his heels as though in triumph at having got rid of the cart. When Ralph came back ten minutes later the horseman was still there, propped comfortably against the gate, smoking his pipe and watching them. Ralph understood that he was staying "a-purpose", as Tacker would have said, in case the horses came to harm in those first moments of freedom. They might kick one another, or rupture themselves in rolling. Soon they would calm down and begin peacefully cropping the grass. He remembered something Jill had said, on May Day, about Mr. Doggett: when there were air raids at night, he would get up and go and sit in the stables, in case the horses were frightened. Poor Mrs. Doggett was left trembling under the bed at home.

He strolled on, and came to the garden hedge. Aunt Lizard would be getting supper. He might just have time to look for the duck's nest in the spinney. He was about to turn back, when a faint sound, a sort of thump, made him stop and peer through the hedge. He thought something moved over there in the grass, under the quince tree; something pinkish-brown. There it was again, caught for a moment in a ray from the setting sun. He leaned forward, holding his breath. What he had seen was the tip of a rabbit's ear. The rabbit sat up, looking round, then sprang down from the bank with a wild caper and danced on its hind feet, as he had seen a tame hare do in play. Then he almost laughed aloud, for the rabbit stood again on its hind legs and hopped, bolt upright, like a kangaroo; two, three, four hops, and down again on its haunches. "Sitting up laughing at you" — he remembered Tacker's words. His hand went to his catapult pocket, but he took it away at once. He couldn't shoot a dancing rabbit. There it was again, prancing on its hind feet, kicking up its heels like the horses in the paddock. He had never seen a wild rabbit do that before. It was so agile that he had doubts about the wire netting. It would probably jump the fence in no time. But he was fascinated. If only Aunt Lizard could see it! Then he thought quickly — where's Cuckoo? The grey cat had been a hunter in his youth, almost living on rabbit. He mustn't catch this one. It was welcome to a few lettuces. They would be ready before the summer holidays, anyway. Peter Quince, he would call it — he was sure it was a buck. Now the rabbit was standing up again, hopping and capering. Suddenly it was gone. Down the burrow? Then, as he watched, something dark loomed up from the hedge behind the burrow, and disappeared again. A cat? But it was so big. A hunting dog? It didn't move like a dog, and it was a different shape, closer to the ground. He thought, but couldn't be sure, that it was long-haired, though not shaggy. Could it have been a badger? He hadn't noticed any white stripe, but he had seen it only for a moment. He remembered a larger burrow in the spinney, that might be a badger's earth. He wandered up and down until dark, and again got up at first light to watch; but he did not see either rabbit or badger — *badger?* — again.

He met Mr. Doggett and the mare at the gate of Fo'c's'les, where they had left the hoe. As soon as Violet was hitched, Mr. Doggett led her out to the cart road again and on past the barn to Sallows, the big field near the lane, with the high thorn hedge where Ralph had thought of looking for butcher birds. There they found Tacker and Silver waiting with another hoe. The two men arranged the work while Ralph stroked Violet's neck. He did not venture to offer any caresses to Silver. Tacker was to take the high "standard" plums and apples. The rows were like fences, no leader was needed to keep the pony straight. Then Ralph heard Mr. Doggett say, "There's my mate waiting. Coop, Violet." He actually nodded at Ralph as he picked up the handles. He meant *me*, Ralph thought, and wanted to dance like the rabbit at this tribute; but instead he took the rein and dropped into a steady plod between the little bush apples, as though he had been a horseman's boy for years.

He was due back at school by seven; there would not be time to work that afternoon. At noon, when the two men tied on the horses' nosebags and sat down by the hedge, Tacker gave him a message from Mr. Riley; he was to pick up his pay at the office, out on the main road. After dinner he borrowed Aunt Lizard's bicycle and found his way there. A girl opened a window and handed him a small square envelope. On it his name was typed: R. Oliver. He tore it open and found a handful of silver and a white slip that said: 14 hours, 9s. 4d. He had done jobs before, but this was his first real pay packet. He had earned all that in three days — enough for a new bike lamp. And Mr. Doggett had called him "my mate"! He went sedately until he was out of sight of the office window, then hurled the bicycle at top speed along the road through the nursery. The dinner hour was just over. The knifehands, with Jill and Sally, were standing at the gate of Fo'c's'les, and he stopped to speak to them. Suddenly the talk died; Joe Lock had ridden up and was standing just behind them. This time he did not avoid the others. He stood for a moment, while they all looked at him, and then said very quietly, in a tone Ralph never forgot, "*They've got her.*" Then he turned his bicycle and rode quickly away. Larry, arriving a moment later, told them that the *Bismarck* had been sunk.

Three days before, with a flourish of trumpets, the German radio had announced the sinking of the *Hood*. Joe's low savage voice, the gleam in his eye, struck the same note. When he was gone, no one had the heart to say the obvious: that won't bring Sid back. For the dead, X still equalled O.

Yet later Ralph would find that, more clearly than reports of the battle and the hunt, the names *Hood* and *Bismarck* called up this green and white landscape of early summer, smells of horses and torn-up weeds and blackcurrant leaves, the feel of the mare's cheek against his knuckles. For the next four years it would be like that. Sieges and battles, disaster and victory, resounding names, Stalingrad, Alamein, Kohima, Caen, were the background to life; but reality meant the spring house, the fields, the bright bitter air of the coast, the fruit trees made and trained and lifted, fruit stocks giving way to root crops, rose fields to wheat and barley. And school life, real enough when he was there, seemed at Beaumarsh like a tiresome interruption. Each time he left for Hertfordshire, he seemed to leave part of himself behind. His dreams of the place were so vivid that they were like a separate life, going on night after night; as though, set free by sleep, he flew straight to the spring house.

Following Aunt Lizard along the headland to catch his train, he stopped to pull up one drooping sock, and looked regretfully across at Sallows, where Jill was now leading Violet. Two months, he would be away. When he came along that path again, the corn in Chequers would be nearly ripe. Looking at the stalks, slim as grass, he wondered suddenly when they would be firm as straws, strong enough for harvest mice to climb up and build their nests. Did mice really do that? He remembered something Aunt Lizard had said about them. He had never seen one of those nests for himself; in Ireland, perhaps there were no harvest mice? It struck him that corn was tall and ripe for only a few weeks in the year. Where did harvest mice live, then, while it was growing? Would they really have time to build a nest and rear their young, before the reaper came? They would have to hurry.

"Hurry," called Aunt Lizard, like an echo. Looking back, she saw with annoyance that he was standing still, gazing into the cornfield. She called again and beckoned urgently. ". . . late," he heard.

Yes, too late now, he thought. Harvest mice, rabbit, badger, horses, they would all have to wait till he could come back. What was it people used to say to him when he was young? — "it won't run away." That was true, anyhow. He moved after her, still looking back; then turned and raced forward, shutting his eyes . . .

CHAPTER SEVEN

Harvestmen

He opened his eyes. He had kept in his mind such a clear picture of the pathway that for a moment he was surprised. Once more all was changed. The long grass on the headland had been cut, and had sprung again in a soft apple-green carpet, sprinkled with white clover. The evening breeze ruffled the little apple trees in Old Park next to the paddock; feathered maidens, he remembered. Against their silvery green, along the headland, grew a tangle of field flowers, vetches, wild pea, scabious and mallows; purple, crimson, lavender and pink. Shakespeare or not, Aunt Lizard would want to paint those. In Chequers the wheat was high and yellow. The heavy heads swayed and rustled with a sound like autumn thistles. He chewed a kernel: hard and crisp already. There was no time to lose. First thing tomorrow, he must start looking for nests in the corn.

Bumping along on his bicycle, he saw a curl of smoke beyond the spinney. Aunt Lizard had been here since the day before yesterday. The house was all ready for him, his bunk made up, the supper laid, a potato pie toasting by the fire in a little Dutch oven she had brought, like a square biscuit tin. He felt a quick pang of jealousy, as though she had stolen a march. No one should be here when he was away, not even for a day or two, not even Aunt Lizard . . . He greeted her a shade distantly, then went to stow the bicycle by the wood stack, and unstrap the saddlebag. He threw the bag on to his bunk, and himself beside it, taking a deep breath.

In May, a small black spider had been living in a crevice in the window-sill. Now he blew softly into the crack, and it ran out. He smiled to himself. As though guessing the reason, Aunt Lizard said, "Old Jim Honeywood was right. We've a plague of daddy-long-legs. Look!" He saw a little creature, with long legs like sand-coloured threads, race around the skirting board. Reaching the sand-coloured matting, it paused, invisible. Ralph saw others about the floor. He said, "They're harvestmen," and, forgetting his grievance, began to tell Aunt Lizard about them.

Last year in the Christmas term, he had found himself, to his dismay, down to give a talk on spiders. These winter lectures at school were designed to instruct the speakers no less than the audience. When he first saw "Spiders: Oliver" on the list, in the headmaster's neat script, Ralph knew nothing about the creatures. He had rarely noticed them, except for a garden spider he had once watched from his bed when he was ill, and the big black ones that sometimes haunted the bath in their Chelsea flat. To be "down for a lecture", he found, was much the same as being in detention. It meant slaving a whole Saturday afternoon in the library, and sitting night after night in the art room, while the sixth formers rehearsed their play, drawing spiders and webs from pictures in *The Wonder Book of Nature*. But he was pleased when he first saw his sketch of a trapdoor spider, enlarged to a monster under the epidiascope. The task suddenly became amusing. Monsters they should have: he branched out among black widows and tarantulas. The ordeal safely over, he had seemed to come across spiders everywhere. He began to be almost as intrigued by them as he was already by mice. Uncle Alfred told him about Dr. Thomas Muffet — father of Little Miss Muffet? — and his book, *A Theatre of Insects*, with its drawings of prancing, twinkling spiders. One Saturday he and Aunt Lizard travelled across the county by bus to see ancient Muffet's Farm, said to have been the home of Dr. Muffet more than three hundred years ago. Aunt Lizard approved of this new interest. She had a way of fostering anything that came under her roof, flies excepted. The harvestmen had arrived in her absence — perhaps through a grating under the west window — to join the house spiders already in possession. He noticed that she was putting down water for them in bottle lids, as she had done in Chelsea.

To Ralph they were a happy omen. Harvestmen, harvest mice — he would find them both. And what about the badger? He would start watching for it at once. He went out as soon as he had unpacked; then reappeared on the doorstep. "Do come quick. Something so queer, in the spinney. Come and listen!"

He led her to the darkest spot among the trees. They groped their way, shading their eyes against switching branches. Ralph clutched her wrist. "There — listen!"

In the darkness she heard a curious croaking or sobbing sound, like a blackbird's distress note; but it was not a bird. They pressed forward, their ankles brushed by rushes, feet sinking in the soft ooze of the underground spring. Ralph shone his torch downward. The call stopped. Ralph gave a cry: something stirred in the beam, with a familiar lurching movement. "A toad! Oh, I bet it's ours! Mr. Crawley, remember?" The torch beamed steadily on its golden eyes. The toad moved out of the beam. Ralph switched it off, and they waited in the dark. No sound came. Could the toad really have uttered that call? Then, as they moved away, it began again, a low monotonous note, more a piping than a croaking. They turned back and found it again by torchlight, and now they could see its throat pulsing as it sent out the plaintive call.

Ralph felt sure he had found his old friend. He resolved to bring him slugs and woodlice every day. They left reluctantly, and went along the track to the field path. Grasshoppers rasped, shrill and invisible, in the moonlight that silvered the wheat. Every dozen rows, Ralph noticed, there was a thread of darkness where the seed drill had missed a row. By going carefully, stepping sideways, he could use these gaps to look for nests in the heart of the cornfield. He knew exactly how they would look, like balls of plaited wheat leaves. He could not sleep for thinking of them. He sat up on his bunk, looking out at the stars. How large and low they seemed here by the sea. He felt that he could put out a hand and touch them.

The sun woke him; not striking low on the window-sill, but shining down on his face from above. Outside he could hear a whirring sound, almost like a reaper; yet it couldn't be that. He leaned out and listened. It *was* the reaper. He was too late, his plan was ruined; tired from end-of-term celebrations, the journey and his starlight vigil, he had slept half the morning.

"Oh," he cried, as Aunt Lizard came in from the garden, "Why did you let me? I wanted to look in the corn — and now they'll smash up all the nests. Oh, why do they have to cut it so soon?"

"But it's ready. Harvest does start early here. In race week, Mr. Riley was saying."

"Is this race week?"

"But for the war. Listen," she went on quickly, "I've been talking to Mr. Riley. Would you like to help with the harvest? They want another hand for stooking."

To help in the field — to handle the sheaves, where the nests would be: that seemed his best chance now to find the harvest mice — if only the machine hadn't mangled them. He ran out to wash at the well. The brick path was warm under his bare feet. He pulled a handful of black currants, hot from the sun, and leaned over to look into the well. The water seemed a long way down. Was it drying up? Tacker said it never had yet; but perhaps they should save water. He pulled off his pyjamas and washed by rolling in the long dewy grass behind the hedge. Wheeling her bicycle from the woodstack, Aunt Lizard called, "Have you been stung? What *are* you doing?"

"Zulu bath. Like in *The Wolf Cub's Handbook*." She clicked her tongue and went off to buy food. He dried by rolling in a sunny patch by the damson tree; the short grass there was like a rough towel. He must hurry. Aunt Lizard had left dungarees on his bunk, with a long-sleeved shirt. How queer of her; he would be stifled in those. He rummaged in his bag for running shorts and singlet, then swallowed a mug of tea that stood ready, and devoured a thick sandwich of hot fried tomato and bacon dripping. He wondered if the rabbit had danced at sunrise. He had missed that, too. Then he remembered that this was only the first morning of the holidays. Weeks and weeks lay ahead.

Mr. Riley was driving the reaper. Mr. Doggett was chargehand in the field, with a team of old hands, Tacker, Harry, Fred and Jake. Each was paired off with a novice — Jill, Tess, Sally, young Bob Doggett and Ralph himself. Mr. Doggett showed them how to handle the sheaves, taking one under each arm and planting them firmly, the tops caught together to make a windproof stook. But, of the young ones, only Sally and Jill proved strong enough to handle two sheaves at a time. The rest were soon ordered to take them singly. Ralph, Mr. Doggett's partner, scurried at top speed in the effort to keep up. For the moment, mice were forgotten; again all that mattered was Mr. Doggett's approval. Once or twice there was a respite, when the binder twine broke and the machine had to stop. Tacker went to help, while Mr. Doggett twisted wheat stems into rough cords to bind the loose sheaves. During one of these waits, he asked Ralph, "How old are you then?"

"Nearly thirteen."

Mr. Doggett grunted. Ralph had a moment's doubt. Was he going to be sent away, as too young and feeble? But Mr. Doggett went on to grumble that Bob was going on thirteen too, and there he was, kept away from work for another year. What was the use of that? he asked. And now they talked about keeping boys and girls at school till they were fifteen. "I'd started in the stables time I was twelve. Fifteen! All they'll want to do by then is drive a blasted tractor, or work in a garage." Ralph listened and nodded, deeply flattered. It was the first time Mr. Doggett had offered him anything like a conversation.

He found himself remembering a scrap of talk, between his aunts, which had haunted him for years. Aunt Lizard had come home one day from shopping and said, "Who do you think I saw in Harridges, working as a lift boy? Little Johnny Kenton, Amy's boy." And Aunt Emmy: "Not Johnny, *working*? But he's a child."

"Fourteen. Well, I don't suppose poor Jock left them a penny."

And then Aunt Emmy: "Wouldn't you think her brother could get the boy into an office!"

That was all. Ralph's aunts would have been shocked to know the feeling of dread that came over him at their casual remarks. To be a lift boy, he thought, might not be so bad; he had often envied them. But to be "put into an office" was a fate he could not bear to imagine;

something he feared so deeply that he could never even ask exactly what it meant. And they spoke as though it would be a stroke of luck! Somehow that increased his depression. Once you were caught like that, you never escaped, he was sure; you could never be a gamekeeper or a naturalist, let alone a gipsy.

But now, standing here in the harvest field, in a golden vista of sun and stubble, the shadow lifted. He began to feel a new confidence. He thought of the pay packet he had brought home at Whitsun. Here they were, he and Aunt Lizard, with a cottage of their own; and here he was, learning to be a farmhand, working outdoors, as he had always meant to do. His birthday came in January — like a horse, grandfather used to say. In a year — just over a year — he would be old enough to start work properly; to start *here*, like Sally. It was a revelation. Away on the brink of his thoughts hovered the cloud, the old fear of losing his father, and having to leave school; but he worked in a dream of independence, warm and reassuring as the sun on his back. His face ran with sweat, his muscles ached, his singlet stuck to his spine, cornstalks and thistles were scratching his arms and legs, but he had never felt so happy in his life.

All the young ones had come out with arms and legs bare; now they were suffering for it. The old men seemed comfortable, even cool, in long shirt sleeves, waistcoats and heavy boots, trouser legs tied with string; Mr. Doggett and Tacker had neat straps for theirs — "Elijahs", Ralph had heard these called. Bob and Sally and the girls kept taking swigs from water-bottles. Ralph cursed himself for not having brought one. Mr. Doggett shook his head at the drinkers, but wasted no breath on them; they had long years to learn sense, his look declared. When the reaper stopped at noon he advised Ralph, "Don't you trouble to bring no water. Only makes you thirsty, swilling away like that. You fetch along a few sticks of rhubarb to chew on."

Ralph lingered, looking among the sheaves, but saw no sign of a mouse. The men sat down in the shade of the spinney and took out bottles of cold tea, packets of bread and cheese, pipes and tobacco. Tacker had a raw onion. Fred strolled down to The Wheatsheaf for a pint. The boys, devouring fish-paste sandwiches, followed him to buy fizzy drinks. Jill and Tess went off to their tomato house. Old Harry took out a great wedge of yellow cake and began cutting small pieces and moistening them with tea. He had lately lost his remaining teeth, and the district nurse kept urging him to have a set of dentures. He would starve without them, she said; but he was obstinate. Now, mumbling away at the cake, he said cheerfully to Ralph, "Cake! I eats cake for breakfast, cake for dinner, cake for tea and cake for supper. I *likes* cake. Lucky, ain't it?"

Back at the spring house, Ralph took a cup to the well. Once started, he drank pint after pint of water, sluicing his scratches and letting the sun lick up the icy drops. He pulled a thick rhubarb stalk, chewed it and spat out the fibre. Mr. Doggett was right; the sharp taste lingered on his palate, and the craving for water was slaked. Fizzy drinks were nothing to it. He pulled an armful to take back to the field.

The house, behind drawn curtains, was cool and dark as a shady wood. Aunt Lizard had gone out again, leaving his lunch between lettuce leaves; thin oatcakes spread with cottage cheese, a ripe tomato from the greenhouse, soda bread and honey. She had made the cheese herself with some leftover pints of milk, a present from the girl on the float: straining the sour milk through muslin overnight, salting it and adding chopped chives from the garden at The Race; their own were not yet ready to pick. Ralph tasted cautiously, then finished the oatcake in two bites and took another. Cuckoo had thrown himself panting on the floor. Ralph took a cigarette from Aunt Lizard's box and lay down, gently pillowing his head on the cat, who flounced a little in protest and then began to lick Ralph's hair. They relaxed together, both watching the little swirl of blue smoke in the dim light. Across the open windows, the curtains hung motionless.

The whirr of the reaper pulled Ralph to his feet. He tore off shorts and singlet, and pulled on the shirt and dungarees that Aunt Lizard had left ready. Then he remembered Mrs. Hooper's saying that, in India, one always kept the windows *shut* in the daytime, "to keep the cool air in". He went round slamming and latching them, scooped up the cat and dropped him under the bushes, then plunged back into the fierce sunlight. But Mr. Riley would not have Bob and Ralph there in the afternoon. Colts shouldn't work all day, he reminded Mr. Doggett; they could come back after tea if they liked. Turned loose, the boys made for the seashore and lay in the reeds, waiting for the tide.

Aunt Lizard had some idea of finding war work to do in the holidays; and at teatime something turned up that was to keep her busy for years. In return for the chives, she had left a small cheese at The Race, with an oatcake and a loaf of soda bread. The owner showed these to a friend who ran a village clinic for mothers and babies. Now the friend called to ask Aunt Lizard if she would come and talk to the mothers and give them new ideas for wartime meals. Aunt Lizard protested that she had had no training: "I can only make the old country things, that we used to rely on, living in the wilds."

"Oh my dear, *yes*." The caller beamed at her. She was middle-aged, with a capable, dedicated air that reminded Ralph again of Mrs. Hooper: the war had brought her a new life. Changing to a serious note, she explained, "We all think of an ordinary dinner as meat and potatoes and cabbage. Soon — I'm very much afraid — we may only have the potatoes and cabbage." She gave them both a solemn look, then smiled again and plunged into details. There was milk to spare in the village; some people had started keeping goats, as well as hens, pigs and rabbits. Cottage cheese would make a splendid change from the mousetrap on the ration. Then, for oatcakes and soda bread, one could still buy coarse oatmeal and wholemeal flour from a mill on the other side of Sussex. Could Aunt Lizard suggest more recipes? Aunt Lizard could and did. Ralph went back to the stooking, leaving them deep in pig swill and home-cured bacon, bean hotpot with scones, potato cakes and rabbit Maryland, dried this and salted that. Work of this sort for Aunt Lizard fitted in well with his own idea of country independence. He liked the notion of her doing something quite different, while he worked out in the fields. In peacetime, of course, she would be painting; that would be all right too.

The reaper went round, the sun sank lower and grew red in the evening sky. When they stopped at last, the men said the field should be finished easily tomorrow. The words brought Ralph's thoughts back to the harvest mice. So far, though he had kept a look-out whenever he had the chance, he had seen only grasshoppers. All the animals in the field, he knew, would be moving towards the centre as the reaper circled. Now there was a huge island left; stupid rabbits would be crouching in it, perhaps Peter Quince, perhaps a hare. Unless they had the sense to creep out in the night, they would all be killed tomorrow — cut up by the machine if they stayed, bashed with sticks if they broke cover. He strolled home and sat on his bunk to think, gazing out at the clear pale sky. Aunt Lizard, in the rocking chair, had Cuckoo on her knee; she was taking "sweethearts" out of his coat. Suddenly she leaned back, laughing: "I was brushing his fur, and a moth flew out. It really did — You moth-eaten old object," she said affectionately. The cat, offended at her laughter, crossed the floor and sprang up beside Ralph.

How hot it was! Heat seemed to radiate from Cuckoo's fur. Ralph took hold of the window bar and swung it to and fro, stirring the air. Cuckoo lifted his face approvingly to the breeze. "Punkah coolie," thought Ralph, and swung harder. The cat spotted something stuck on the window jamb. He reached up to touch it with his paw. A tiny black object dropped to the sill. It was the little spider, dead. Ralph was amazed at how sorry he felt. Then it dawned on him that he must have killed it himself, when he slammed the window after lunch. Things were always getting killed, he thought in dejection. How could he save those creatures out in the wheatfield? He asked Aunt Lizard suddenly, "Do you know a spell to make it rain?"

"A spell! What do you mean? 'Kill a spider and it will rain tomorrow'?"

He was startled. "'Kill a spider' — why did you say that?"

"Well, I don't know. I heard it somewhere once."

"Would it count if you'd killed one by accident?"

"Heavens, I don't know. We don't want rain at harvest, surely?"

"I should like," he said slowly, one finger touching the dead spider, "I'd like it to be fine all the morning, and then rain cats and dogs, just when Mr. Riley got to the last bit."

He had meant to go out and walk round the field again; but sleep overcame him all at once, at the supper table, so that he could hardly finish his soup and stumble into bed. Next moment, it seemed, the sun was shining again. The morning was still and brilliant. No chance of rain, he thought; yet, when they gathered in the field, Mr. Doggett was shaking his head and muttering, "Too bright too early." Work began with a swing, but soon Ralph felt himself flagging. As the morning wore on, a heat haze dulled the sunlight. The air became close and heavy. Arms and legs ached; flies hovered tormentingly. In the distance, once or twice, Ralph thought he caught the low rumble of gunfire; it was thunder out at sea, the men said. After the dinner break, Mr. Riley let the boys stay on. Banks of purplish cloud rolled up from the south and gave zest to the work: they were racing the storm. Then it was on them in a flash; rain burst over them like a wave. They dropped their sheaves and ran for the barn. Ralph flew home, in case Aunt Lizard had left the windows open, but she was there. Through the window she saw him coming and hurried to let him in. He checked the bicycles by the woodstack; they were safely covered. In that short distance he had been soaked, his hair plastered to his skull. It was almost dark indoors, between flashes of lightning. Downs, fields and spinney were hidden behind a glassy waterfall of rain. It thundered on the roof in waves of sound, like a high wind, ebbing for a few moments and then gathering fury. Lightning flickered, thunder crashed, heavy drops sluiced down from the eaves, bouncing and splashing on the sills. From the south window, Ralph saw the quince tree blown into a whirl of grey leaves. Dead flowers like brown tassels blew from the Spanish chestnut; the leaves streamed with rain. There would be no more reaping today, he thought happily. Quite a spell, after all, that one about killing a spider! He turned to look at Aunt Lizard. She was writing at the table. Beside her were bunches of sage, thyme and balm, bought from a market garden, to be hung up to dry in paper bags. She would make a good witch, he thought, with her bright brown eyes and long brown fingers, her bunches of herbs, her cat, the birch broom by the door, the cauldron over the fire . . . She looked up and met his smile. He asked quickly, "What are you writing? More spells?"

"Oh . . . recipes."

"Aha. *Fire burn and cauldron bubble* . . ."

She laughed. "As a matter of fact — I've just had a message from some women's club. The Wild Hill Sisterhood. Now *they* should be a coven!"

"And they want you to join?"

"Well, they want me to go and talk about soda bread."

He wondered what he could do tomorrow; but he need not have worried. Before the day was out, two more jobs had been lined up for him.

The air was cool after the storm, but the skies did not clear. Evening set in grey and chilly. Ralph brought in wood and made a fire. They put potatoes to bake in the oven and settled to beggar-my-neighbour as though it were a winter night. Drips of rain made the fire hiss now and then. In the autumn, Ralph thought, they would have chestnuts at the door, ready for roasting.

"Cones!" said Aunt Lizard suddenly.

"What?"

"They're lovely to start a fire in winter." She put down her cards. "Ralph, you remember that pinewood — on the way here — when we saw the weasel?"

"Stoat."

"I dare say. Well, it wasn't far from here. Do you think you could find it again? A few sacks of cones would come in very handy."

"But will there be cones now? In summer?"

"They're a summer crop. Last year's, you see, just fallen. You could go tomorrow; why not?"

Before bedtime the rain ceased to patter on the tiles. He wandered out into Chequers and across the stubble. He tried to go barefoot, to keep his sandshoes dry, but quickly pulled them on again; the stubble felt sharp as knives. The patch of uncut wheat lay draggled in the dusk, flattened this way and that by the storm. The hidden creatures were reprieved, he felt sure. It might not be cut for days. Perhaps Tacker would have to finish it with a reaping hook.

The air smelled of wet straw, wet yarrow, sweet briar. Poking about in the hedge, he tracked down a briar bush by the scent. He thought of the gaps in their own hedge, round the skeleton hawthorn stems, gnawed bare by rabbits. He would take some briar cuttings and plant them there. As he picked a piece to show Aunt Lizard, someone came walking softly along by the hedge. It was Mr. Riley, on his way to the observers' post.

"Hello," he said, "blackberries already?"

When Ralph said, "Sweetbriar," Mr. Riley shone his torch on the briars and looked carefully at them. "H'm, yes. Good stock. Seen any more about? Or .. what d'you call them — dog roses?"

"Oh yes. Hundreds." He was surprised. As the manager seemed to be waiting, he added, "There were lovely ones by the shore, and that lane up to the downs. Oh, and white ones, in our spinney."

Mr. Riley asked, as Aunt Lizard had done, "Do you think you could find them again? Well, here's a job for you. The hips will soon be getting ripe. Look around, when you're out on your bike, and pick a few, the best you see. Keep them separate, you know, and label them, dog roses, white briar and so on. And bring them along to the office. Then we'll pick out what we want, and you can go back later for more. Mind you mark the bushes — bits of coloured wool or something."

Still Ralph was mystified, until the manager explained. No rose stocks could come in from abroad. Anyway, for the next few years, they would be growing other things. But the war wouldn't last for ever. "We don't want to lose all our roses, whatever the war ag. chaps say. I thought we might raise a few briar stocks from seed, and bud them in our spare time, and save what we can for the peace."

Corn harvest, cone harvest, rose hips; then there would be wild crabs to gather for jelly, sloes for sloe gin, blackberries for jam, so long as the sugar held out; mushrooms to be dried and stored in jars, haricot beans to be picked and shelled later.

Once, on holidays with Aunt Lizard, there had been smells of paint and Indian ink. Now the smells were of pine needles and cones, herbs, damson cheese and seething jam, peeled shallots, hot vinegar and tomato pulp. Ralph found the pinewood and spent several mornings stuffing a sack with cones, to be tipped into a barrel which Tacker found for them. The trees were set with small green cones; dry cones strewed the ground below, and the wide grassy path bordering the road. Each morning a party of children on horseback cantered by, otherwise he had the wood to himself.

While the barrel filled up with cones, the store cupboard, too, was slowly filling with jars and bottles; purple jam, red tomato sauce, green mint jelly, dark brown chutney, and one jar of horse radish root from the garden, dried and grated — mixed with human skin, Ralph complained, sucking his knuckles after his turn with the cheese grater. Dwarf haricot beans ripened in the vegetable patch; green quinces turned pale gold. Beyond the hedge the tallest almond trees were heavy with green nuts. In the spinney, too, white nuts were ripening on the hazels; and one day, in a pasture by the shore, he found a walnut tree. Aunt Lizard said that walnuts, like mushrooms, were a farm crop: he must get leave to pick them. When he tracked down the owner in a pig yard, the man looked astonished at his request: "Mostly," he said, "they just come and get 'em" — adding thoughtfully, "Then Nailer has a bit o' sport." Nailer, an ugly cross-bred terrier, leered up at his name, showing wicked teeth. Ralph decided to forget the walnuts; they wouldn't be ripe for weeks, anyway. He and Bob Doggett competed for mushrooms in the home paddock, but Bob was usually the winner. Ralph got up at dawn, but he would linger by the garden hedge, looking for the rabbit.

He looked in vain; all the rabbits seemed to be gone from their burrow. Had Cuckoo caught them, or scared them away? No: as he grew older, Cuckoo had lost his zeal for hunting. It struck Ralph that nowadays he hardly ever saw the cat out of doors, unless he or Aunt Lizard were in the garden. Even then, Cuckoo seemed nervous and jumpy, fidgeting and glancing over his shoulder, or staring into the hedge as though some other creature might be hidden there. Could he be afraid of the badger? One evening, while Ralph was staking tomato plants and Cuckoo was taking the air, he saw the cat jump and stiffen, arch his back and gaze fiercely into a clump of rhubarb; and then Ralph did fancy that a dark shadow moved under one of the giant leaves, merging into the shadows of the spinney. He found nothing there. But next morning an odd thing happened. Aunt Lizard hung out the cheese bag to drip from her clothes line, while she swept the house. As soon as her back was turned, the cheese bag vanished. She found it on the other side of the garden, the muslin ripped to pieces and most of the curds gone. The bag, swinging two or three feet from the ground, had been dragged from its hanger. Would a badger really do that, and in broad daylight? How quick, how cunning, how agile it must be. She was vexed for her lost cheese, and Ralph for his lost chance: oh, to have seen such a feat! But he had been miles away on the downs. He had marked a sloe tree for later visits — father, on his last leave, had left a bottle of gin in the flat — and brought home a sheaf of rowan boughs with glistening red berries; but at these Aunt Lizard shook her head. Merren McKay had tried rowan jelly and said it was *weirsh* (a good Scottish word) and a waste of sugar.

Now Aunt Lizard was launched on her new career. The sisterhood talk was successful, and her name appeared in a local paper. Ralph came across it by accident, wrapped round a piece of haddock, and could hardly wait to get home and read aloud: " "Miss Izard invited each member to sample her bread and cheese. This was muck enjoyed." "

"Printers," she said, "can't always resist."

"No, nor reporters, listen: 'When the speaker had finished the audience sang, *Now thank we all our God.*' " He had heard father say that the youngest reporters had the job of rewriting news from local clubs.

The outcome was more flattering. Letters began to arrive from all over the countryside, asking her to give talks to women's clubs in villages round about. Sometimes she borrowed a pony and trap for the journey; then Ralph went along to hold the pony. More often she travelled by bus or bicycle, while he rambled about at home by himself, or went swimming with Bob and his friends on the incoming tide.

One evening, he strayed into deep water. He was out in the main channel when cramp struck him. It had happened once before, in the swimming bath at school; but this was more frightening. His legs felt numb; he was helpless. He writhed in panic, doubled up and sank. Coming to the surface, he shouted for help, tried to reach a moored boat, shouted again. The other boys were chasing and ducking each other a dozen yards away; they shouted back laughing. He went down again, felt the water singing in his ears, and knew nothing more until he came to his senses on the shore, coughing up water. Red anxious faces hung over him. Just in time, Bob had realized that he wasn't playing, and hauled him out. "You didn't half holler," they said. "And you fought old Bob like a wildcat. Look at his black eye." Bob grinned and blushed. Ralph felt weak and sick from cramp and muddy water, and full of shame at his whole performance. His teeth chattered, he turned blue with cold. But Sally, who always carried matches, lit a fire of dry reeds and driftwood on the bank, and soon he was warm again. He had no intention of telling Aunt Lizard what had happened; so it gave him a jolt to find her already home, looking out for him, calling as he came through the gate, "There you are. Are you all right?" Blast, he thought, someone must have gossiped already. That was the worst of the country. He hung about outside, scraping mud off his bicycle tyres. She came and watched; presently she said, half laughing, "You know, a funny thing happened an hour or two ago. I was coming through Brookfield . . . and I thought I heard you *calling for help*. I stopped and looked everywhere. Wasn't it queer?"

He bent over the wheel, muttering something. A small shiver went down his spine. Brookfield was five miles away. When he looked up she had gone. No point in worrying her, he thought; he would tell her some day. But for years he could not bring himself to do it.

On May Day it had seemed surprising to have a whole day to himself; now it happened quite often. Aunt Lizard would set out early to reach some distant gathering, leaving Ralph to buy and cook their supper. One afternoon, passing a bookshop in the town, he stopped to admire a bird book in the window. The dustjacket showed the head of a cock pheasant, gleaming blue and green, encircled by other heads, swallow, chaffinch, kingfisher, bullfinch. The colouring was perfect: that meant the book would be expensive. Still, he had his harvest money, and more to come, besides what he would earn by picking rose hips. He went in to ask the price. The shopman was busy, and while he waited Ralph picked up something else; a small red book, *Sussex Flora*. No pictures hardly; only one page of faint watercolours, and a map of Sussex. It seemed an odd sort of flower book: no descriptions, either; just a list of flower names and place names. "Green hellebore," he read. "End of Lordington wood, by Brooksnap. Pheasant's Eye. Shingles near first sluice bridge, Eastbourne, Impatient Ladies' Smock. Shady woods; very rare. Hedge bank by roadside E. of W. Grinstead. Pale two-flowered Narcissus. Forest meadows near Horsham. Star of Bethlehem. Dane's Wood, far from any dwelling. Oxlip" — wasn't that one of the Shakespeare flowers Aunt Lizard had done? One of those now lying on the bottom of the sea? He felt sure it was. She would have to paint it again. She would want one to copy. "Oxlip, Ashling Wood." Why — this was a guidebook! It was just what she needed. What other flowers had he found for her, that last spring at Nine Wells? Early purple orchis, primrose, anemone, violet — but they had all those in the spinney. Wild daffodil: that wasn't so common. He looked it up, and found a whole list of woods and copses. Should he copy them out? But there were so many others. He might come back and buy it for Aunt Lizard's Christmas present.

Turning the pages, he saw a note about bilberry pies and puddings. Where could you pick bilberries? In a dozen places, it seemed. "West Harden heath" — that wasn't far away. Aunt Lizard had given one of her talks in a village called East Harden. It struck him that the book might be useful for harvesting, too. In the index he found cranberry, cherry, wild medlar, wild pear. And roses: whole pages of different kinds. Yes, he must buy it, and keep it hidden until Christmas. Meanwhile he could use it himself; starting now, with bilberries. He found the shopman standing with a patient smile at his side. How long had he been there? The book cost five shillings; he had only twopence left. Forgetting to ask about the bird book, forgetting the sausage meat in his saddlebag and the tomatoes at home in the Dutch oven, he took *Sussex Flora* in his hand and set out for West Harden heath.

More than fifty years had passed since the author noted bilberries there; 1887, he read on the title page. Yet when he reached the heath, late in the afternoon, there they were still; mats of red and green leaves, with tiny purple berries. It took a long time to pick enough for a pudding. He found an old cap in his saddlebag, and lined it with dockleaves to hold them. As he toiled away, he kept hearing tiny sounds like matches being struck, from clumps of gorse near by: ripe seedpods exploding in the sun. He picked a handful to sow in the hedge at home. Sweetbriar and gorse were Aunt Lizard's favourite scents. He found ripe blackberries too, wrapping them in leaves; and some other purple fruits, smooth and glossy, which he could not name. He picked a few to show her. Thirsty as he was, he would not allow himself any of these, but chewed sorrel leaves instead. He would be late home, as it was, by the time he had filled the cap with bilberries.

The sun was gone behind the downs when he turned towards home. He wheeled his bicycle up a steep hill — gradient one in five, he guessed — came into sunlight again, and again lost it in the deep winding lanes. When he came within sight of Beaumarsh, the sun showed only a rim of orange beyond the creeks. A long straight road took him from west to east along a high ridge; half-way along it was a lane running south, down to Beaumarsh. As he neared this, he saw another bicycle approaching quickly. A woman was riding it. She looked rather like Aunt Lizard, thin and upright; a moment later he saw that she *was* Aunt Lizard. It struck him that she might have been anxious, and come out to look for him. He put on a spurt; they met at the turning. He held out the capful of bilberries, to forestall reproaches; but she cried, "Oh Ralph! Did you come looking for me? I'd no idea I'd be so late." He said handsomely, "Doesn't matter. How were the hags?" They rode home together. Unpacking his juicy cargo, unlocking the door, Ralph laughed, "*Put on the pan, said greedy Nan* — I'm *famished*." Aunt Lizard retorted, "I don't suppose she said, *Let's wash up before we go* —". The fire had died hours ago. The tomatoes in the oven were still firm. While Ralph relit the fire and put a little water to heat in the cauldron, Aunt Lizard stuffed the tomatoes and set them down by the blaze. There were enough bilberries to line four cups. She added a spoonful of honey to each, poured in a sponge mixture and put the cups in the cauldron. Ralph banked the fire with cones. He could find plenty more. They ate the tomatoes, then played chess for an hour while the cups gently clinked and rattled in the pot. Both were beginners at chess. The game proved odd and interesting, each being left at last with king, queen, and one pawn. They gave it up and ate their puddings, while the cones glowed red as strawberries, and an owl hooted from the spinney.

August went quickly by. Already summer was passing. Swifts no longer wheeled and shrieked overhead. The stooks in Chequers were carted and stacked, Bob leading Captain and Ralph leading Violet across the stubble. The men forked the sheaves on and off the carts. Mr. Doggett and Fred Buckler built the stack. It was shrouded in tarpaulins and left to wait until threshing time. Going out at dusk, Ralph saw the dark outline against the sky, like another house. A house for rats and mice, perhaps. For harvest mice? He had never seen one after all, nor a trace of the beautiful plaited nests he had imagined. Yet he could not give up hope. It struck him that, when at last he found a mouse, he might keep it for a while, if he had somewhere safe; not a cage, but a big enclosure where it could run wild.

Couldn't he build a sort of chicken-run, and plant it with corn, to be ready?

At once the idea gripped him. He would make it in the spinney, where Cuckoo never went, disliking the damp ground there. He spent several hours in the dell, building the run from the remains of Tacker's rabbit-wire, fastened to hazel rods with staples, and roofed over with netting securely tied. One side was made to open like a gate. He went out and gleaned steadily in Chequers, bringing back an armful of wheat stalks and ears. He scattered a handful in the mouse-run, and stored the rest behind the woodstack. The run was shaded by hazels, carpeted with moss; it was ready and waiting. Still he found no mice, though he searched day after day in The Oaks field, round the edge of the red-gold wheat that would soon be ready to cut.

On his way down there one morning, he saw Joe and Ted Lock working in Hammers with Jill and Tess. He went over to watch. They were budding the last of the peaches, Ted told him. He and Joe carried bundles of long shoots, clipped from trees they had made in other seasons. Next year's "wood buds" showed as tiny green specks on the bark. A twig would be cut from one of the shoots, this year's leaves trimmed off, then a single bud cut out. Each was mounted on a slip of bark an inch long, with a thin layer of green tissue behind the bud. The sharp knife made a T-shaped cut in the stock, the bark was lifted and the bud inserted, resting firmly in its niche. Each operation took only a minute or two, and the men went on, leaving Jill and Tess to finish it off; binding bud to stock with raffia and daubing the bandages with pitch. As usual, Ted was not too busy to let Ralph try his hand. Afterwards he marked his own stock with a peeled twig; he would come out later and put a better mark — plant a red pencil there, perhaps — so that in April he could find it again. If the bud had "taken", he would buy the peach tree later on. They were Sea Eagle buds on plum stocks, Ted explained. The salt winds would make them into sturdy trees: Seaforth trees were famous. They might be trained into fans, like the peaches and nectarines he had seen growing on ancient garden walls. If he came along to Fo'c's'les in a week or two, Ted added, he and Joe would be on to training trees, and he would see how it was done. "We'll make a knifehand of you," he promised. Ralph knew this was meant for chaff, but it fed his secret new assurance.

Bullrush field was being cleared for ploughing. Fred and Harry grubbed out rose trees and tangles of climbing roses, thick with flowers, and piled them into heaps, to be burned later on. Only a few bushes were left; they would be sold in the autumn. But that wasn't the end of the roses. In the autumn, with the briar seed, he would start the cycle again.

In the autumn . . . but it was autumn now, he thought. Overnight, it seemed, the season had changed. There was a new sparkle in the air. The early sun drew a light mist from the grass. Walking under a windbreak of poplars, he thought the shadow of a butterfly went floating across the path. He looked up and saw that it was a yellow leaf. It hovered for a moment, caught in an eddy, then sank to the ground. There were scarlet cuckoo pint berries in the ditch, scarlet rose hips in the hedges. He did not need *Sussex Flora* to find them, or the glossy dark ones in the downland lane, or the little orange hips from white briar roses in the spinney. He filled a chip basket over and over, tilting the hips into separate lots by the potting shed. He helped Jill and Tess to squeeze out the rose seeds, packed in gold fluff and unexpectedly sharp, pricking the fingertips. They were sown in boxes of damp sand and packed in a frame. Ralph borrowed a box to sow the gorse seeds, mixing them with seed from briars, broom and fox-gloves. He was sorry the rabbits had gone, but glad too; now he could make a better hedge.

Blackberries and haws were ripe in the thick hedge between Fo'c's'les and The Oaks. The wheat was cut, and for several days he worked at stooking, then again at carting for the rick; and then the corn harvest was over. There would be no harvest home supper at Seaforth, but on market day Tacker, Fred and Jake disappeared into the town on a spree of their own, drinking all day in the market taverns: "a day for the king," they called it.

Now, with a kind of quiet autumn sadness, Ralph felt the holidays slipping away downhill. The weather, the misty mornings and gentle sunlit afternoons underlined his mood. As he picked blackberries in Fo'c's'les, swallows gathered on telephone wires, and butterflies lazed about the warm hedges; furry red admirals spread their wings to the sun, and once a clouded yellow passed, on wings the exact colour of the clouded yellow apple leaves. The Lock brothers were training young apple trees along the wire fences, for cordons and espaliers. And, with the other knifehands gone, Jill and Tess were making their first attempt, turning two-year-old peach trees into fans: planting a trellis of canes, choosing the strongest shoots and coaxing them to lie flat and take an upward slant like the spokes of a fan, before they were tied into place. As he listened to the four of them, Ralph found himself beginning to know a cordon tree from a fan, or a feathered maiden from a dwarf pyramid. He read the labels, Golden Eagle, Lord Napier, Bellegarde, Waterloo, and wondered who had thought of these dashing names. Only that morning, he had learned that the term "maiden tree" was romantic, not rustic; he had taken them to be "maden trees", as in "boughten cake". Then, reaching for an apple from an old tree in the hedge, Jill said, "I suppose *we* can have these, if the foxes did."

"Foxes?"

"Yes. Fred says the foxes ate the windfalls, when they used to live here, before the earths were stopped." Seeing his puzzled look, she added, "You knew this field was called Fox'ls, didn't you?"

"Oh! — oh, yes, of course." Quickly he rearranged the spelling in his head.

That was a day of surprises. Helping Tess to plant the canes beside her second tree, Ralph swooped to pick up something from the ground; a scrap of china, but not like the ones he had found in Little Stint. It had not the same smoothness or pure colour. He began telling the girls about those scraps. Jill said, "Oh, yes. You mean bits of the Roman villa."

He stared at her.

"There was one here, with a coloured pavement, but it got broken up before the — you know — the antique people found it. They're always ploughing up bits of tiles in Little Stint and Bullrush. There's a whole lot of them in the abbey museum, if you want to go and look."

A Roman villa . . . Ralph felt he had known already that there was something special about those fragments. Now, idling in the sun, picking blackberries, stalking a butterfly, watching the knifehands, he fell into a dream. Perhaps there had been an orchard here, by the villa, with peach and apple trees. (Did they have peaches, in Roman times?) Then he began to think of the man who had lived in the villa, seeing him as a Roman soldier, a centurion, like one in a book at school, in silver armour over dark green tunic, with helmet and crest, the vine staff in his hand. Vines: were there vines here too, as well as peach trees? Or were the sea winds too cold? He pictured the Roman as an exile from the south, striding about this orchard, longing for Italy. He had an idea that this might be all wrong, that not all Romans in Britain were Roman-born, or soldiers either; but never mind that.

The swallows twittered overhead, the picture grew. Marcus, he might have been called. *Marcus in the North*: a good name for a poem. Lines began to form in his mind, rather like the verse of *X Equals Nought*, but his own this time: "*Gladly stream the swallow legions south* . . . No, not *south: forth*, to rhyme with *north* . . . *Grey winds cry loud* . . . *a loud sea echoes them* . . . ." No, he would start with a spring verse, something about the peach trees blossoming, then summer, *then* sad autumn, the sun dying . . . like a sunflower withering . . . and the swallows gone.

Shouts came from across the hedge, where Bob and some other boys were hunting rabbits with the dog called Nailer. Bob was calling them to look at something. He pretended not to hear; he didn't want to see a wretched mangled rabbit. More shouts; Jill and Tess went over, and came back looking cross.

"Cruel little devils," muttered Jill, sitting down again on a box beside her tree.

"What was it?" he asked, lounging on the grass.

"Just a nest of mice they'd smashed up. Harvest mice."

The words cut through his reverie. For a second he looked so stricken that, as he jumped to his feet, she grabbed him by the arm.

"Don't go. They're all dead now. That dog —"

But he tore his arm away and ran. The boys were standing about by the hedge. One held the remains of the nest they had found, made of dry grass, built in a clump of teazles in the ditch. The dog was still chewing and worrying at something. They showed Ralph the nest. He looked at it, then threw it down and ran off.

"If only you'd a-told us," Tacker said that evening, as they dug potatoes in the garden; and again, "If I'd known, I'd have had them all on the look-out. Mice! I daresay we might have found you a dozen."

Ralph went on digging beside him, turning up the dry crisp earth. Potatoes, clean and smooth as russet apples, tumbled about as they shook the withering haulms. His last harvest; he remembered that first day of the holidays, when the time had seemed endless. Now it was over, and he had missed so much. He had never seen the badger, he had missed —

"Threshing time," said Tacker. "That's your best bet. That's when I've seen them little mice, mostly. You come here when we've got the tackle, and — Mice! Gor, if I'd known you wanted them —"

"Will the thresher come soon?" Ralph interrupted, knowing the answer.

"October, November, maybe."

"Yes. Well, I'll be at school, won't I?" he said, savagely forking up another root.

"Mind you don't bash the taters about." Then Tacker began in a reminiscent tone, "When I was a nipper, I wanted to go to the races, but 'twas always a school day, so —" Ralph waited, thinking, Yes, yes, so you played truant, so you caught it next day, you told me before, what's that got to do with — suddenly he saw the point.

"— so they'd bring along their own umpire, and this fancy wicket keeper of theirs, you see, the umpire was his old dad. So all the afternoon it'd be, "How's that, dad?" — "Out, my son. Well played, my son". Our chaps'd get wild, but 'twasn't a bit of good —"

Ralph looked up in surprise. Wicket keeper? Umpire? Then he saw that Aunt Lizard was standing beside them.

Nothing more was said about the thresher; but, as Tacker closed the gate, Ralph went close and whispered, "I'll get a postcard, shall I? And address it to me, at school, and leave it with you — then you could let me know — 'How's that, dad?' "

" 'Out, my son'," Tacker said smartly, like a password, and Ralph heard him laughing to himself as he vanished into the dusk.

CHAPTER EIGHT

Harvest Mice

Ripe apples, crimson against the pale blue sky, covered the twisted trees of an old orchard by the railway line. The May Day frost had not touched them, Ralph thought; yet the orchard seemed forgotten except by the birds. The downs were smoke-blue, watercress beds deep emerald, ploughed fields soft cocoa brown like the inside of a puffball. In the hazy sunshine, hedges were bright with maple leaves, red dogwood twigs and bryony berries. Perched in the guard's van on his bicycle, watching the familiar countryside go by, he felt that in a few hours he had travelled from the grey of early winter back to mellow autumn.

In a few hours . . . it was only yesterday morning that the postcard had come. It seemed a lifetime. Tacker had written just "Sat." and today's date; but, when the card was handed to him after breakfast, Ralph felt himself colouring guiltily, as though everyone — the postman, the head boy who took in the letters, the master who sorted them — must have read it and guessed what the message meant. His fears were confirmed when another boy caught sight of it. This boy, a newcomer put in Ralph's care when the term began, had been a bugbear ever since. An alert rabbit-faced child, all ears and spectacles and twitching nose, he had arrived without a trace of homesickness or shyness, primed with ideas for practical jokes, learned from books. He was doggedly working through his list; the alarm clock in the first-form cupboard, the chalking of the mistress's chair, the white mouse in her desk, the desk lids glued down, all had already been endured. Incredibly, his name was Madden. Word had gone out that, because of his youth and innocence, he was not to be too drastically suppressed just yet. He remained delighted with himself; it was Ralph who blushed for him. Now, heedless of any code about other people's letters, he said blithely, in ringing tones, "What a short postcard. What do they mean, 'Sat.'?" Ralph quickly turned the card over, then stuffed it into his pocket. No one else had noticed anything. Escaping from Madden, he went straight to the library, empty at this hour, and took out a book of road maps. He measured the distance to Beaumarsh with his thumbnail. Eighty miles, about. But if you caught a train at Guildford, you could be there in just one more hour — there, at Beaumarsh, where they were threshing tomorrow; where Tacker and Bob Doggett and the rest would be looking out for harvest mice. Tomorrow: but of course he couldn't go. He had a moment's vision of marching into the headmaster's study to explain, and ask for special leave. Flip might have brought it off. There were times, like this, when he missed Flip badly: but he felt he could never manage it for himself. And yet, he thought, the request wouldn't be outrageous. Tomorrow was half-term Saturday, and a holiday. In the morning there was a bicycle paper chase, and he was one of the hares. Aunt Lizard had written that she couldn't get away to the spring house; but she would come in the afternoon to take him and Madden out to tea. Suppose he asked Aunt Liz to take them to Beaumarsh, instead of to Hatfield or St. Albans? But, he realized, there would never be time. She wasn't bringing her car, she had no petrol. Long before they could get there by train, it would be dark and the threshing over. Still, Tacker might have got a mouse for him. They could stay the night: why not? The house was there, waiting. It was a waste to leave the place empty. Then, with a shock, he looked up to find Madden at his side, watching him with interest. He said sharply, "What are you doing? You aren't allowed in here."

"I came to look for you. Please would you sharpen my pencil?" He turned a wide-eyed look on the book of maps; a knowing look, Ralph thought. But that was silly: the child had nothing to be knowing about. He had no hope of getting to Beaumarsh . . . had he? Still, as he got ready for hare-and-hounds at odd moments during the day, pumping his bicycle tyres, tearing up a great bag of scent, he allowed himself to pretend that he really was going. He tested his lamps. The two hares would be leaving in daylight, after breakfast; but, after all, they might lose their way and get benighted, as in *Tom Brown*. Stealthily as a hen "stealing" its nest, he pocketed a sausage at dinnertime, a rock cake at tea, a baked potato at supper. Extra food always came in handy. Rail fares would have been the problem, if he *had* been going to Beaumarsh; but, on his return to school, he had forgotten to hand in his harvest money. It was still in the bicycle toolbag, wrapped in an oily rag. At bedtime he thought again of asking permission; but instinct was against it. If he told anyone about the mice, they would never come true. He got into bed intending to sort out his intentions quietly, but he fell at once into a deep sleep. Waking before daybreak, he was up in an instant, as cool and clear-headed as though he had planned every detail; gathering clothes and tiptoeing to dress in a bathroom, then down to the bootroom for coat and shoes. He left his cap, but slung the bag of scent over his shoulder. Holding his breath, he slid back the bolts on the side door, and was out in the damp laurel-smelling darkness, with not a star to be seen, but no rain either; and round to the bicycle shed. He had left his bicycle in the first rack by the door, trouser-clips on the handlebars: he had long trousers now, and a good thing too — they made him look so much older. He had a bad moment as he closed the shed door again; a gust of wind caught the corrugated iron of the shed roof, and shook it with a clatter like a stage thunderstorm. He waited for a window to go up, for a shout, "Who's there?" But nothing happened, except another gust, and another clatter; and he realized that the roof must have been doing that all night. He mounted and rode beside the laurels, side-slipping dangerously on soft mud, but making no sound. Outside the gate at last, he turned south and rode at top speed, keeping to the lanes, by-passing villages, running before the wind like a racing yacht.

Rain clouds followed, but he outran them. For an hour he saw no one but a farmer, ploughing by tractor headlamps. Dawn broke through bars of crimson. He remembered to leave a little scent now and then. Crossing a railway bridge, he was challenged by a home guard patrol, and showed the bag of torn paper, gasping, "Paper chase". They laughed and let him go. Even Flip could not have managed better. Then he had his biggest stroke of luck. On the edge of Buckinghamshire, pausing at the roadside to eat his rations, he was engulfed by a Canadian army convoy, also taking a brief halt. Someone offered him a cigarette. Someone else asked where he was going. His heart in his mouth, he said recklessly that it was half-term, and he was going home. A moment later he found himself and his bicycle stowed away in the back of a truck, speeding in convoy down the black roads, past bleak windy fields where land girls were topping and loading sugar beet, through pinewoods and over heathery commons, until they dropped him at a railway station in the middle of Surrey.

The stack in The Oaks was already threshed; away in the distance he could hear the sound of an engine from Chequers. He pressed on down the lane, waved to the Lock brothers — planting fruit stocks in Hammers — and swished through drifts of brown sweet-smelling poplar leaves, along the farm road. Bullrush and Chequers were newly ploughed. By the barn stood a caravan, home of the travelling engineer. A pleasant whiff of hot oil reached him from the engine that drove the thresher. The dishevelled stack no longer looked like a house. They were all there, hard at work, just as he had pictured: Tacker and Mr. Doggett on the rick, cutting twine and pitching sheaves; Fred and Harry building the straw stack; Jill and Tess, coifed like nuns against the clouds of dust, raking away at the chaff that poured out under the machine — careful not to stand upright for fear of being scalped by the racing belts; Jake and Jim Honeywood bagging the grain. Ralph came to stand near, watching eagerly. At any moment one of the little mice, flushed from its winter nest, might scamper out of the corn. Dust drifted over him. He sneezed, but never took his eyes from the rick. He came nearer, and the driver waved and shouted at him to stand back. Suddenly the sound of machinery died. Mr. Doggett and the driver conferred, and Mr. Doggett called, "Twenty minutes". In the silence, the men climbed down, too stiff and grimy to talk. The girls stretched, shaking out their head-wrappings, wiping dust and chaff from their eyelashes, writhing as it worked down their necks and through their socks. It was knocking-off time, but the tackle was there, the weather was good: no question of leaving until the stack was done; but everyone would be glad to finish this dirty job. Then Mr. Riley drove up with pay-packets, and a crate of bottled beer. At once there were grins all round, as though a schoolmaster had produced a hamper of cakes. Ralph caught up at last with Tacker, waiting while he tilted a bottle.

"Thanks for the card. Have you —"

"You got it all right, then."

"Yes. Have you —"

"They let you off then." Tacker took another swig.

"No, I played truant. I say, have you seen —"

Tacker lowered the bottle, whistled through his teeth and shook his head, laughing delightedly. "Cor, you'll cop it when you go back. Get the cane, won't you?"

"They don't cane you at our school, we have to dig the garden instead." This time he brought out in a rush, "*Are there any harvest mice*?"

But Tacker was unaccountably deaf: trying his knife on his thumb, shaking his head and grumbling, "This knife o' mine wouldn't go through a rotten apple. Left my stone over your place, too. Just by your woodstack, I left it." He looked at Ralph, who said dully, "I'll fetch it, shall I?" He could see why the old man was putting him off; he had found no mice, and didn't want to disappoint him. So he had come all this way for nothing; or had he? There was still the afternoon.

When he reached the garden, he forgot the mice for a minute. Here was something new. The woodstack was still there, but now it was enclosed in a neat shed. He unhooked the door and stepped inside. Tacker's billhook hung on one wall, spade and forks on the other; Tacker — he was sure this was Tacker's handiwork — had rigged up a shelf at the back for things like paint tins, garden lines, the trowel, the whetstone. His bundle of gleanings was still safe, tucked between two logs. Then he saw something else, on the ground between the stacked logs and kindling wood: a small apple barrel, like the one indoors that he had filled with cones. It was covered with fine wire netting. Could Tacker be keeping his ferret in here? He stooped and peered through the wire. The barrel was lined with straw. He heard something move with a small quick rushing sound. Cautiously he lifted the wire.

What he saw made him cry out in surprise. A mouse, the size of an acorn, sat in the middle of a grey sunflower head, munching seed. It was reddish-brown, with a long soft tail. A dormouse, he thought with a leap of joy; but how tiny it was . . . and then: "It's a *harvest* mouse," he breathed to himself, and broke into crazy soundless laughter. For months this little creature had rustled in and out of his dreams; but this wasn't a dream. (And clever Tacker, crafty old fox, sending him for the whetstone!) He wanted to skip and jump, to rush out and fetch the others — but only for a moment. The first dizzy excitement over, he sat down on the chopping-block, gazing at the mouse. It seemed to catch sight of him; but after a slight pause and turn, as though to make for shelter, as though asking itself, *Need I stop eating?* — it stayed where it was, nibbling away, one dark eye fixed on him. He did not stir again, even when the straw parted and another mouse appeared. As it moved, he saw the white underside, the colour of barley, and the way its tail curled round, like a hop bine or a bindweed shoot. It climbed up into the sunflower, sprawling for a moment on the edge, tiny body stretched, supple as though it were boneless, made of fur and elastic. It took a seed, darted away and sat in the straw, nibbling rapidly, like a squirrel with a fir cone. Ralph put up his hand to take an ear of corn from the gleanings; then he thought of the mouse-run in the spinney. Securing the wire lid, he picked up the barrel, carried it out to the run and laid it on its side, like a Nissen hut. He took away the lid, went back for the gleanings and strewed them about the run. Again he sat down to watch. For a long while there was no sound, but presently he caught a faint scurrying, and a glimpse of red-brown fur, the colour of the wheat in The Oaks. He could see why Gilbert White talked about "red mice". Of course, the wire run wouldn't keep them in, the mesh was too big to imprison such tiny mice; but he hoped they would stay for a long time, perhaps for the winter. Then next year they would have young ones. He would sow corn for them; he would find a dormouse, too, perhaps. The spinney would be a sort of preserve, like a bird sanctuary.

At length something penetrated his thoughts; not a sound, but a silence. The threshing had stopped. He realized that the sun was low down behind the trees. How long had he been here? With a last long look into the barrel, where the mice remained in hiding, he made his way back to the field. As he came near, he remembered Tacker's stone, and stopped short; but threshing was over, they were all packing up to go, covering the straw, loading sacks into a lorry. Tacker gave him a look and grinned. Ralph began to stammer his thanks.

"Good job I'd got a spare wi' me," Tacker said, tossing a whetstone in his hand. "I'd an idea you might find something over your place to keep you busy. Turned 'em out of the stack first thing this morning."

"They're in the spinney. Come and see." But someone was calling Tacker; he went to help with the tarpaulins. Ralph strolled over to look at the engine. Wiping his hands, the driver nodded to him and said after a while, "Not many of these left nowadays. They'll be going out after the war, I expect. Same as windmills and watermills — and that little house over there." He nodded towards the spring house. Seeing Ralph look puzzled, the man added, "Built for a threshing house, first off, I bet that was. Ever wondered why you find them little round houses on farms?"

"*Do* you? I didn't —"

"Fitted up with machinery, they used to be. A horse'd walk round and round, like a turnspit. Horse power, they still talk about, don't they? Precious few horses now, though. Fewer still after the war." He picked up his coat, nodded again and went whistling off to his caravan.

The little house, that had seen so many changes, smelled homely and pleasant: a blend of distemper, cones, herbs, wood ash, and a strong new whiff of apples. Tacker had picked their small crop and laid them out on newspapers. Sunlight filled the west window. Ralph lit the fire, drew water and hung the kettle on its hook. He had no food left but a beetroot sandwich, bought at the station. He swallowed it in two bites, grimacing at the wishy-washy taste; a pity Cuckoo isn't here, he thought. Beetroot was one of Cuckoo's treats; others were melon, asparagus and pickled cherries. But he didn't want to think of Cuckoo now, any more than he wanted to think of Aunt Lizard, Uncle Alfred, school . . . He inspected the store cupboard. Hungry as he was, he did not quite fancy eating jam or chutney without bread. He found a small tin of baked beans — that was much better. He opened it, meaning to heat the beans in a pan, but their enticing smell was too much for him. He devoured them cold, with a teaspoon; roast turkey would not have tasted better. At the back of the shelf he had another lucky find: a packet of flat rye biscuit. He spread the squares with crab apple jelly and crunched his way through them; like eating birch bark, he thought. Their dryness made him thirsty. The kettle boiled and he made tea. He had no milk or sugar, but there was a pot of honey in the cupboard; he would try a spoonful instead of sugar. Stirring the mixture, he strolled out of doors. He found a black wrinkled damson on the tree. It tasted sweet as honey. The quince leaves had changed again from silver to pale gold; dark gold fruits hung among them. Bright green grass by the gate was covered with brown chestnut leaves, small flat nuts, greenish burrs. He sat down under the tree, where he had sat on that far-off April night. A yellow husk dropped with a splash into his mug of tea, spilling out two small nuts. He fished them out and ate them. Sitting in the quiet autumn evening, with no sounds but the patter of a withered leaf, the whistle of a robin, the distant cry of a sea-gull, he touched a peak of happiness. He had taken a journey, and found what he had set out to find.

A small mew, then a touch on his hand, made him start up. A black cat rubbed itself against him, and sat down a yard away, watching him. He was sure he had never seen it before. It was a huge cat, with a gentle and friendly air. It came again to rub against his foot. Stroking it, he had an odd feeling that *he* was the stranger, the visitor, and the black cat his host, politely making him welcome. The black fur was long and thick, sleek to his touch; the coat of a well-fed animal. It must have come over from one of those cottages in the lane, Ralph decided — perhaps after rats from the stack. It looked too meek and mild for a hunter; but cats, he knew, could look deceptive. This thought had hardly entered his head when a noise made him jump: a rustling and crashing in the tall almonds across the hedge. He was just in time to see a grey squirrel run down a slim trunk, pause for a moment with lifted head, and bolt into the spinney.

He had heard a good deal, in the summer, about grey squirrels and their raids on village gardens, and how they played havoc with the unripe fruit and nuts. As fast as they were trapped or shot, others swarmed in. One gardener had rigged up electric wires to try to save his wall cherries, but in vain; the squirrels seemed to enjoy skipping about the wires, taking small shocks cheerfully as they nipped off the May Dukes, Napoleons and Morellos. This was the first Ralph had seen here for himself. Now, as he watched, the squirrel darted back, nose black with earth from burying something, ran up the nearest almond tree, sprawled along a slender bough, bit off an almond and again ran down to the ground. Sitting upright, tail waving lightly as a plume over pricked ears, it bit off the end of the husk; then away into the spinney, and out again. Back and forth it skipped, each time following the same routine; never attempting to eat the nut, but always biting the tip, then running away out of sight, and back at once, as though afraid to waste a moment.

It struck Ralph that the nursery owner might want the almonds for himself; or he might have let Ralph pick them for a Christmas cake. He began to bombard the squirrel with chestnut husks. It ran down a stem with a nut in its mouth, and paused, four feet splayed, eyes bulging, tail jerking angrily. He glanced at the cat. All this time it had remained sitting at his side, green eyes narrowed, watching the squirrel intently; now something tense and fierce in its look made Ralph whisper, laughing, "Go on boy — catch him!" The result amazed him. Obedient as a dog, the cat hurled itself forward. The squirrel turned tail and raced back up the tree, the cat at its heels. Grey fur and black, they were lost to sight among clashing boughs; then the squirrel flumped to the ground and tore into the spinney, the cat in pursuit like a black streak. He heard a rustle from the spinney. Would it catch the squirrel? Would they fight? He followed along the edge of the field, and saw a flash of white under an oak tree on the corner. He stood still, then moved quietly nearer. A jay was hopping about under the oak. It looked alert and cocky as the squirrel; in colour it was like a Siamese cat, black, white and buff, with a cold pale blue eye cocked at him. It did not give the alarm, but went on foraging among the dead leaves, picking up acorns. Was it burying them, he wondered — making a winter store, like the squirrel? He stood watching, hoping it might shed a blue wing feather. Then he strolled back to the tall almonds, searched for a nut and picked it. The husk was yellowish-grey and smooth, with a sheen like worn suède. He cracked it with a stone and nibbled the wet brown kernel, but did not care for its bitter flavour. He scrambled through the spinney to the dell, and as he came near the mouse-run, he thought he heard a faint scampering noise from the straw; but when he peered in there was silence. He lingered, while shadows crept through the trees and drained all colour away — yellow of ash and hazel, dim blue of scabious, rank green of undergrowth. Now it was dark under the trees. All sounds had died. And suddenly, as he stood there, his own situation came home to him: he had played truant, he was eighty miles from school, he had no money left. He must start back at once; he would have to keep going all night. And when he got there, what sort of reckoning would there be? For the first time it struck him that people wouldn't simply be wondering where he had gone, and when he would be back. They would be searching for him. They might even have told the police he was missing. True, he had laid a trail of paper, fairly and squarely, all the way; but, he saw now, that would seem a flimsy excuse to Uncle Alfred. Crossing the garden, he heard footsteps beyond the hedge. Guilt made him apprehensive. Perhaps it was only someone going to the village? No, the steps had turned off, they were coming to the gate. Panic seized him. Could it be

Uncle Alfred, or a policeman? He ran forward, then stopped dead. It was Aunt Lizard.

For a moment he could not believe his eyes. They stared at each other in silence. In the twilight she looked very pale. Her steady gaze was disconcerting. At last she said in a distant voice, "I suppose you know you may be expelled."

Just in time, he stopped himself from retorting, "Then, can I come and live here?" Reality, cold and dreary, flooded over him. He looked at the chestnut tree, trying to remember how happy he had been a little while ago. How could he have felt like that? He must have known all the time how it would end. He was silent under her breathless questions: "Ralph, are you mad? What does it mean? When I told you we couldn't come this time? You're old enough, surely — ?" and then, on a pinnacle of exasperation, "Why not *ask*?"

Because, if you tell, you don't get your wish. Because I wanted to come by myself. Because I couldn't risk it, in case they said No — and that, he saw, was the true answer. He *had* to come, to see the harvest mice; but only he would allow that. He had gone about his own business, like a grown-up person; but to others he was still a child. They could even take away the spring house; it wasn't really his. He said in despair, "What am I going to do?"

Not answering, she walked slowly past him into the house. He followed and saw her glance round the shadowy room. He knew that she too wanted to stay. She knelt down and spread her fingers over the hot ashes, almost touching them, and said wearily, "We must catch the next train, of course."

After a pause he asked, "How did you know I was here?"

The asperity came back into her tone. "Fortunately — one of the boys told me."

"They can't have! Who?"

"An intelligent child called Madden."

"Madden!" He was furious. "I didn't breathe —"

"At first they thought you'd gone off early on the paper chase. They found some traces —" He nodded. "Then when you didn't come back by dinner time — can't you realize how worried we were?"

"I never thought of that, honestly I didn't. You *know* I can take care of myself."

She was silent.

"What about Madden?"

"Well, I came to take you out this afternoon. I suppose you'd forgotten? And *he* told me you'd had a postcard, with a Sussex postmark, and something about 'Sat.' He waited to get me alone, he said you'd be wild with him" — she smiled in spite of herself, thinking of Madden, so important and mysterious, hissing and beckoning. Suddenly they were both laughing.

"Good for him."

"But not for you, Ralph. I give you fair warning —"

"I know, I know, 'off with his head'." The laughter had banished his gloom. He flashed out accusingly, "*You* said — when you trespassed at Versailles, after some flower or other, bog bean — and they shouted at you and you pretended not to hear — I heard you tell

Merren your motto was, *Get to the flower first and hear the shouting afterwards*!" And, at her stunned expression, he saw that he had scored. Before she could speak he went on with a rush, telling her about the mice; then about the mouse sanctuary, the postcard, the thresher, Tacker's little joke about fetching the whetstone. "And there's a grey squirrel here, oh and a great black cat from somewhere — d'you think the mouse-run will be safe? Come and look, I'll take the lamp off my bike —" He broke off. She was not looking at him, but at something on the sill beside her bunk; a small dark object like a fir cone. As they watched, it moved. A mouse leapt on to the curtain, ran up and huddled for a second on the rod, then sped along it, down the other curtain and out of the door.

"It's all right," he said, "only a fieldmouse."

"Mouse sanctuary, indeed," said Aunt Lizard, sounding so like her normal self that he gave a sigh of relief and began to fill his pockets with apples.

But all the way back — in the train, in the tube, in the train again — she was silent and thoughtful. He knew she was on his side now; and that this would not help him. At school, just the same, the skies were going to fall. Aunt Lizard had telephoned the headmaster from Beaumarsh; ominously, she would tell him nothing about the conversation. She gave him a meal at The Race: from now on, her manner implied, he would find himself on bread and water.

Arriving late at night, he found himself in fact, to his surprise, in the sanatorium; a thermometer between his lips, a cup of invalid food at his side, and matron hovering with a grave face. No stormy reception could have been so disconcerting. Also, it nipped in the bud his faint defiant hope of a sensation in the dormitory. Next morning he was still apparently in quarantine, but too drowsy at first to care. He slept and slept. No one but matron came near him, and she spoke briefly, asking only clinical questions. There was no sign of bread and water. She brought him ordinary meals, and looked in surprise at the empty plates, as though he were really an invalid. Next day it was the same. He began to grow uneasy. He ventured at last, "I'm not ill, you know." She looked serious, she did not answer. He added pertly in desperation, "I'm just shamming." She retaliated with a dose of bromide, which he loathed. He spent the day playing dominoes by himself. Next morning he was allowed up; Uncle Alfred sent for him, questioned him, and demanded as Aunt Lizard had done, "Why not ask?" His explanations were lame; reaction had set in, he almost wished he had never started all this. He was sent back to the sanatorium. There was nothing to do there: nothing to read, apparently, but *Uncle Tom's Cabin*. No one offered to play a game with him. He begged for pencil and paper and passed the time by sketching the little mice from memory. This cheered him at once; again, the whole thing seemed worthwhile. But next morning the sketches were confiscated. The headmaster had them, matron said.

And still the skies did not fall. Still his conduct seemed to be looked on, not as a crime, but as a curious illness: a "crise de nerfs", suggested mademoiselle, bringing his tea when matron was off duty. "Brainstorm" he heard once, in low tones, from matron in the outer room. The idea was disquieting; if only — he found himself thinking — if only they would stop all this fuss, set him free, fine him half a term's pocket-money, give him twenty or thirty rows of digging — wartime equivalent of "lines" — confiscate his bike, anything, and let him get back to everyday life — he would never risk this sort of embarrassment again.

Could this have been Uncle Alfred's intention? Not for nothing, perhaps, had he been headmaster for twenty years; and not for a moment did Ralph suspect his dilemma: torn between respect for enterprise and the need, for their own safety, to keep the young within bounds.

Sentence was postponed another day. When it came, it was typical of Uncle Alfred; not expulsion from school, or exile from Beaumarsh, but two weeks' detention with hard labour. He must give a lecture on harvest mice.

CHAPTER NINE

Running Deer

Ralph came warily along the muddy path from the barn, wheeling his bicycle. Now and then he paused to listen for peculiar sounds from the spring house. For once, he was in no hurry to arrive.

Two days earlier, Aunt Lizard had rung him at school: "Ralph, I hope you don't mind. I'm bringing a baby to stay with us for Christmas."

"A *baby*? Oh, good lord, must we?"

"Well, yes." It was an orphan, she explained. The parents had died in Germany, in a concentration camp, soon after the baby had been sent away to England. She had met the grandparents in a shelter last year. Now the grandmother was ill, and she had offered to bring the child to Beaumarsh for a week, to give her a rest.

He saw that he could not object. He countered, "I hope you won't mind, I'm bringing two white mice to stay as well. I'm looking after them for someone."

Her dismay was an echo of his own. "Must we? More mice? I feel like Bishop Hatto. Well, mind you bring a strong cage."

He was balancing the cage on his saddle now. Inside, the two white mice took turns to spin on their playwheel. He thought of the harvest mice, and wondered if they were still in the mouse-run. Leaving the visitors in the woodshed, he ran to the spinney. He had often wondered if that black cat, or the grey squirrel, might have tried to get at them. No, the wire netting was intact; but the mice had disappeared. The straw inside was sodden, husks picked clean of grains; the sunflower head lay there like an empty black honeycomb. They would be nesting somewhere near, he thought. He would come again and search for them. He dawdled back to the house, and listened at the door. Still he heard no wailing or babbling sounds. The infant must be asleep. Fetching the cage again, as though to lay stress on his schoolboy detachment, he opened the door and went in. Aunt Lizard, busy at the table, turned to greet him in happy surprise; she had not expected him yet. He kissed her with an air of reserve, and looked quickly about. He could see no pram, cot or high chair; nothing unusual except a folded camp bed against one wall, and a high fireguard round the hearth. Cuckoo lay stretched full length like a caged tiger inside the guard.

"Where's the baby? — not come yet?"

"Oh . . . he was after a spider." Stooping down beside her bunk, she said, "Tommy, come out." A mop of dark curly hair appeared from under the bunk. A small child wriggled out and brought something for her to see, held carefully in one shut hand. It was a large house spider. She said, "Ralph, this is Tommy Mordecai."

The spider dropped to the floor and vanished like a shadow. The child crouched, looking for it. Ralph murmured, "I don't call that a baby."

"You're three, aren't you, Tommy? — What would you call him, then?"

He said softly, laughing, "I'd call it a brat."

Low as he had spoken, he was taken aback when the child lifted his head, showing a pale delicate face and brilliant eyes, and gave him a look of quiet awareness; then turned again to watch the spider. He felt reproached, and produced the mouse cage as a friendly gesture. Tommy rose and stood looking into the cage, beginning to smile with pleasure. Aunt Lizard said, "What are their names?"

"They haven't any yet. They're pedigree mice," he added impressively. "The big one's the buck."

"Ralph! You don't mean they're a pair?" She clicked her tongue. "You'll have swarms of young in no time."

"No we won't. They're father and daughter."

"I'm afraid that won't deter them. Mice don't trouble about prohibited degrees, or tables of affinity."

It was her turn to receive a penetrating look. Ralph seemed about to say something, checked himself and went out abruptly. Returning to her work, she thought, Of course, he didn't know what I was talking about.

Adults who say this to themselves are apt to be wrong. Aunt Lizard was mistaken now. Ralph knew a great deal about tables of affinity, for a reason that might have startled her. The phrase had dogged his thoughts lately, and no doubt, in her odd way, she had picked it up from him. The whole thing had begun on the Sunday after half-term. Young Madden had taken to Aunt Lizard; and as he walked to church with Ralph he suddenly asked, "Do you think your aunt will get married to your father?"

Ralph was amused. "Don't be wet. How could they?"

"Why not? It would be a good idea. Then she'd be your mother."

Was he serious or not? Ralph gazed down at his ward, too astonished to snub him. "But don't you see? — they're *relations*. It's all on a list in the church porch. 'A man may not marry his grandmother' —" He saw Madden open his mouth to say, "Well, she's not —" and rapped out in a flash of irritation, "Why don't you pipe down?" Madden shut his mouth again and looked downcast, increasing Ralph's annoyance. A ditty he had heard somewhere began to jig in his head: *Bricks without straw, bricks without straw, A man may not marry his mother-in-law. Needles and pins, needles and pins, when a man marries his trouble begins* . . . or someone else's trouble, perhaps? He felt a pricking sensation like mental pins and needles. As soon as he reached his place in church he flipped through a prayer book and found the Table of Kindred and Affinity. Thank heaven, there it was in black and white — or black and yellow, for the prayer book was an old one: "A man may not marry . . . Sister, Wife's Sister . . ." and there on the other side: "woman may not marry . . . Sister's Husband". He felt reprieved, and let his eye wander on to the fascinating complications of "Husband's Daughter's Son" and "Wife's Brother's Daughter". But half-way through the service an unpleasant notion jolted him. He turned to a prayer for the Royal Family. As he had feared, it ran: "... our most gracious Sovereign Lord King Edward ... our gracious Queen Alexandra ...". He knew that laws, like kings and queens, could change in the course of time: this one might have changed years ago. But the idea was too absurd! Father was father, Aunt Lizard was Aunt Lizard. Still, he was so bemused that he forgot to listen as usual for the prayer about "the hands of our enemies", with its forthright petition, "asswage their malice and confound their devices ...". On the way back to school, he waylaid matron, singling her out from the flock like a skilful sheepdog, and asked, "If someone's mother died — his father couldn't get married to her sister, could he?" Dejection returned when she failed to reassure him at once. She hesitated, pondered, then asked, "Didn't they pass a law called" — *diseased wife's sister*, it sounded like; he was too appalled to say any more.

Until now, the idea of such a marriage had never crossed his mind. Had it crossed *theirs*? He could not swear that it hadn't. And the more he considered it, and the changes it might bring, the less he cared for it. They all got on very well as they were. Nowadays, as a rule, Aunt Lizard treated him like another adult. Father did not. When they were apart he felt that he and father were close friends; together, he was not so sure. Reluctantly, his thoughts slid back to the beginning of one holiday, their last at Nine Wells, just before the war. Father had come over to Ireland on leave, and Ralph had looked forward with pride and excitement to their meeting; for a year, since he joined the navy, they had hardly seen each other. He knew that in the past father had been disappointed because he did not shine at games. Gymnastics he liked, or anything that involved climbing and jumping; and that sort of thing, he realized, did not count beside cricket or football. But these holidays, while awaiting father's arrival, he had been helping grandfather to train a pony for a jumping event at Nenagh show. Ralph would never make a first-rate horseman; but, though nervous, he had light hands, and could steel himself to enjoy the jumps, at least when they were over . . . besides, the pony was called Squirrel, and the name made her seem playful and frisky, not hostile and tricky like so many of her kind. Ralph treated her with unwonted confidence, and Squirrel behaved demurely. They did so well that grandfather said, teasing, "B' God, if you go on like this, we'll have you riding at Dublin in no time." Fatal words; elated, certain that for once he was doing something father would thoroughly approve, Ralph had run to greet him, and burst out at once with an account of the morning's work in the paddock. But, instead of looking pleased, father had said coldly — his heart still sank as he remembered it — "I'm afraid I'm rather out of touch with all that", and had gone into the house without another word. Ralph saw too late where he had mucked it: he had sounded uppish instead of just keen. The holiday never quite recovered from this unlucky start.

Aunt Lizard, he knew, wouldn't have misread him like that. Only — supposing they *were* married —

mightn't she become less of a companion, more like father? He had heard that married couples did grow alike, just as horsy people got to look like horses. In any case, they would be taken up with each other — wouldn't they? — and he would simply be in the way. He saw himself left behind at school while they spent father's leave together at the spring house.

Staring into the cage, but not thinking of the mice, Ralph heard Aunt Lizard calling him to tea. Thankfully, he realized — I needn't really worry about any of it now. Father's next leave was weeks away, in March; nothing could happen before then. And tomorrow was Christmas Eve. He had a thousand things to do.

They all went early to bed. Tommy slept without stirring, but Aunt Lizard and Ralph passed a wakeful night. The nameless pair in the woodshed, more active than ever in the dark, kept up a steady thrumming, a night-long marathon on their playwheel. Again and again Ralph woke to hear its whirr and thud through the wall, beyond Aunt Lizard's bunk. Once, in the small hours, she groaned aloud: "Tomorrow night, we'll take that wretched wheel away."

He whispered back in apology, "I think they're just trying to keep warm."

"Nonsense. They have good fur coats."

Christmas Eve dawned bright and cold, with hoar frost thick on trees and grass. Ivy leaves in the hedge were stiff to the touch, like artificial leaves, sparkling silver over dark green. Ralph picked trails of them to wreath the window-sills; in a few moments they were limp again, glossy with dew. He thought he would go straight away to Wild Hill woods for holly. Tacker had fixed this with his friend the head forester. At home they wouldn't need much, with only two pictures and one pudding to decorate; but Tacker said the villagers were glad of all the holly they could get for the church.

He shook out the breakfast crumbs on the path, and stood for a minute sniffing the frosty air, so sharp that it made him gasp. Two cock birds, robin and chaffinch, at once took turns to fly down and feed. They were tame because Tacker fed them. From separate points they challenged one another, the robin "ticking" and the chaffinch answering him with a metallic "chink-chink". They looked pretty and ferocious, like little toy soldiers; the robin one of Wellington's men, in white trousers and scarlet coat; the other, in steel-blue helmet, acting as though the world were made for chaffinches: Ralph had heard people say this about the Germans. Admiring them, Ralph thought of the bird book he had seen last summer in the town, and of the pound note father had sent him. Now he could go and buy it. And he must find a present for young Tommy. Last night, when the child was asleep, Aunt Lizard had shown Ralph what she had brought for his stocking. In long quiet days at the wardens' post she had made two soft toys, rabbit-like creatures, from old scraps of fur; and Aunt Emmy had knitted him a scarlet jacket. What else would he like? So far Ralph had seen him take an interest only in the spider, in Aunt Lizard's wireless set, and in chatting to Cuckoo through the fireguard; but Cuckoo remained out of reach, declining to become a soft toy. Ralph went indoors to consult Aunt Lizard, but she was preoccupied, gazing at the table on which her morning's work was spread: onions and herbs to be chopped, a duck to be stuffed for tomorrow; she had even found an orange to garnish it, and the peel must be grated to flavour something else. Then there was a rabbit to be stewed for today's dinner, and soup to make, and a damson jelly for the child, and brandy sauce for the Christmas pudding, last of her pre-war stock. Next year, if they were spared, the pudding would have to be made with beer and prunes and grated carrots. Blackberry tarts and mince pies she had brought from Chelsea, the precious mincemeat eked out with chopped apple. Ralph snatched up a tiny bottle of brandy and held it over the spiders' water dish: "Let's give the spiders a Christmas treat, shall we? Just a drop. They might dance a tarantella. Like this . . . You'll see them," he said to Tommy, "dropping down all over the place, dead beat, using six of their legs to mop their streaming brow." But Aunt Lizard, in no mood for trifling, rescued the bottle and sent him to the shed for potatoes. When he came back, Tommy was playing with something on the floor. Ralph wandered across to see what he had found; a bit of brown tape, he thought at first. Tommy held it up. It gleamed and rippled in the firelight; it seemed to twist itself like a gold bracelet over Tommy's wrist. As Ralph stared, the bracelet moved again, writhing and swaying in the child's clutch. Ralph cried, "A slow-worm!" Tommy sprang up and ran towards Aunt Lizard, his face alight with excitement. Ralph tried to take the slow-worm, but Tommy backed away, holding it firmly. Ralph gabbled, "It must have come in the grating — it may have been here weeks — isn't it a beauty?" Aunt Lizard looked dubious. Cuckoo was staring from his cage. Ralph appealed to Tommy, "Don't squeeze it, don't hurt it. Let's put it in the barrel with the cones, then it'll go to sleep." He scooped out cones into the wood box. Tommy leaned over the barrel and let the slow-worm glide through his fingers, down into the hollow among the cones. They hung there together, watching it gleam in the dusk below. Ralph grinned across at Aunt Lizard. Not a brat, he conceded silently: another boy. He urged, "Can he come up to the woods with me?"

"Not on your bicycle!"

"No, no — on yours." She had fitted a child's seat, with footrests, to her carrier. Still she demurred, thinking of army trucks hurtling along the main road. Guessing this, he promised to keep to the lanes. Tommy meanwhile had disappeared; when Ralph went out he found him already planted on the bicycle. Aunt Lizard brought his outdoor things, and fastened the safety-straps about his waist. They crossed the main road and went uphill through winding lanes; past a wood where Jill said wild daffodils grew, and Bob Doggett said there used to be two notices, "Beware of man traps" and "Beware of spring guns"; past a keeper's gibbet with twenty-nine grey squirrels; and on between flint walls and beechwoods, until they came to a side road with steep mossy banks. They hid the bicycle behind a tree and walked down a straight green ride, between hazels flat as trained trees, covered with small grey catkins. The ride ran into a dark fir plantation, and Ralph picked up a dead gold-crest, a wisp of feathers, ash-grey and olive green, light as a butterfly. It must have died in last night's frost. He would skin it for the school museum. Coming out again into sunlight, they went on, skipping and running, deeper and deeper into the wood. Presently they passed an enclosure like a pheasant breeding pen, with high wire fences. Ralph could not see any pheasants; but a fallow deer, browsing among rows of seedling trees, lifted its antlered head to stare at them. That must be a sort of paddock for tame deer, Ralph whispered, like his own mouse-run at home. The stag was eyeing them nervously, poised for flight, tail switching; and they hurried by on tiptoe, so as not to disturb it. Now, just ahead, they found the copse that Tacker had described. Here and there, above the chestnut scrub, the woodmen had left an oak sapling, a twiggy crab tree, or a holly crowned with green and scarlet. Tommy reached up to peel an ivy tendril downwards from an oak tree; a delicious sensation, like the forbidden sport of unpicking wallpaper. Ralph swarmed up a holly trunk and began to pull red-berried sprays and throw them to the ground. Both were so busy that they did not hear a motor van coming along the ride, until the driver, spotting Ralph, braked and shouted angrily. Ralph lost his nerve and jumped, biting his tongue as he hit the ground; but it was all right, after all. The driver was Tacker's friend the forester. When Ralph had gathered up the holly, he put them in the back of his van to take them to the lane.

Primed by Tacker yesterday, on his way from the station, Ralph lost no time in asking about dormice; were there any hereabouts? The forester, as though trying to jog his memory, said he hadn't seen any lately, now he came to think about it. As the van bumped along the ride, Ralph added, "Are there many deer in that pen? We saw just one as we came along."

The response to this was unexpected. The driver swung round in his seat, glaring at Ralph: "You saw a deer *where*?" The van rocked, branches scraped the windows.

"In that wire place — you know —"

Before Ralph could say another word, the forester turned abruptly round, straightened their course and accelerated. The van skidded in dry wheel ruts, bumped and swayed on grassy verges, tilted between the two. Ralph clung to Tommy, and they laughed together, but silently. There was a rather grim look about the set of the driver's head, though they couldn't see his face. The wire fence came in sight, but before they reached it the forester braked and cried, "Look there!" Head high, forefeet tucked in, the deer came over the wire with inches to spare. It landed lightly as a squirrel, swerved and bounded away down the ride. The driver started in pursuit. Faster and faster they went, running now on smooth short turf. A blackbird flew screaming out of the hazels and skimmed down the ride before them, just behind the deer. They ran into the dark fir tunnel. When they came out at the end, deer and blackbird were gone. The forester stopped the van and turned round to say, "Deer pen? You know what that's supposed to be? Tree nursery. You know what that high wire's for? To keep the blessed deer out. Tcha! Like trying to keep the blessed foxes out of blessed chicken coops . . ." The deer had come from another estate, he said. A herd of them, with one white doe, frightened by a deer shoot, had crossed the downs to Wild Hill. Now the poachers were after them — a fine time he had had lately, what with that, and soldiers knocking off pheasants, and diddycoys after holly and Christmas trees. He fell into a brooding silence. All the way to the lane, all the way back to Beaumarsh, Ralph saw the curve of the deer's leap, its flying feet that hardly seemed to touch the ground, its coat like pale bracken in the sunlight, the rise and fall of the blackbird. He remembered it all day, and thought of the white doe wandering somewhere in the forest.

The village church was a scene of busy preparation. In wartime, because of the blackout, it was used only by daylight; so, while the decorators were at work, bickering quietly in low voices, the choir children had had their final Christmas practice. It was just over when Ralph and Tommy arrived. The young singers came tumbling down from the choir loft at the back of the church, stealing into the aisles to look at the holly, stifling irreverent laughter as they dodged the verger, Mr. "Invasion" Toon, who was trying to banish them.

Old Mr. Toon had won his nickname only eighteen months ago, but he would never lose it now. Soon after the fall of France, the village had been alerted one evening, first by air raid sirens and then by the tolling of the church bell, the warning of invasion. Soldiers, wardens, local defence volunteers, farm men with billhooks, retired fishermen with boathooks, all had turned out to look for enemy parachutists. Rumours swarmed like bees. No one knew who had given the signal. Cornered at last in his belfry by a raging army officer, Mr. Toon explained with dignity, "I thought, as soon as them sirens went, I had to ring my bell." Now, seeing Ralph and Tommy by the door, he hurried out to take the bunch of holly and dismiss them; but the lady from the clinic noticed Ralph and swooped down the aisle with a message for Aunt Lizard. Looking round a minute later, Ralph was just in time to see Tommy disappearing through a door behind the font, attracted by strains of organ music from above. Ralph sped after him, but Tommy was up the stairs like a monkey. Reaching the loft, Ralph found him standing beside the organ, watching the player's hands. The elderly organist looked round with a kind vague smile and went on playing. Afraid that the child might set up a wail if he were removed, Ralph let him stand there. For ten minutes he did not stir or lift his eyes from the keys. When the music ended, Ralph carried him down the stairs. He did not protest, but hung limp, looking back, like a child in a trance.

They crossed a wooden bridge over the mill stream, where it ran foaming out to the shore. In a narrow lane behind the church they found a small shop, and paused to look in the window. A few toys were on view: a golliwog, a home-made wooden cart, a mouth-organ.

There would be more choice in the town, Ralph decided. Back at home, they found that Aunt Lizard's thoughts were still in the oven. Stopping only for toast and soup, which burnt Ralph's bitten tongue, they set off again. As he had promised, Ralph made a wide detour through quiet byroads, then wheeled his bicycle through the crowded streets. At the bookshop, he was disappointed; the bird book had gone two days ago. And the biggest toyshop, near the Wax Gate of the abbey, had little that he could afford. When he asked doubtfully, "Look, Tommy, would you like that tank? Or toy soldiers?" the child nodded towards the abbey and whispered, "One of those."

"One of what?"

Tommy was listening, his head turned away. Faintly through the stone archway came the sound of the abbey organ. Tommy darted a smile at Ralph.

"An organ?" Ralph smiled back. "Well, you see, they're a bit expensive." Then he remembered the village shop. "Would a mouth-organ do? You could play tunes on it, anyway." Tommy now began trying to wriggle out of his harness. When Ralph unbuckled it and lifted him down from the carrier, Tommy gripped his hand and pulled him towards the gateway. They left the bicycle and walked through the cloisters, over flagstones that were gravestones of deans and canons, through a high door standing ajar, into the dark abbey. In the afternoon light, the west window glowed with rose and blue like a kaleidoscope. Candles flickered on the high altar. The rest was echoing space and darkness. Ralph grasped Tommy by the collar, fearful of losing him, and groped his way to a seat. The organ pealed, an unseen choir sang, and again the small boy seemed to listen entranced. Outside again, they wandered through narrow back streets. Already dusk was falling; here and there, in lighted cottage windows, were little fir trees decorated with cotton wool snow, coloured figures cut from Christmas cards, silver stars saved from crackers. They went through another high arched gateway, past the abbey school in the gatehouse, mounted and freewheeled down a lane past the abbey orchard, now a close with houses and long gardens. Ralph wondered if the monks had known about budding and grafting; or did they grow fruit trees from pips and stones, as he used to do himself? He wondered, too, what names they had given their fruits: Beurre Hardy, Cox's Orange? Not Waterloo, anyway, or Victoria either. The lane ran down to an ancient mill, where lay brothers had once ground corn to feed the monks and their pilgrim guests. Aunt Lizard had read out bits about the abbey from a book she had found in the summer. A stream flowed from the mill, through open parkland, to the old fishpools. In the blue wintry twilight, the place was deserted. Mists rose from the water. They heard the quack of a duck, and a splash that might have been made by a fish, or a water rat, or a moorhen diving. At the far side of the park they came out into Fishpool Lane, and went through Orchard Street back to the country roads. Then the back tyre flattened with a puncture, and Ralph had to walk the last half mile. Perhaps the flints in the abbey mill lane had been too hard on it.

Supper was ready when they reached home; the house smelled of baked potatoes and orange biscuits. But Ralph remembered that he had still Tommy's present to buy. Aunt Lizard asked, "Where are you going now? I've fed Sir Walter and Miss . . ."

He looked at her.

"— Your pedigree friends outside. Boiled chestnuts and birdseed I've given them, and they're nicely bedded down in straw."

"And you've taken their wheel away."

"Oh dear, yes."

"All right — look, I've something to get in the village. I shan't be long." He accepted a hot potato to keep him going, and ate it as quickly as his sore tongue allowed. Warming his hands on the fireguard, Tommy said, "He's going to buy me a mouse-organ."

"Who is?" Aunt Lizard asked.

"That boy. Ralph."

"I should hope," she said clearly, raising her voice a little, "that Ralph has more sense than to buy you any such thing." He grinned at her and went out. The bikes were bewitched, his own tyres were flat; he ran, suddenly afraid that the mouth-organ, like the bird book, might have gone; but this time he was lucky. It was still in the window, the shop still open; these worries over, he felt he could afford the five shillings he was charged. He wandered down to the green beyond the church, playing the mouth-organ softly to try it out. The tide was high, running up round the bench where the old men sat on sunny days. The creek gleamed under a clear white sky. Low down in the west there were long shining strands of primrose colour and pale green. The swish of the mill race seemed much louder now. He could hear the sea clapping with a hungry sound on the wooden piles below the boathouse. Back in the village street, all was blacked-out and silent. The Race and the other houses had disappeared behind drawn blinds. A thin frosty breeze stirred the bare chestnut branches. He shirked the dark field path, and was glad to reach Seaforth yard, to hear the horses munching and stamping in the stable, Silver rubbing his halter on the manger, Mr. Doggett whistling and working away at something by faint lantern light in Captain's stall. A stable wasn't a bad place to be on Christmas Eve, he thought, facing the lonely road through the nursery. Stars flashed and glittered overhead. The east wind was bitter, whistling through the young trees that gave no shelter to the wayfarer. The poplars stood up like broomsticks; a dead leaf fluttered somewhere, like teeth chattering. How cold it was: the bones of his feet felt bruised from the hard ground. By the gate of Bullrush field he stopped to get his breath, and caught another sound, a queer rhythmic beat, high up, coming in from the sea, but not aircraft. Could it be a great bird of some kind? It was circling, coming lower. Frozen, he stood looking up. Something glimmered in the air just above his head. He saw the white flash of wings. A shining thing hovered for a moment in the starlight, then veered with a graceful dipping movement and was gone. The hoarse wing beat died away. He felt himself gasping and tingling, as though from an icy plunge. Only a swan, he told himself, flying down to Bullrush pond. He had startled it, that was all. For a moment he had half thought it might be something else. *What else*? He longed for the moment to come back, strained eyes and ears in vain, and went indoors at last reluctantly, shutting out the huge mysterious night where anything might happen.

Soon the impression faded, dispelled by light and warmth and sudden aching hunger. Tommy was asleep in the camp bed. Ralph and Aunt Lizard talked in whispers. She brought out the stocking to be filled; the mouth-organ went in the toe, then nuts and an apple, then the soft toys. It was hung on a nail at the end of her bunk, where the child could see it as soon as he woke. Ralph hid *Sussex Flora* under his pillow, ready for the morning. Tonight all was quiet in the woodshed, not a mouse stirring; but Ralph was awakened by rustling and shrill squeaks. He jumped up, then realized that it was morning already, and the squeaks were Tommy's. He slid down under the blankets, shutting his eyes against the candlelight, trying to recapture sleep. Behind him came the piercing smell of methylated spirits, a low steady roar from the primus, the chink of teacups; then more rustling of paper. He heard Tommy say quietly, "Oh, look," and Aunt Lizard, "What is it?" Then Tommy again, in triumph: "Ralph hasn't any more sense than you said he had," and a shrill cascade of notes from the mouth-organ. Sleep banished, he rolled over and sat up. Parcels were piled beside his bunk. The paper felt chill when he touched it. He hesitated, then slid out of bed and went to rekindle the fire, piling apple twigs and cones on the white ashes, and driftwood from the shore. Flames leaped up, burning blue and green, smelling of tar and resin. He rubbed ashy fingertips on Cuckoo's fur, raising electric sparks. Back in his bunk, he attacked the first parcel. And now, had he not been past the age of mouse-like squeaks, his performance might have matched Tommy's. Inside was the bird book he had coveted; a miracle, he thought, for he had never mentioned it. He turned the pages slowly, fingering the crisp tissue paper protecting the coloured plates; a barn owl at the nest, pheasants in a woodland ride, partridges on a heath. Finding Tommy at his side, he tilted the book so that the child could look without touching; but Tommy was intent on the mouth-organ. He blew a few notes and said doubtfully, "My organ doesn't go like . . . those other ones?"

Ralph groped on the sill for his penknife. Slowly, he cut a page. "What other ones? Oh, I see. It's not a real one, that's why."

"It's *not* a real one," protested Tommy, meaning to contradict.

Untying another parcel, Ralph explained, "You see, they were church organs — oh, I say!" A paintbox came into view; a student's box, with tubes of colour to mix for himself. Another package contained brushes and a palette. Aunt Lizard had bought them from a girl who had hoped to go to the Slade School, but found herself in the women's timber corps instead. Now he could paint his own coloured plates — starting with the dead goldcrest, then the robin and cock chaffinch.

Sipping his mug of tea, he watched Aunt Lizard unwrap her book. He had waited four months for this moment; her first raptures were drowned by the mouth-organ, but he saw that they equalled his own. Cuckoo mewed at the door, and was released. Outside, as he appeared, the robin ticked. Ralph blew out the candle, jerked his curtains back and scrubbed with his sleeve at the misty pane. Feathers of cloud, pink and grey, floated in the east. From his old paintbox he would have used rose madder for that sky, and a touch of vermilion. He opened the last parcel; a long-desired toolkit. He and Aunt Lizard sat still, absorbed in their presents. Tommy blew and listened and blew again. Ranging between the two, he said, "I'll have to go and play my organ in church?" Ralph said absently, "Yes, of course you will." Aunt Lizard said, "Tommy, where are your slippers?"

It was mid-morning when they missed him. Ralph was in the spinney, putting chestnuts in the mouse-run, when he heard Aunt Lizard call. He came to the end of the garden. She called again from the doorstep, "Tommy should have his topcoat on." Ralph looked about for the child, wandered over and put his head in at the door. "Where is he, then?" Aunt Lizard was at the table, busy with the duck. She whirled round: "But — he followed you out. Isn't he still with you?" Their eyes met, he saw hers widen in alarm. There was no sign of the child in garden or spinney. She gasped, "I'll run down to the lane — you go that way — the path —" Ralph flew along the headland calling,

"Tommy, Tommy." By the edge of Old Park he stopped to look around. Something fluttered low down on the barbed wire; a scrap of scarlet wool, like the tags he had used to mark the wild rose bushes, but this was new. And there, in the mud, was the print of a small wellington boot. He bent down to make sure, and stood up to scan the horizon. Far away he saw a flash of scarlet like a holly berry. Thank heaven, there he was, right away over the field, making straight for the sea wall. He had a long start. Running and calling, Ralph saw him reach the wall, saw him clearly for an instant on the skyline; then he vanished. Fear seized Ralph again. Supposing the tide were up, as high as the wall — supposing Tommy had fallen in? He might be sucked out into the deep channel, his cries mistaken for a seagull's, or unheard because people were at church. *Church*! With a shock, he recalled Tommy's remark about the organ. Then, with a surge of relief, he saw the scarlet jacket reappear, bobbing up the steps by the boatyard and on along the wall. Yes, he was making for the church — he must have fancied the wretched mouth-organ would sound different there. Gaining the wall, Ralph saw that the mud flats were uncovered, the tide far down the bay. There was still the dangerous mill race; but he didn't think Tommy would hang about on the bridge. No such luck . . . He had disappeared, he must be in the lane already, passing the shop, the inn, the churchyard wall. Ralph called again and again as he ran, hoping someone might hear and stop the runaway. No longer alarmed for Tommy's safety, he was filled with new misgivings. What would happen if the brat *did* make his way into church, in the middle of the service, and start that racket on the mouth-organ? Heavens, he would disgrace them all. I *must* catch him, Ralph thought, with inward curses. He met no one in the lane. Here was the lychgate, but still no sign of Tommy. The porch was empty; the door stood a little way open. From inside came a smell of hassocks and bruised leaves, the drone of a familiar prayer. A printed notice said, *Of your charity pray for the sick*. He felt sick himself from panic. He pushed at the heavy door and slipped inside. The verger, standing at the foot of the aisle, looked sideways, frowning. Next moment he stared indignantly as Ralph tiptoed forward, past the font, towards the stairway to the loft. Tommy, he was sure, must have got up there unseen. Oh Lord, prayed Ralph, let me be in time. The parson's voice had stopped; the congregation rustled to its feet. *In Quires and Places where they sing, here followeth* . . . He reached the door, but too late. "Invasion" Toon had moved swiftly; unfortunate as ever, he barred the way. Ralph tried in a frantic whisper to explain, but Mr. Toon stood firm, collection plate clasped like a buckler to his chest. Ralph saw that it was no use. He couldn't knock the old fool down. He had done his best, and Mr. Toon had scuppered him. Now let Tommy rip. He pictured the child, bright-eyed, confident, standing by the organ. No one would see him in time, no one would stop him. Torn between dismay and hysterical laughter, Ralph sank down on a bench and waited, covering his ears.

But the sound that followed was not, by a hair's breadth, what he feared. One strange blast he caught from above, before the organ swamped it with a high jubilant phrase. The choir swung unsuspecting into their carol. Of all the congregation only Ralph noticed the alien note behind the melody. Standing up, light-headed with relief, he heard the rest of the worshippers join in:

O, the rising of the sun,
The running of the deer,
The playing of the merry organ,
Sweet singing in the choir.

Because of all this, they sat down later to an unexpected Christmas dinner: roast potatoes, braised celery, orange salad, artichoke chips and sausages. The pudding, the brandy sauce were safe; but, while they were out in search of Tommy, the duck had vanished without trace.

CHAPTER TEN

Badger

It seemed quiet at the spring house when Tommy and his mouth-organ were gone. The new year came in, still with clear cold weather. They breakfasted while the full moon was setting, a round white lamp, behind the spinney, and drank their tea in the afternoon as they watched it rising behind the abbey tower. Then came a change. Mists hung over the fields until noon, and closed in again after an hour's faint sunshine. From the west window, the spinney appeared and disappeared before their eyes. One minute Ralph could see the church steeple through the greenish pallor of ash boughs; then the mist returned, and the branches, dripping with dew, might have been the edge of a great forest. The downs they did not see for days. The mist seemed to muffle sound as well. The birds were silent; even the white mice seemed subdued. Ralph imagined himself and Aunt Lizard cut off from the world, becalmed in a clipper, stormbound in a mountain hut, cruising in a submarine — but without tedium or danger; snug as bears in a winter den.

Without danger? Sometimes he remembered the stolen duck. They might have one enemy at least; but he pushed this thought away, especially at night, when the thief might have returned, might be lurking outside. The idea was menacing, like a thin howl in the dark. On Christmas Day, when they returned to find the duck gone, and Cuckoo prowling wild-eyed about the room, Aunt Lizard had said lightly, "Oh, a stray dog, I expect," and let the subject drop. Still, Ralph knew she must be as puzzled as himself. He waited to consult Tacker; then, as their friend did not appear, he armed himself with the billhook from the shed, smuggling it indoors each evening, and hiding it away under his bunk. It was the best he could do for the moment; he was not yet allowed an airgun.

If Aunt Lizard noticed this precaution, she gave no sign. And in the mornings, when the hidden sun made the mist gleam like an oyster shell, when he could hear the milk pony trotting, and sometimes the men calling in the fields, he felt inclined to scoff at his own fears.

Aunt Lizard believed in dispatching housework as soon as they were up — "the worst bit of the day, and then the best," she would say. So by breakfast time the room was swept and dusted, milk fetched, water drawn, mice fed, firewood stacked by the hearth, a loaf of soda bread in the oven. Then they lingered over coffee and toast, dipping into books, mixing new colours, talking of plans for the spring, when she would go ahead with her Shakespeare paintings. She could start soon, she said, with catkins for Mercutio's hazelnut. On her list, too, she had various kinds of fruit blossom, quince, medlar, apricot, crab. Why not pick some buds now and bring them indoors, Ralph asked; then she could make an earlier start? But she thought that forced flowers wouldn't do, they might look pallid and fragile. One morning, searching in Shakespeare for Perdita's flowers, she exclaimed, "Do listen to this. It's all about budding:

> *. . . we marry*
> *A gentler scion to the wildest stock,*
> *And make conceive a bark of baser kind*
> *By bud of nobler race . . ."*

Then in another play she found a gardener complaining of a "disordered" springtime,

> *When our sea-walled garden, the whole land,*
> *Is full of weeds; her fairest flowers chok'd up,*
> *Her fruit-trees all unpruned, her hedges ruined . . .*

The language differed a little from that of Ted Lock and Tacker Brooks; yet, Ralph agreed, they had told him just the same sort of things. Leaning over to take the book from her, he found himself skimming a dialogue that seemed, when you got down to it, all about pruning, topping, tying, pest control and bark ringing; knifework, in fact. And it hadn't changed much since Shakespeare's day. Then perhaps the monks had practised it, long before, in the abbey orchard; or even Marcus and his gardeners, here at Seaforth, centuries ago?

Ralph, in turn, began to read Aunt Lizard snatches from his bird book. Attracted in the first place by the pictures, it was some time before he reached the text. When he did so, he found that the writer, a bird-loving clergyman, had set out to show that birds couldn't really be divided into sheep and goats, "beneficial and mischievous", but were usually both: the jay, detested by gamekeeper and gardener, devoured "large numbers of mischievous insects"; the starling fed on "mischievous grubs", the kestrel on "highly injurious caterpillars", the sparrow on "highly mischievous beetles", and so on. Even the bullfinch, most destructive of all, might, the writer pleaded, "play the part of a natural disbudder, and help to prevent the evils of overgrowth and unduly heavy fruitage." Pleased by these arguments, storing them up for future use, toasting an apple and watching it sizzle, Ralph asked lazily, "if you were a bird — which d'you think you'd call a parson? Beneficial or mischievous?"

"Beneficial, of *course*. Think of your Selborne curate — and all these reverend botanists."

"Still, a bird wouldn't care about botany."

"Not even," she laughed, "that beneficial bullfinch?"

His favourite illustration, showing pheasants in a wood, was rather like one of the pictures on the wall; youthful efforts of Aunt Lizard's, made over to Ralph and brought from Chelsea, at his request, with the rugs and the rocking chair. One showed a pale green lion, among rocks and shadows — a detail, she said, copied from a famous picture. She was a little mysterious about the other, a woodland scene, refusing to say where it had been painted. Like the picture in the bird book, it made him feel that he was there in the wood, not looking at a flat painting. Sometimes, too, reading the lists of names in *Sussex Flora*, he fancied that he could see the places named, Cut-and-lie Wood, Packhorse Lane, Spider Gallop, Starvecrow Wood and Starvemouse Plain; as though the vicar, remembering each one for himself, had written his thoughts into the pages. When Ralph tried to explain this feeling, Aunt Lizard told him about a painter she had known, who drew an imaginary landscape for a book jacket — iron gates, an avenue of trees, a distant park. Half hidden among the trees he put a small building like a summerhouse, with a domed roof. Meeting the author later, he was astonished at being reproached for not calling to see him, "when you did your sketch for the jacket". Puzzled, he explained that he had made up the scene, after reading a chapter or two; in fact, he had no idea where the author lived. At that, the literary man looked at him oddly and pressed him to come. When he reached the place, a cottage in Gloucestershire, the author took him straight up to his writing-room. The window looked out on the very scene he had painted; iron gates, a lime grove, a disused roadway thick with leaves. In the distance he saw a small domed ruin: an eighteenth-century ice-house.

Outside the mist drifted, the bony trees loomed up and disappeared. Ralph thought of the hovering thief, shivered and turned his back on the windows. Leafing through the flower book again, he came on some paragraphs at the end. One, headed "Peas Earth-Nut", was about a wild pea growing on the coast, in cornfields, or along their edges. He remembered the wild pea flowers he had seen on the headland, when he came home for the summer holidays. Could they be the same? The book said that their roots were good to eat, tasting like nuts; and that they looked like dead shrivelled mice. Someone called Gerard, it seemed, had written that the roots were like "domesticall mise", with long tails. Should he search along the field path, and dig up some to taste? But perhaps, he thought, Aunt Lizard had had enough, just lately, of "domesticall mise". He turned a page, and came to a note reprinted from a newspaper, about a boy who had died from eating belladonna berries. Three other children had escaped, "they had eaten less freely of the glossy purple berries". He had flicked over the page again when a thought struck him. He turned back, staring at the lines, trying to remember something. Aunt Lizard spoke to him and got no answer. She touched his arm, and he looked up.

"I said, it's time for your maths. What *is* the matter? You've gone quite green."

He said hoarsely, "Those berries" — and thrust the book into her hands, pointing to the headline, "Belladonna Poisoning." She read, with a frown of perplexity. Before she had finished, he urged, "We'll have to chuck the whole lot out. All our blackberry jam."

"I don't understand a word. What can you mean?"

"In the summer — that day I went after bilberries." He screwed up his eyes in the effort to remember. "I picked a lot of blackberries as well, and then I found some things, "glossy purple berries", like it says there. I wondered what they were, and I put them on top of the blackberries to show you."

"Well?"

"Well! That's all. I never thought of them again. What did we do with those blackberries? I bet you made them into jam. It's nothing to laugh at," he insisted. "*Don't you see*, they're deadly poison? — we can't eat any more bramble jam, in case it was *that* lot?"

"I'm afraid," she said, "it's too late to worry. We had the last spoonful on Christmas Eve."

The blackberry tarts! He was silent, thinking of what might have happened, of headlines in the local paper, "Three Poisoned in Lonely Cottage". But Christmas Eve was days ago. They would hardly fall ill now. He fanned himself dramatically with the book.

Aunt Lizard said, "Ralph, how *dreadful* of you."

"I know. And I've eaten pots of it. I never felt a twinge. Why not?"

"Well, let it be a lesson to you. And, now, talking of lessons —"

In the term ahead, Ralph was faced with two examinations: one for a place at a London day school, at present in wartime quarters in north Devon, the other for a scholarship to a boarding school. Both goals were rather hazy in his mind. He had not given much thought to either, except that he liked the idea of going to Devon. The other school was in Hertfordshire, not far from his present one, in a countryside he knew quite well, and this too had its attractions; but scholarships, he realized, were not won every year. He was really taking this second exam for practice — as an exercise, Uncle Alfred said; no one would worry if he didn't succeed. The two exams, in fact, were hurdles to be got over somehow, and then he would have his reward. It had all been arranged in father's latest letter; Rollo would be at Portsmouth in March, he would have a week's leave, he would come to Beaumarsh at last and see the spring house. He and Ralph would have a week together, he wrote; then he would take Ralph back to school for sports day. So much for the flap about his marrying Aunt Lizard! — she would be in London, and they wouldn't even meet, except perhaps for an hour or two. Father was taking over her car "for the duration", and would pick it up in Chelsea to start with. The whole plan seemed to belong to those glorious hopes that mustn't be thought about beforehand. First, the wretched exams. He had orders to do two hours' mathematics every day. While Aunt Lizard cooked their early dinner he struggled with theorems, equations or decimals. "Problems" he rather liked, and looked forward to teasing Aunt Lizard with today's: "A train starts from Point A at midday and travels at a uniform speed of 40 m.p.h. towards Point B, 200 miles down the line. Another train starts at Point B at 1 p.m. and travels at a uniform speed of 60 m.p.h. towards Point A. At what time will they pass each other?" A sum like that made sense, he thought; one could picture the two trains rushing towards each other. Aunt Lizard, in her solution, would literally picture them: she always had to draw her answers as she went along. He coped less readily with cubic feet of water flowing into tanks ("calculate the depth after three hours") or with vast walls being papered at so-much-and-three-farthings per square yard; but decimals were his chief enemy, the decimal point still, despite many explanations, an exasperating riddle. His thoughts strayed away to father's leave, to the wonderful time they would have here. And sports day; this year he might have a real chance in the high jump and the hurdles. He would start practising at once.

He spent the afternoon making a jumping-stand by the spinney: two bean poles, with nails to hold a lathe. Feeling optimistic, he set the nails up to five feet high. The take-off was slippery; he strewed it with ashes and practised until dark. The next afternoon he rigged up four hurdles in a row along the grass path through the garden. The mist was so thick that by teatime he was jumping blindfold. Again he had a curious notion that someone, or something, was watching him, and went indoors rather hastily. In the night, waking with a start, he thought he had heard the latch click on the garden gate. Could it have been a dream? Peering out, he could see nothing; and in the morning he found no footprints except from cat's paws: Cuckoo's paws, of course. Still, by afternoon he grew uneasy again, and decided to rig up a man trap of some sort. In the barnyard, behind a barrel, he had noticed a tangle of old rusty barbed wire, mixed up with wire netting. Dragging it clear, he hid the jumble behind the woodshed to wait until night. The wind had been rising all day, the mist was gone. Now he had a clear view of dark fields and downs; the gale was combing withered leaves out of the hedge and scattering them in the air. On his way to the village shop for Aunt Lizard, he found waves pounding over the harbour wall, dashing spray against the cottage windows. He raced up and down along the wall, dodging the waves, and reached home soaked. Aunt Lizard promptly forbade this game — "You might be swept away and drowned." Going out at nightfall, he could hear the tide running up the marsh a mile away. The gale was so strong that he was glad of the sheltering hedge and spinney, as with gloved hands he set his trap: wedging the barbed wire tightly against the gate on the inside, and hooking loose strands of wire round the gateposts. He was not proud of this makeshift device, but it would show, at least, that they were on the alert. If anyone tried to open the gate, he would have a tussle, and they might hear him. If he tried vaulting it, he would find himself snarled up in the wire.

He persuaded Aunt Lizard to sit up late: they would hardly be able to sleep in this storm. The wind howled in from the sea, boomed in the chimney, roared in the Spanish chestnut tree. Nodding over the chessboard, Ralph thought at length that it was wailing like a cat; even Cuckoo thought so. He rose from the hearth, arched his back and switched his tail. Suddenly he sprang on to Aunt Lizard's bunk, thrust himself between the curtains and pawed the glass, growling as though strangers were about. Ralph listened. There was the sound again, a strange anguished mewing that died into a long wail. Cuckoo took up the note. Ralph and Aunt Lizard were on their feet together, Ralph grabbing his torch while she turned out the lamp and opened the door a crack. An icy draught swept in. They stood waiting for a lull, and with the lull they heard once more a pitiful caterwauling. Ralph shouted, "There — it *is* a cat!" and rushed to the gate, to the man trap. At his feet he caught a thrashing noise, then a low growl. In the torchlight, horrified, he saw a black cat throwing himself from side to side, a front paw caught in the tangled wire. He quailed away from the light, howled as though in agony, bit and tore at the wire. Throwing the torch to Aunt Lizard, Ralph bent to help, but she cried, "Wait, he'll tear your hands to pieces! Run for your gloves!" He ran, but not for gloves; he brought his old coat, flung it over the cat, dragged the wire free, and, gathering up the whole armful — the cat still struggling, spitting and snarling — he staggered into the house.

A strange hour followed. They crouched on the hearth, Aunt Lizard holding the cat while Ralph worked away by lamplight and firelight with pliers from his toolkit. The trap had worked all too well. Jumping down from the gate, it seemed, the poor cat had caught his near front paw in the mesh, and a rusty barb, crooked like a fish-hook, had gone into the pad. As he struggled, his long fur had been caught in a dozen places; it was matted with blood where the barbs had made sharp gashes. Releasing the wounded paw was torture. While Aunt Lizard held his head and hind feet, muffling them in the coat, Ralph snipped and picked at the wire, murmuring distractedly over and over, "Poor puss, poor pussy, poor fellow." The cat leaped, whined and snarled in terror, but she clasped him firmly. At last it was done, and Ralph set to work on the other barbs, snipping off chunks of wet, tangled black fur. He saw thankfully that there were no more deep wounds. Now he was free. They sat back, expecting the cat to spring up and away at once. To their amazement, his fear and anger vanished. He licked frantically at the injured paw, then sat up, peering round. After a moment, as though realizing that they were friends, he relaxed and settled down to lick steadily at the paw. Aunt Lizard brought warm milk. Cuckoo, who had been watching avidly from a distance, now came near. The black cat glanced once at him, blinked meekly, then stretched out his head and lapped from the saucer. After a few laps he went back to licking the paw, and Cuckoo retired.

Now that the wire was gone, the creature seemed quite tame and gentle, allowing them to bathe his wounds without protest, and even to put on iodine; but he would not let them touch the paw. The wound should be stitched, Aunt Lizard thought. Tomorrow they should take him to the vet, and then try to find the owner. She added, "How good he is now. Really, he might be at home."

Ralph said, "I think he *is* at home." He told her about the cat that had come to tea with him in the garden, the day of the harvest mice. This was the same cat, he was sure: "I thought then, he seemed to belong here. I believe he's been here all the summer, living wild in our garden. Cuckoo knew, what's more." He hesitated, then admitted, "Do you know something? I believe *he* was my badger, all the time."

Early in the morning they set off for the vet. The invalid, tied into Cuckoo's travelling bag, lay quietly at first in Aunt Lizard's bicycle basket; but, as they came to the main road, he took fright and struggled so frantically that she dismounted and carried him in her arms to the bus stop, leaving Ralph to take the bicycles home again. The wind had fallen; the morning was mild and calm. He coaxed Cuckoo out of doors for a walk, to save hard feelings, and also to watch for Aunt Lizard's return. Perched on the barnyard gate, he could catch a glimpse of buses on the distant main road. From the town, there were three an hour. With mounting anxiety he counted seven; then Mr. Riley's car pulled up at the gate in the lane, and Aunt Lizard got out. Cuckoo ran along the farm road to meet her, but he stopped all of a sudden and scooted back towards home, evading Ralph; he had seen that once again she was carrying the black cat. A stranger was approaching along the headland. Cuckoo caught sight of him, seemed to lose his head completely, and swerved into the field among the fruit trees. Aunt Lizard called, "Go after him, Ralph — he'll be lost!" It was easier than catching the pig; Cuckoo lay down, panting, after a while and allowed himself to be caught. Aunt Lizard had taken her burden indoors; when Ralph got there she had come out again and was talking to the stranger by the well. Ralph dumped Cuckoo into her arms and ran to see the invalid. In the doorway he pulled up short. The black cat lay quite still on the hearth. Its eyes were shut, head lolling, one lip wrinkled back, showing its teeth. It was a corpse.

He backed away. Afraid he might burst into tears, he fled over the garden into the spinney. The vet must have "put it to sleep". Then it must have been badly hurt. All my fault, he realized. But why had Aunt Lizard brought it back? That was cruel: it wasn't like her at all. He remembered how kindly the cat had greeted him that day in October, when they were alone together. It had been so friendly, purring and rubbing round, and then haring after the squirrel, the minute it was told. He felt it would have been his own cat, as Cuckoo was Aunt Lizard's. Badger, he could have called it. Now, because of that idiotic trap, it was dead; and he would have to bury it as well.

Another thought struck him — could he bear to skin it, like the goldcrest? To have it for a rug, beside his bunk? Was *that* why Aunt Lizard had brought it back? He shuddered; yet the idea was intriguing. He turned back along the field path, hung about a few moments longer behind the hedge, then wriggled through and went to peer in at the west window.

The corpse was sitting up, licking its paw.

Coming in a minute later, Aunt Lizard explained, "The vet had to dope him. He put in five stitches. No use bandaging it, he said, just let it heal. He'll soon be well again."

Badger, still doped and languid, blinked up at her from Ralph's knee, green eyes narrowing to bright chinks. Ralph said eagerly, "Oh yes, and we can feed him up. He can have all my milk. And let's get a rabbit, he likes them." He thought swiftly, ruefully, of Peter Quince: no wonder the garden rabbits had disappeared.

"And another duck, I suppose," she said drily.

"The Christmas duck? *Him?* Oh, he can't have — I'm sure he never did!"

But, within a day or two, Ralph had to admit that the puzzle was solved. Living wild, Badger had become a ruthless and cunning thief. No food was safe from him. Aunt Lizard had only to turn her back for a moment, and half a pound of sausages vanished from the table. Another time, a basin of dripping was licked clean. It was easy to see where the cheese bag had gone, back in the summer. Each time, Badger looked up at her blandly from his place by the hearth, refusing to understand reproaches. After that, he was given no more chances.

Aunt Lizard, for her part, had to admit that in other respects he was faultless; gentle and meek, clean in his habits, endlessly tiring his long glossy fur, treating the ruffled Cuckoo with respect. From the first, it was obvious, he knew his place. All Cuckoo's spits and snarls he met with his patient, submissive blink, never raising a paw; yet without any loss of dignity. When Badger went out, Cuckoo would rush to take his place by the fire, retreating with a low growl when Badger sidled in again. Badger was twice Cuckoo's weight, yet he never offered to retaliate. Nor did he show any desire to resume his outdoor life. The weather had turned bitter, the garden was covered with snow. He spent all his time on Ralph's knee, or curled on a bed of sacks which Ralph made for him by the hearth.

"He's determined," said Aunt Lizard, "not to go on his travels again."

"He's not a wild cat," Ralph pointed out, "just homeless. He *was* homeless," he amended, and looked at her anxiously. Only two more weeks were left of the holidays. What then? Despite many inquiries, spread far and wide by the milk girl, no one had claimed Badger.

"I know," she said, answering the look, "but what are we to do with him? We can't keep him, it's too hard on Cuckoo. You can't take him back to school. We can't just turn him adrift."

"But couldn't he go on living here? As a garden cat? Tacker would feed him, I'll pay. I want him here. Do let me." Still she would not say yes.

At Nine Wells there had been four old farm cats, Tinker, Tailor, Soldier and Sailor. Aunt Lizard drew the line at Thief. Even without an extra mouth to feed, without Badger's raids, food was a problem. Yet, as Ralph said, he did not expect duck every day. He ate gratefully whatever was offered, porridge, beans, mashed potato, soaked dog biscuits; no pet could have been more accommodating. Soon, no doubt, he would return to mousing and rabbiting out of doors — and he must be coaxed to keep out of the spinney. Ralph assured himself that all would be well. Badger was his.

He had reckoned, however, without Badger himself. As Aunt Lizard had noticed, his ambition was to remain a hearth-rug cat; and within another week he had found a hearth of his own.

Merren McKay, arriving one day to tea, looked down at him in astonishment: "Whatever is that? A bear cub?" Badger raised his head and blinked at her. Ralph told her the whole story, starting back in May with the "badger" and Peter Quince. She said, "Ho, that's the sort of cat I need. A waste of time, my garden is — what the rabbits skip, the rats snap up." Hastily, afraid Aunt Lizard might take the hint, he steered her on to other topics, telling her about Tommy Mordecai, about the deer at Wild Hill; then about the deadly nightshade jam. He ran to the shed and brought in the cage with Sir Walter and Miss. They reminded one another of past encounters at school, when he was Madden's age. As she sat there in the rocking chair, dressed as an air raid warden — she had come straight from Portsmouth — she looked just as he remembered her from those days, plump and laughing; with her fresh colour, her good blue eyes and forthright ways, she was more like his idea of a farmer's wife, or a sailor's breezy daughter, than a teacher or a warden. Badger seemed to share his approval. When Ralph came back from stowing away the mouse cage, the black cat had settled his ten-pound weight in her lap, fraying her trouser knees with his claws. For the first time, he produced a raucous purr. She stroked his ears and refused to have him dislodged. During tea, as the talk moved on to next term's plans, Aunt Lizard mentioned the decimals. At once Merren offered to help. What luck, she said; she was on an early shift. She could come up by bus each afternoon. Brushing aside Aunt Lizard's protests, brushing scone crumbs from her blue serge bosom, she took out a notebook and pencil and gave him a lesson then and there. Ralph knew at once that the decimal point would have to yield up its secret. In five minutes he understood for the first time exactly why 0.5 meant a half, and 0.25 a quarter, and 0.125 — unlikely as it seemed — an eighth. After three more days, with Merren still rocking away quietly, Badger on her knee, the notebook propped on Badger, Ralph hanging over her shoulder, the whole business was clear. Not only would he never have to worry about it again: he could not remember why it had ever puzzled him.

On the fourth day, Merren arrived on her bicycle from her downland cottage; she had just started a few days' leave. It was dark when she set off on the long ride back, but she said she was used to it; she would be home in an hour. The snow was gone. Ralph went with her as far as the field gate, Badger trotting behind; he had taken a great fancy to Merren, who brought him a small package of horsemeat each day from a shop near the dockyard. Turning to go in, when Merren's bicycle lights were out of sight, Ralph could not find the cat, but knew that Badger wouldn't be lost. Sitting with paints and sketchbook, he kept listening for Badger's modest signal at the door, but at bedtime the black cat was still out. Ralph searched the garden by torchlight, finding no sign of him, and roamed along the path to the barn, tripping over molehills, calling and listening. Badger did not come. Aunt Lizard said, "Don't worry. I expect, now he's better, he'll start to hunt again." Still, Ralph could not help worrying. Badger might have strayed into another trap — a steel trap, this time. He got up before dawn, hoping to find the cat on the doorstep; he was disappointed.

Aunt Lizard went out shopping. He would not go with her, but paced about, longing to see the great black creature winding in and out among the almonds, or jumping on to the barnyard wall. He could see the men far off in Hammers, lifting fruit trees. One of them might have seen Badger. Setting out to ask, he met the postman bicycling towards him along the farm road. To his surprise, the man called, "Telegram for Mr. Oliver!" Ralph thought he must be joking, but the man held out a yellow envelope addressed to Ralph Oliver, The Spring House, Beaumarsh. He tore it open — could it be from father? — and gazed at the message. He found himself blinking like Badger. He could not take it in. Merren had sent it, two hours ago, from Fitching post office. He read again: "Badger safe with me stop very welcome stop here stop shall I return him Merren McKay." He sorted out the stops. It was "reply paid", the postman said, care of Fitching post office; but Ralph could not wait. He would be there himself, up at Merren's cottage, fetching Badger, in an hour. But how in the world had Badger got there? Merren, he knew, wouldn't have kidnapped him on purpose. Besides, he had seen her go. It was a mystery, far stranger than the missing duck or the decimals. He darted back for his bicycle and Cuckoo's travelling bag.

He knew the steep path up the yew tree valley was too slippery for use in winter. Merren had said she would go "the long way round"; to Fitching village, then up the downs by an old coach road, along the hilltop, past the tumuli and an old polo ground. Asking his way from a hedger-and-ditcher, a group of children in a school playground, a tractor-driver munching bread and cheese at a headland, he came out at last on top of the downs. The day was bleak and cold. Black heather stalks hissed in the wind. The far-off sea creeks had a steely glint, the abbey tower looked like a grey fungus. He passed the tumuli, that were older than the abbey, older than the Roman villa; but he could not stop to explore them. He left the flint track and ran on along narrow paths through the heather, through a little wood, on to Merren's cottage standing on its own, miles from anywhere; a gamekeeper had last lived there. Merren saw him coming and hurried down the path to meet him, full of apologies. Badger had followed her to the main road, she said. Dismounting to let some traffic pass, she had found him beside her, rubbing round her ankles; but he wouldn't be caught. At last she thought he had turned back — then, to her dismay, a mile or so on along the lanes, she heard him crying in the distance, and waited for him to catch up. Again, when she tried to pick him up, he retreated. That went on until she got to the foot of the downs, and it seemed too late to turn back; then he let himself be caught, and sat quite peacefully in her basket while she trudged up the hill.

They were inside Merren's kitchen now. It was dark, except for the glowing bars of a coal range. Ralph's eye went straight to something like a black fur cushion, curled against the oven door. He dropped to his knees, crying "Badger!" The cat lifted his head, blinked, then tucked his nose back into his fur. Merren, still apologetic, said Badger seemed tired after his long trot;

besides, he had already killed a rat in the coalshed. Ralph hugged him, laughing and teasing: "Why, Badger, Badger, don't you know me?" Badger did not respond. He stirred, sighed, wriggled, and at last got up, stretched himself and strolled, with the air of a person at home, to an armchair. He sprang into it and sat washing. When Ralph tried to pick him up he went stiff, with a little mew of protest, and made as though to bite.

Ralph would not stay after that. Let him rat if he wanted to, he told himself furiously: let someone else warn Merren about his thieving ways. Riding recklessly down the stony track, he thought, She's nursing a viper, and giggled in spite of himself. But on the flat road, facing the long dispiriting homeward trek, he could not laugh. The wind blew keenly; there was sleet in it. Sad and disillusioned, numb with cold, he hurried on through the mirk, impatient to tell Aunt Lizard that he had found his cat, and that Badger, the meek, the affectionate, the grateful — Badger had cut him dead.

CHAPTER ELEVEN

Molecatcher

That month they were grateful for the sun and moon. Ralph felt he had never really noticed either, before he came to live there. Never before had he watched dawn and sunset on a wide low horizon, and grudged their loss in dark or misty weather; or waited for moonlight so that he could more conveniently go out after tea. Now the days were growing longer. Every evening the first cry of the brown owl, down in Beaumarsh village, came a little later. Once the owl flew over to perch in the oak tree by the spinney, and sat making small purring and trilling sounds. Listening, Ralph thought he understood how gamekeepers felt about owls. He loved to hear this one, but he did not want it hunting in the spinney.

This afternoon, while he practised hurdling, he noticed a man in the distance, walking slowly along the pathway from the barn. Every few yards, he paused and stooped down — to tie a bootlace, Ralph thought at first; but he came on, still stooping, walking, stooping again. No bootlace would come undone as often as that. Ralph watched him curiously. Something in his movements recalled a warren keeper he had known; but this man was a gipsy-like individual, carrying a spade over his shoulder, and what looked like a handful of long twigs, as for budding and grafting; or *dowsing*, perhaps? He realized that he had seen the man before. Hadn't Aunt Lizard spoken to him, by the well, when she brought Badger back from the vet? Just then, he heard her calling him in, to help re-hang the curtains. She had lined their blackout stuff with some cottagey curtains of Aunt Emmy's, with roses and parrots, to look more cheerful after dark. It was dark when they had finished, and the man was gone.

In the morning, going to fetch the milk, Ralph found a row of bent hazel wands among the molehills beside the path. They were fastened in hoops, such as he had seen in gardens, protecting part of a lawn where fresh grass seed had been sown. What could they be protecting here? He had heard of a gamekeeper's sowing parsley seed to attract hares. That might be it; or were the twigs some kind of springe? They didn't look like rabbit snares. He thought he would watch for the man, and ask him. Just before dinner, he slipped out to walk round the garden and spinney, taking the white mice along for company. The day was springlike; a missel thrush sang, bell tits called. He came out on to the field path, and saw that the man with the hazel twigs had been here this morning; now there were hoops in the turf beside the spinney. As before, they were straddling fresh molehills. He bent to look at one of them, put out a hand, then hesitated. Once, he had meddled with a rat trap set by the school gardener, and had nearly lost the top of his forefinger. The steel snapper had caught it with a lightning slash, designed to break a rat's neck. The finger was still flattened at the first joint, close to an older scar where a dormouse had bitten him, and next to the thumb he had sliced on May Day. He looked from his scars to the springe, then prodded the twig gently with his toe. At once a gruff voice called, "Hey, you. Leave that alone."

He jumped, and looked round. The man was sitting at the edge of the spinney, spade and twigs beside him, with a bundle of ironware of some kind. He wore a patchy-looking greyish jacket made of fur — ponyskin? catskin? — which blended like a keeper's coat with his surroundings. Moving nearer, Ralph saw that he had one blind white eye; the other, blue and watery, glinted fiercely at him. He was not smoking, or eating. He seemed to be simply sitting there, watching his twigs. Ralph said meekly, "I just wondered what they were."

"No business o' yourn."

Ralph had another twinge of longing for Flip. He remembered those rat traps at school; they had been set by the hen-keeping gardener, to protect his young chicks. A surly character, he had refused to have frog spawn in the greenhouse, and would treacherously throw buckets of it down the drain while the owners were in class. However, Flip had pointed out to him that rat traps could easily be sprung by accident, unless someone kept an eye on them when he was at work elsewhere. The man knew blackmail when he heard it, and after that the spawn was unmolested. He even let Flip keep a newt in the greenhouse tank. A protection racket, Uncle Alfred said when he heard of it. Ralph would have liked to try the same gambit now, but he knew he lacked Flip's self-confidence. He was more likely to get a thump for his pains — what Bob Doggett called "a haymaker" — than to find out anything that way. As usual, he would have to ask Tacker what the twigs were for; but Tacker had not appeared since Christmas. He was laid up with rheumatism, the milk girl told him next morning. On impulse, he asked her who the stranger could be. She laughed at his description. "That's not a gipsy. That's Bert Monk, the molecatcher."

Of course! He remembered now. The hazel wands were old-fashioned mole traps; and the iron things were modern ones. And the jacket was moleskin — he might have known that. He had caught a mole once, but it bit him and he had dropped it. The girl was chattering on, full of information: "Bert Mink, they call him now. Everyone says he's making a fortune." Once, farmers would pay him a few shillings to clear a farm, or perhaps give him twopence a tail. Now, rich furriers from London were paying "pounds and pounds" for the skins. People would give anything for a fur coat. "No coupons, you see, they buy the skins first, and then get them made up." Molecatching, she added, used to be just a sideline. Bert had always been a well-known poacher, and he still did a bit that way, people said. (Ralph thought of the deer and pheasants in Wild Hill woods.) He had lost his eye in a fight with some keepers — "though he'll tell you it was a sniper in the last war."

I wish he *would* tell me, Ralph thought, weaving his way home with the milk can. What a pity he had rubbed him up the wrong way yesterday — if he had been more tactful, they might have gone moling together. If Bert Monk had been a *mole*, though, there wouldn't have been a wrong way: he remembered the short fur, with its silvery sheen, too close-fitting to be ruffled when the mole was hurtling up and down tunnels. Was that why people wanted moleskin coats — to wear in air raid dug-outs? He considered this sally, and thought again of Flip. *He* would have thought it fairly funny. What a time they could have had here together. Still — next time, father would be here.

A little later he had a surprise. Coming home from an errand in the village, he opened the door, and there was the molecatcher himself, taking his ease by the fire; talking away to Aunt Lizard while he ate his lunch — pheasant sandwiches, no doubt — and drank a glass of Tacker's beer. He nodded affably to Ralph, as though meeting him for the first time. Ralph gathered that Aunt Lizard and Bert Monk had met somewhere before; and then, that his first guess had been right, Bert Monk had once been a gamekeeper. But Aunt Lizard steered the talk away from the past, on to his present trade. Looking at Cuckoo, he began talking about a cat he had had, that actually killed a weasel: "not a great savage tom cat either. A pretty little longhaired thing she was, looked fit for nothing but lapping cream, but a fighter all right. Take on a rat any day. Well, this weasel came after the moles —"

"Oh, do they hunt moles?" Ralph exclaimed.

"Listen, I'm a-telling you. I was setting mole traps, and the weasel come up out of a run. The cat got hold of it by the neck, and I hollered at her, thinking she'd bitten more than she could chew, but she hung on, and shook it like a blessed ratter, and jumped to and fro over it, and in a minute or two the weasel was dead as a nit. Died of rage, I always say." Again he looked appraisingly at Cuckoo, who, even in his palmy days, would never have tackled a weasel. Ralph felt impelled to say loyally, "Cuckoo once *growled* at a keeper that he thought was going to shoot him. The keeper laughed like anything, when he told us."

Presently, with infinite care, Ralph began on the subject of mole springes. "You set them in the tunnels, don't you? But I don't quite see how they catch the moles?"

Still good-humoured, Bert Monk told him that each springe had a noose on the end. He demonstrated how it worked. The minute the mole got his neck in the noose, it sprang up and strangled him: a deadly engine.

Aunt Lizard laughed suddenly, then explained, "Mole-strangling sounds like a Mummerset joke."

"I dare say. Well, it won't be one for long. Not many chaps nowadays know how it's done, nor how to dig them either. It's all these shop traps now."

"Dig them — ?" asked Ralph.

"That's it." He finished his beer and got up to go. Outside, he took something from the fork of the damson tree — an ancient mole corpse — and put it in his pocket. Ralph said, when he was out of earshot, "Phew! He won't skin that one. It's practically a fossil."

Watching the man lope away past Little Stint, and across the lane into Flint Walls field, he wanted to follow, but judged it best to let well alone. If Bert Monk wanted company, no doubt he would say so.

Late in the afternoon there came a rap at the door. When Ralph opened it, the molecatcher thrust a limp dead rabbit into his hands and made off without waiting to be thanked. This was the first time Ralph had skinned a rabbit for the pot. He found it easier than the goldcrest.

Next day, his luck was in. Coming from hurdle practice, he saw Bert in the distance, leaning against the barn wall, his spade at his side. Going nearer, Ralph saw he was watching a fresh mole-run. Ralph tiptoed up as lightly as possible: "Are you going to dig it out *now*?"

"Not time yet. Another twenty minutes." Ralph eyed him doubtfully: was that a joke? Bert saw the look but said nothing. Ralph pursued,

"You mean, you know what *time* it'll come along?"

"Near enough. Every four hours they feed, like humans. I've heard moles'll die inside twelve hours, if they can't feed. Dozens of worms they get through in a day. Thirsty little beggars, too. You'll find them in your copse in a dry spell looking for water." Ralph leaned beside him. Presently Bert straightened up, holding his spade in both hands, knees slightly bent, watching the ground. Ralph thought he saw a flicker of movement in the turf between two molehills; but the molecatcher kept still. Another movement, and he took a new grip on the spade and lowered it, but again without moving his feet. It'll get away now, Ralph thought: he's waited too long. But the next moment Bert made a swift scooping movement; something flew through the air and landed on the turf. It would have scrambled away, but a quick rap finished it. Poor mole: but Ralph could not help admiring the catcher's neatness. Seeing this, Bert became talkative again.

"Ain't no good jumping on a mole first time you see him move. That's why you can't train a dog to this game like you can to ratting. It's like the snipers in the old war" — Ralph's gaze went in fascination to his blind eye — "first move you see him, second move you take aim, and then the third you nabs him — flick him right out with your spade, because by that time he's right up near the surface. If you go for him the first or second time, he's too far down."

"Supposing you miss him?"

"Then you can try later. He'll be up after worms at the end of four hours, if he's still in the same run."

"Or you could set a trap?"

"Could. But they can spoil the skin. Besides, the old mole, he's clever about traps. You have to go one better. Now I always carry some flat bits of iron when I go trapping, to block the way round. If I didn't, I might find the trap empty, and the mole's been underneath. Or I give it a rub over with a dead'n. He smells it, and thinks he's got a trespasser, and then, if you're lucky he'll get in a fury and blunder in before he can stop himself." Still, Bert insisted, the mole was no fool. "People talk as if moles were daft as well as blind, but I tell you they can see with their ears and hear with their noses, and they're crafty as anything barring a fox. You look at a mother mole. She keeps her family in a great hullock, and I've found them places many a time, but never a mole inside. You can come up as quiet as you like, and dig into the nest like lightning — it's not a bit of good. Old mother's heard you coming a long way off, and she's got hold of her young ones and carried them off. And the place is such a maze of tunnels, beggared if you'd know where to look for 'em next."

He was going down to set springes in Fox'ls, and Ralph would have gone with him; but Aunt Lizard appeared, suggesting that they might cycle into town to see a film. He had a moment's suspicion that she was keeping him away from Bert Monk — because he was a poacher? — then he forgot about it.

The day had again been mild and quiet; but, coming out of the cinema, they found the wind had risen, a shrill north-easter that blew them home. Dark clouds were looming up, and the air was frosty. On the field path, the wind seemed to cut them to the bone. They had had to put out the fire before leaving, and the house felt dank. Ralph was soon in bed, watching firelight on the ceiling, listening to the wind outside; but warmth seemed slow in returning. Next morning he woke feeling out of sorts. The ache was still there in his bones, and in his head as well. He got up and sat by the fire, but he was restless. Aunt Lizard looked at his heavy eyes, put her hand for a moment on his forehead, and sent him back to bed.

It was 'flu, she thought. For three days he was not allowed up, and he did not mind. He was not particularly ill, but he felt dull and tired of life. What a way to end the holidays! The weather outside reflected his mood. Sky and fields, drained of colour, lay drab in the bitter wind. Aunt Lizard disappeared for long stretches of time, searching far and wide for an orange or a lemon for him, but without success; he had to make do with blackcurrant tea. On the fourth day his temperature was down, he had a streaming cold and wanted to grumble at everything. He could not eat. She dived into her stores to tempt him with onion soup, a mushroom omelette, a toffee tart made with black treacle; piled the fire with logs, and taught him to play bezique. Next day she had promised to give talks in two villages some miles on the other side of Fitching. Someone in the nearer village had asked her to lunch, and would drive her to both places afterwards. Now she did not want to leave Ralph, but he insisted that he was quite recovered. The day rose bleak and sunless, with thin scurrying snowflakes; too cold for another snowfall, he thought, and sighed. He had hoped to be really snowed up, cut off by great white drifts; too late now. The holidays were gone.

He had thought he would enjoy some hours alone; but, as soon as Aunt Lizard was out of sight, he found himself thinking with dismay of the long hours ahead. She had left wood and water for the day, and had fed the white mice, torpid in their cage outside. He pottered about, fiddling with the fire, making cocoa which he did not want. Nothing to get dressed for, even. He remained in pyjamas and his old coat, but felt slatternly and good for nothing. Time, that usually passed far too quickly, now seemed to crawl. Cuckoo, curled on the other bunk, slept resolutely. Slow-worm and spiders had disappeared. He looked at his algebra, but could not bring himself to open it. He did not want to read or paint. The wireless seemed dull; he switched it off. The wind moaned in the chimney. He thought again of the endless empty day, and was glad to see a gang of men arriving in New Barn field to lift fruit trees. At least he could hear their voices, and catch glimpses of them through the hedge.

A knock at the door; Tacker put his head in, with a message from Mr. Riley — they were a hand short, would he like to come and carry trees? His face lit up.

"I'll be out in a minute, Tacker!"

"Bring your bike, then." The door shut.

For a moment conscience pricked him. Tacker, just back himself, didn't know he had been ill. But he had made no promise about staying in — Aunt Lizard had simply assumed he would want to. Well he couldn't. He'd rather die of pneumonia than spend another hour by himself. Pneumonia? . . . grandmother used to threaten him with that, when he started paddling too early in the year. He brushed the thought aside and began pulling on long trousers, socks and gumboots, straight over his pyjama trousers — the best garb for cold weather, Jill had said. Hearing this on a summer day in Fox'ls, he had laughed; today he could see the sense of it. He put on three jerseys and the old coat on top of them, stuffed the pockets with clean handkerchiefs, poured a scalding mug of cocoa and drank it down, put up the fireguard, patted Cuckoo and opened the door. A blast of sleet met him. As a sop to thoughts of Aunt Lizard, he rummaged in a trunk for his sou'wester and put it on. Then he was out in the arctic weather, running over the field to join the gang.

Winter was another harvest time at Seaforth. The tree lifters worked in threes, two digging with flat-bladed grafts, the third pulling the tree, timing his pull so that it came up gently with roots unbroken. Ralph and Sally raced to and fro carrying trees to the nearest path, where Joe Lock sorted them into lots. Joe carried a wad of papers, dog-clipped together, ends flapping in the wind. The night before he had gone through the day's orders, making lists for each field. As fast as one batch came out, he was calling for another: "Ten standard Bramleys" — "Fifteen bush Reverend Wilks" — "Twenty pyramid Conference" — "Two half-standard almonds" — "Six standard walnuts". The last would be a longer job; they were five-year-old walnut trees with tough roots. Harry, Ted and Jake were left to it while the rest cycled on, to lift great whipping plum trees in Sallows, then more bush apples; then into Little Stint for bundles of gooseberry bushes and pungent-smelling blackcurrants; on down to Bullrush for the last roses, then into Fox'ls for fan peaches and cordon apples. Tacker followed with Violet, loading trees into the cart. Then, to Ralph's amazement, Tess arrived looking proud and wary, leading Silver. She had been working with him for a week now. Sally grinned: "Sooner her'n me." The grey pony had tried his best to bite or trample her, but hadn't succeeded yet. She kept nimbly out of his way, Ralph noticed. When she had to lead him on, she would approach soundlessly from behind, sheltered by his blinkers, and take the rein with a firm grip, close to his mouth, so that he could not turn and bite. It was a day-long battle, but Tess seemed to be enjoying it.

Oddly enough, Ralph felt better in the open than he had done indoors. He had no time to feel cold; they were kept on the run. Whenever there was a moment's pause, Sally lit a fire of dry grass on the path; not for warmth, though they toasted their fingers a second, but for amusement, to see the grass flare up and wither. The flames were the only speck of colour in the grey landscape. At dinner time Ralph sped home, made up the fire, drank a cup of soup, put the bean hotpot to warm for supper; and out again into the wind, under a dull sky, ragged clouds and flurries of sleet. In Bullrush and Fox'ls they had been sheltered, almost warm. In Hammers there were no windbreaks. The wind flowed over them like icy water. The lifters paused now and then to blow on their fingers and flail their arms. They said, "Bitter," and then, inevitably, "Bitter, sir? I don't mind if I do." Despite the weather, the atmosphere was cheerful, and Ralph was thankful that he had not stayed moping indoors. Old Harry, nibbling a mouthful of cake, was chaffed about his new false teeth, and took it in good part: "That blamed nurse says I've got to *clean* these." Two or three of the young men had a private slogan which they exchanged whenever they met. When Ralph asked Ted what it meant, he looked taken aback for a moment, and said, "Well, it's a bit broad" — then explained; using, Ralph noticed, exactly the words that a schoolmaster would have chosen. The older men had none of this fluency; but perhaps they did not need it. Their own ribaldries, if any, were not for this company. Ralph never heard Tacker, or George Doggett, or old Harry, make a doubtful quip, however mild, in front of boys and girls. From the old sea-dogs, again, one might have expected to hear a few salty oaths; but if Tacker or Fred Buckler knew any, they were not produced for his benefit.

Bert Monk wandered by, earthy mole-traps jangling, a bulging sack slung over his shoulder, and stopped for a word with them. No one chaffed him — he was not one of themselves — though Jim Honeywood lost no time in muttering to the boys, "Bet he's got some good moles in that sack. Feathered 'uns, with long tails." Once or twice Ralph had heard a cock pheasant in the kale across the road. He wondered if Bert had set springes for them; a raisin on a horsehair, perhaps. He had heard about this trick years ago, from two gipsy boys at a village school. The pheasant, according to them, would swallow the raisin and choke to death on the horsehair; Ralph himself could never quite swallow this tale.

Before he went on his way, Bert came and stood beside Ralph and Sally as they crouched over one of their little fires. Sally bent low, blowing on the flames. Bert said to Ralph in a muttered aside, "So *she's* not married agen?"

Looking up, he met the glare of the molecatcher's eye. The question startled him, as Madden's had done three months ago.

"Who? Oh, Aunt Lizard!" He laughed. They were all determined to marry her off! "Oh, no, she's never been married."

"Married to that Dane chap though, wasn't she?"

"Oh! Oh, yes, I see." The foreman was calling, "Look alive," and he did not wait to point out the mistake. It was Aunt Emmy, of course, who was Mrs. Dane. Bert must have met her, as well as Aunt Liz. Where? He would ask Liz tonight.

Darkness came down early, and they followed the carts to the packing shed, the high Dutch barn opposite the stables. Coming in from the gloom outside, the place seemed almost gay. Electric bulbs swayed gently in a draught, shining on mountains of yellow straw, on Captain's burnished coat, and the few bronze leaves still clinging to trees and bushes stacked in bays around the walls. George Doggett waited with the big tumbril to take another load to the station. The air smelled of sap and straw, the rafters echoed with whistling. The lifters joined the packers; for their journeys to distant gardens and orchards, the trees had to be swathed in straw, roots and all. The tall ones ended up like giant wine bottles in straw flasks. Fans and espaliers were lashed to flat wooden "cradles". The packer would first lay down a row of strings, then a thick layer of straw, then the bundle of trees; he drew the strings tight, and there it was, another neat parcel, ready for the tumbril. Joe gave Ralph a bunch of currant bushes to pack; minutes later he was still struggling, covered in straw. Meanwhile, Joe himself had packed a seven-foot sheaf of plum trees, smooth as thatch, not a wisp out of place, as easily as tying up a bunch of snowdrops.

Jill, the checker, raised a cry, "Belle de Louvain!" and called Ralph to help search for it.

"What's lost?" he asked Tess in a whisper. "An apple or a rose?"

"*I* thought it was a song she wanted them to whistle."

Everyone would be working overtime. At five, Ralph joined the girls at the water tap. They washed in snow-cold water, brushed one another down and took turns with a comb, before bicycling down to The Race for tea. As soon as they entered the guest house, Ralph saw why they had made him tidy up. Coming from the barn and the wintry fields, he saw the place with new eyes; the blazing fire, soft carpets, glossy tables and glossy magazines, hyacinths and china, buttered toast and chocolate fingers, all were like something from another life, strange and luxurious. He saw why Tess came here each day to brace herself for the seven dark miles home. She said, "I look forward to it all day. When I leave home it's pitch dark and freezing, roads covered with ice, I keep skidding about, and I don't see a soul for five miles, and I think, only twelve hours from now I'll be sitting by the fire in The Race, reading *Theatre Arts*."

"Who do you see, after five miles?"

"Oh, I meet a dear little man in a blue cap, like a Dutchman, and we call out 'Marning'. At least, I don't see him, of course, but I did in the summer, and now I hear his boots on the road. If I don't, I know I'm late."

Ralph suddenly remembered that Aunt Lizard would be back. He had barely time to reach home, shed his top garments and top grime, relight the fire and lay the table. To Aunt Lizard, pinched from her journey, the house seemed warm. At supper, when Ralph passed his plate for a third helping, she looked pleased, then incredulous: "Why, Ralph — I do believe your cold's *gone*."

Pausing, a forkful of beans in his hand, he realized that this was so. Wind and weather had blown it away. For hours he had not given it a thought.

She said pleasantly, "Nothing like a day indoors, in the warm, to cure a cold. Is there?" He was going to agree; then noticed her looking at something on the floor by his bunk: his gumboots, flung down in haste, plastered with mud and straw. Swiftly he said the first thing that came into his head. "Shall I tell you something? Bert Monk's got you and Aunt Emmy mixed up. He thinks *you*'re Mrs. Dane!"

For once, the red herring diverted her. She looked quite put out, saying sharply, "Oh! Has *he* been here?"

"He — well, I saw him this afternoon. He asked if you'd married *again*, too!" He repeated what Bert had said. She agreed, "How funny." Looking at her plate, she added, "And? What else did he want to know?"

"Nothing else. I say! D'you think he really wants to marry you himself?"

Composed again now, she smiled back. "Barkis is willing? No, I'd say Barkis is wedded to his moles."

"Still, they say he's nearly a millionaire."

But she would not go on with it. She began to collect the dishes. Kicking the gumboots out of sight, Ralph yawned and dropped on to his bunk, almost too drowsy to finish undressing. And now he wished no one had started all this talk about her marrying — father, or anyone else. What would be the sense of it? He followed this old hare for fifteen seconds, then he was asleep.

CHAPTER TWELVE

Hurdler

As the open car spun along winding roads among the downs, Ralph sang to himself under the hum of the engine. The marvellous day had come; trapped in the long weeks of term, he had never really believed that it would. Here they were, he and father, on a bright March afternoon, speeding towards Beaumarsh. The downs were pale green, combed by the wind. Russet leaves lay thickly on beechwood floors, under straight silver-grey beech trunks. A russet cock pheasant raised its brilliant head to watch them from a hedgerow, nonchalantly, as though aware of the close season, and unaware of poachers. A yellowhammer called. "That's Fitching down, Dad, where Merren lives." Looking up at the dark yews and junipers, he thought of Badger stalking among them. There were so many things to tell. "I say, Dad — at Christmas there was a cat —" His father asked at the same moment, "Which way here?"

"Oh — left." Just in time he stopped himself from adding companionably, as he would have done with Aunt Lizard, "Right might have been better." There were no signposts, of course, but he remembered this road vaguely, from his excursion to East Harden heath.

He must be careful, though, he reminded himself; must keep his head, and keep his mouth shut; mustn't say anything to annoy father. This was going to be the best holiday they had ever had, the first for six years in a home of their own, not at Nine Wells or in some hotel: a whole week at the spring house together. Beforehand, the sense of responsibility had sometimes terrified him; but, now that they were on the road, excitement soared above his doubts. Nothing could go wrong.

He glanced sideways at father: fair hair, broad shoulders, bright grey eye, head cocked slightly, listening to the engine — this was the first time he had driven Aunt Lizard's car — old tweed jacket and polo-necked sweater; Ralph had long ago stopped hoping that he might arrive at school in uniform. He wished he could look like that himself, not thin and dark like his mother's family. Still, he might change. By the time he was old enough to be called up —

"Anything coming your side?"

They were approaching the point of a V-fork. Ralph glanced back along the parallel road to his left; he could see as far as a bend, thirty feet or so away. "No, it's clear — still clear —" an army truck skidded round the bend — "No, wait!" Father had braked already. The truck shot past; there was just room for it. Father raised his eyebrows, half smiled and said nothing. They drove on in silence. Ralph found himself struggling with familiar sensations: rebellion, and then depression. That wasn't fair, he thought. It was clear when I said so. The truck must have been doing fifty. Never mind, he didn't say anything, I mustn't think about it, it's going to be all right. Wait till we get to the spring house. He looked down at his wrist watch, father's present, already worn over two hours. Half an hour more and they would be there.

Something else he mustn't think about: the scholarship exam. If those exams had been hurdles, he had crashed at the last fence. But it was done now; it was over. Whatever they all said when they heard about it — and sooner or later, he supposed, it would all come out — no regrets could bring back his lost chance, or unwrite what he had written. What *had* he written? No, no, not now — forget it quickly. But if only he could go back and have yesterday over again . . . He shivered slightly. They were running on the shady side of the downs. Father glanced at him, slowed down, dragged a scarf from the back and threw it to him, moving slowly while he wound it round over his blazer. No loose ends, he warned Ralph. Some famous woman had broken her neck, driving in an open car with a flapping scarf. Listening to this tale as they gathered speed again, Ralph forgot about yesterday. They came out again into the bright afternoon, driving past woods thick with last month's catkins, past flashing ruffled ponds and a windmill, through meadows bordered with thickets of orange willow withies. At the level crossing they had a setback; a goods train was clattering back and forth. The gates remained shut, the minutes ticked past. He could feel father growing impatient.

"Ralph — where's the nearest road bridge?"

He jumped. "Over the railway?" He thought quickly, wondering if the delay were his fault, bringing them this way. With relief, he remembered the map.

"Oh, miles down the line — about six miles." Father nodded and lit a cigarette. Ralph leaned forward to look at the rails gleaming in the sun, straight as a Roman road. Somewhere down there was the orchard he had seen, that day in October. He wondered if anyone had ever gone there to pick the apples, or if the birds had swiped them all. How did you get to the place, anyway? He couldn't remember any road that seemed to lead there. As he thought about it, something clanked in the signal-box; the gates swung open, they were through, running along the main road, then down the lane. "That's The Oaks, where I went harvesting. Fox'ls, oh, there's George Doggett — there's Tess and Silver — we'll see the spring house in a minute. There! D'you see, out beyond the barn? Turn off here — oh, the gate's open. Look, that's the spinney, where the mouse-run is. That's New Barn field — spring wheat, it's going to be, now we've cleared the trees, and barley in Chequers . . ." They drew up by the barnyard. Ralph could hardly wait to be out of the car.

"Oh — but aren't you bringing your case? I'll carry it. I've only got my kitbag, and the rations, and the egg-box —" Four pullets' eggs, he had bought from the school gardener, and all sorts of stuff from the cook. He ran to pull out the case, but father stopped him.

"Just a minute — leave it, leave the lot. Let's have a look at this place of yours first."

They were actually walking along the field path, just as he had imagined. Here was the house. He tried to see it with father's eyes; longed to ask at once, "Is it what you expected?" — restrained himself, ran on to the niche in the well, brought out the key and unlocked the door. "Here we are, Dad — come in."

Father stepped over the threshold, bending his head slightly, looked quickly round and exclaimed, "Good God! Is this it?" He laughed, standing in the middle of the room, looking immensely tall, amused and — with some other expression in his face that Ralph shied away from reading. He added, "Well, well, so this is the spring house," and seemed at a loss for words. Ralph prompted him — "You didn't expect it'd be like this, did you?" Father shook his head. Ralph pursued, "It's a bit like a ship's cabin, isn't it? All compact and — you know — small, and —" He paused. Father said, a shade grimly, "I do know. Well —" Again he smiled and glanced round.

"Wait, I'll do the fire in a second, then it'll be warming up, then I'll bring the gear in. I'll put the kettle on, we can have tea first, and poached eggs, I thought, and muffins." He had never tried making muffins by himself, but he knew how they were done. "Oh, but —" he hesitated, then begged, "Could we just come to the spinney for a minute? Before it starts getting dark? I want to show you where the harvest mice" — He stopped; father did not seem to be attending; but the next moment he turned to say, "Yes, of course, old boy. You lead on. Let's see it all." They circled the hedge and took the path into the spinney.

"Mind, it's a bit soggy." It was more than soggy; it was a quagmire. They squelched through, jumping from one tuft of rushes to the next, and came to the drier ground above the dell. Hazel boughs clashed in the wind, pollen blew about like pepper. Here was the mouse-run. Father caught him up as he stood looking at it. Ralph was dumb; father said in a bluff, hearty tone:

"So, that's the mouse-run. Any mice there now?" Ralph shook his head. He could not speak. Something was going wrong. There was nothing to see, after all; only wire netting, sodden moss, old straw. Why on earth had he brought father here? He muttered angrily, "Now we'll go back." Father moved as though to take his arm, but he dashed ahead, letting a hazel branch fly back. Father put up a hand and caught it. Ralph gasped, "Sorry. I didn't mean —"

"No harm done. Where now?"

Not answering, Ralph led the way back to the path. He stood there with his face to the cold wind, his back to the sunset, gazing at the small dark hump that was the spring house. He thought in panic — Fool, fool. What on earth have I done?

He had brought father to this awful God-forsaken place, to waste his precious leave in a hovel, in the middle of ploughed fields, in winter — to eat scratch meals, and drink smoky tea, and — what would they do all day? What *was* there to do — how on earth did he and Aunt Lizard pass their time? He had no idea. He ran on to the house, flung open the door and went in. It was getting dark, it was cold; the firewood might be damp, it would take hours to get the place warmed up. Why, why had he ever started this? Aunt Liz shouldn't have let him — she knew what father was like, but she had left him to cope by himself. Of course, he saw now, she had never really liked the place either. She had only pretended, to humour him. He felt choked by dark and bitter thoughts.

A step; father was standing just behind him. "Ralph." Quiet, decisive voice.

"Yes?" He waited, calmly now, for what he knew was coming.

"Should you mind very much, old boy — if we don't stay here? You see —" Ralph interrupted, "I don't mind a bit, I don't want to stay, I can't stand this place!" and walked out of the house and away, without another look, to the waiting car.

The moment they turned their faces towards the town, the holiday really began. Constraint simply melted away. Father admitted that he had telephoned earlier for a room in a hotel beside the abbey — "Just in case we changed our minds, you know" — where they sold his favourite draught beer. In peacetime, he added, the beer would have had to be weighed against the bells; but now, thank heaven, the ringers had other things to do. Ralph was charmed by this man-to-man approach, wild with relief to be rid of his awkward mistake, and so easily. They laughed together, speeding away from the dank misty countryside, the silent cottage, towards civilization, good fires, deep chairs, roast chicken and iced pudding. The hotel was old, but antiquity was kept in its place: copper warming-pans on the oak panelled walls, electric blankets on the beds. After dinner, playing cards by the fire, they were joined by two brother officers. It was late when Ralph went up to bed, giddy with sleep and ginger ale, feeling a head taller and five years older than usual. His shadow, six feet high, reeled across the landing; a grandfather clock seemed to click its tongue in disapproval before it struck twelve.

And the spell remained unbroken. At breakfast next morning he had a moment's panic, when father suggested a ride on the downs: "You'd like that, wouldn't you?" He realized — I haven't ridden for two years! Supposing I've forgotten how? Supposing I get a bolter? — but, knowing the plan was meant as a treat, he could not say any of this. He did point out that he had no jodhpurs, and no coupons, but this was met with an easy-going, "I dare say we can manage that." He was glad to relax again in this aura of confidence and competence; and, before he could picture further disasters, he found himself in an outfitter's, standing in front of a long mirror, absorbed in what Aunt Lizard called "a trying-on match". There was a slight hitch when father picked out a pair of buff-coloured jodhpurs for him, while he had set his heart on a smart stone-grey, like those worn by the Irish boy who had ridden Squirrel at Nenagh. But it was all right. While father tried on breeches for himself, the old shopman murmured discreetly to Ralph, "Which do *you* prefer, sir?" Ralph pointed out his choice, and presently heard his ally commending it successfully to father.

At the stables, though he did not realize it yet, he found another ally in the riding master, James Seaton. Keyed up and apprehensive as he was, it seemed amazing luck to find himself mounted on a kind, gay little horse which looked spirited enough to do him credit, but which — he found in the first few minutes — he could manage easily. He took to James straight away, with his thin tanned face, fine-boned as a fox's, and shrewd eye that had summed them up in a brief chat, while he spoke of the horses, the war, the weather, and pointed out bridle paths on a map. This, father soon remarked with amusement, had been a gesture of courtesy; the two horses took them firmly by the novices' route, over field paths and parkland to the top of the downs, downhill by a grassy ride beside a pinewood — familiar at once to Ralph as the conewood — and back along quiet lanes, splashing through spring floods called "lavants". In the stableyard, feeding Rory and Conker with sugar lumps brought from the breakfast table, Ralph saw James Seaton watching him with approval; had he known it, he had passed a test. James had no use for boys and girls who jumped down and made off without a word to their mounts; they were only fit, he would say, to ride bicycles, and would doubtless treat those with more respect.

On Saturday they took a longer ride. Stopping for bread and cheese at a country pub, while the horses rested in the stable, they shared a table outside in the sun with Tess; she was on her way to watch her young man play in a football match. The east wind was keen: she would have a bleak time of it. Glad to have escaped cheering the Saturday match at school, Ralph sympathized with her; but, she said, it would have been much colder, planting cuttings in Little Stint. At this, father spoke of a letter in *The Times* from a farming expert, who said that every man, woman, horse and tractor in the countryside ought to be working a seven-day week: what did Tess think of that? Tess considered — "It *sounds* quite right, of course. Only — I wonder — would it mean more *work*?" At rush times like harvest, or ploughing, or threshing, or tree lifting, people worked overtime anyway; but that was special, like a short sprint. "If you did it all the year round, you'd just get tired and slow. Or tireder and slower. I should, I think, and so would Silver. He's always vile on Saturdays."

"Well," said father, "I hope you'll write and say so."

"*I* write? To *The Times*?" She looked astounded.

"Why not? Who could be better qualified?"

Taking this for irony, she said, "All the same . . . even soldiers don't work every day, all the time. Look at those village dances they keep getting up, for searchlight men."

"And," said Ralph impudently, "sailors on leave, hacking about —"

"Exactly. Mind you say that in your letter."

She laughed. "Well, all right, I might try. But they'd never print it. Land girls are a joke, you know, like clippies and snoopers and — and gas masks."

"All the better. Editors like a joke."

They rode for the next three mornings, through woods and lanes, along windy downland tracks. Once, on a smallholding, they watched a farmer sowing barley broadcast, throwing fistfuls right and left from a long basket slung round his neck — the first and last time Ralph was to see this in England. On their last day they took sausages and apples in their pockets, caught a bus to Cold Shaws village and climbed a windmill hill. The crossed sweeps of the mill were gone, the place a gaunt ruin; but a tractor-driven plough was circling it, turning up the ancient turf into brown and white furrows. They watched the clouds of seagulls for a while, then walked on through budding copses, lit a fire and toasted bread and sausages on peeled sticks. In the distance they could hear the sound of a billhook. A few minutes' walk brought them into a great clearing, dotted with hazel stubs. Over the twiggy brown floor grew young leaves of primrose and foxglove, old patches of reddish woodspurge. A man was working in the pale sunlight, making a hurdle. Split hazel rods had been set in a row of ten holes in a plank; bent over his work, the man was weaving hazel strips in and out; like weaving a paper mat in a kindergarten, Ralph thought, looking at his deft horny fingers. Close by was a woodland hut, a tarpaulin on four poles — that must be for wet days. His open-air workshop smelled of sap from chips of wood piled thickly on the ground, and brushwood smoke from his fire, a ring of blackened flints, with a kettle slung on three sticks. Brushwood and hazel rods were ranged in neat piles all about. Ralph saw an axe, a billhook, a slasher; tied upright to a tree was a measuring rod, marked in chalk, like the ones that Jill and Tess had used for topping and grading the almond trees. Half a dozen hurdles were stacked against an oak; beautifully trimmed and finished, the brown bark glossy, the split sides fading from cream colour to pale fawn. Father and Ralph would have passed by, so as not to disturb him; but the hurdler seemed pleased to straighten his back for a smoke and a chat. He told them he had bought and cut ten acres of seven-year hazel in the winter; now he was starting to make the hurdles. He had been a hurdler all his life, and all his family, away back. Oh yes, there was always a demand, no fear of that; they used hurdles nowadays for all sorts besides sheepfolds: fencing town gardens, for one thing, now the railings were gone. His son Dick was away at the war — a soldier in India — but he'd be back, and plenty of work for him.

Ralph interrupted suddenly — "Oh look! A kestrel."

All three looked up at the black spot overhead, with its quivering wing-beat. It gave a sudden swoop, and again they saw the delicate hovering motion, like a humming-bird hawk moth over a flower: "after young rabbits," the hurdler said, "or it might be a mouse." Watching Ralph watch the bird, he told an anecdote from his son's last letter. "They'd been at some army caper or other, and Dick sprained both ankles at once, and he was hobbling on crutches for a week or two. Well, one day they were all lined up for dinner, out in the open this was, and Dick'd just got his plate in his hand — a bit awkward, with the crutches — when, swish! down came a kite one way, straight out of the blue, and swoosh! down came another — and there he was left gaping, with his plate empty, the grub all gone, clean as a whistle. Must have spotted he was fair game, crocked up like that. 'Dad', he wrote, 'I wished I was back in Coldmill Copse where the ruddy birds know their place.' "

From hawks and kites the talk went to rats and mice. The hurdler, like the Wild Hill forester, could not remember seeing a dormouse lately; but if Ralph liked to come and sit down anywhere in this copse, and keep still, he might see wood mice playing about. As they talked, Ralph noticed a bumble bee on the tarpaulin. He touched it, but it felt stiff — dead? or asleep? It was furry, like a tiny black mouse, sandy-striped. He tipped the matches from his box and put the bee in their place, pocketing it carefully.

The old craftsman bent to his hurdle again, and they went on. Looking back, father said thoughtfully, "A long long way from the war." Ralph said, "I *do* wish I could get a dormouse," and noticed that father gave him a sharp look. He began to explain his plan for a mouse sanctuary in the spinney; but father did not respond. He had grown silent and preoccupied. Ralph dried up, and they walked for a while without speaking. They paused by a stile at the end of a wood, and father said abruptly, "You know, Ralph — I'm a bit worried about you."

"Worried?" he faltered, taken by surprise. "Oh — why?" He looked at father, then looked away, thinking, Don't tell me why. I can guess.

"This fauna business. Mice, and so on. Don't let it get out of hand, will you?"

At the curt tone, he felt all their new camaraderie slipping away, and could only mutter sullenly, childishly, "How do you mean?"

"Well. It's really a bit of a mania, isn't it? All this prowling after wild beasts — harmless enough as a hobby, of course. But — don't let it interfere with school work, will you?"

He was silent, fiddling with the lid of the matchbox, feeling telltale colour mounting to his face. Of course! That was it. Someone, Uncle Alfred, Aunt Liz, had told father about the harvest mice. That wasn't fair, it was all supposed to be done with, he'd slaved for hours on the beastly lecture. Damn them, they're always like this, he thought: pretending to be friendly, then swooping down on you. Father said now in a serious tone, "Rather an important year for you, isn't it?"

He nodded. Those exams! What's he going to say, when he knows about *that*? Hell to pay . . . besides, he thought, it's not only the exams. Father really thinks it's all a bit wet, "this fauna business". He would have liked a son like the games captain at school — or like Flip; who, seeing the heath for the first time, had said at once, "A good place to land parachute troops." Ralph himself had been going to say, "A good place to look for adders." He felt the searching glance again, the pause, waiting for him to answer. Nothing to say; yet he knew father had been decent all this time; never once asking about the papers, let alone needling away, like some parents — "How did you get on? What sort of questions? And what did you put?" Uncle Alfred was the same: no post mortems, he decreed. But that made it worse. He had let them down, and soon they would have to know. Should he tell now, and get it over? No, he couldn't. He couldn't even remember what he had said. He hesitated; father waited a moment longer, then added, "Well, of course we must wait and see. But I hope —" he broke off, gazing downhill into the distance with keen long-sighted eyes. "Isn't that a bus, away over there? Come on — we might just catch it."

They raced down the slope. They were miles from a bus-stop, the bus would have gone past, but father hailed it and it stopped. Running into low sunlight, while father talked to the conductress, Ralph shut his eyes. Now he couldn't escape: in dazzling colours, behind his eyelids, he seemed to see word for word the idiotic things he had written.

It was on the last afternoon that it had happened. Up till then, the two exams had not seemed as bad as he expected. Even the maths had been a bit better than he had dared to hope. Then at the end of the scholarship exam came that history paper; the final hurdle before the holiday. The goal in sight, he had begun to feel lighthearted, but answered the shorter questions carefully and soberly. Last of all came an essay (*Allow 30 minutes*) — and then he lost his head: "Describe a day in the life of *one* of the following: A novice in a mediaeval monastery; a City apprentice in Elizabethan times; a sailor in Nelson's flagship . . .". There were others, but he never read them. Instantly, with the word *monastery*, he had a vision of Tommy and himself exploring on Christmas Eve; he saw the abbey, the mill, the orchard, the fishpools. A novice, he knew from *Puck of Pook's Hill*, could have been an ordinary schoolboy. He remembered some of the things Aunt Liz had told him about the monks: two meals a day, five baths a year, bed at six in winter, eight in summer; a fire in the dorm from All Souls to Easter; stone walls, so cold that they slept in their robes . . . suddenly the whole thing was clear in his mind: the boy novice stealing out of the dormitory at dawn, a spring night, fire burning low — past the snoring monks, out to look at his night lines in the stream; then playing truant all day from the gatehouse school, going to help in the orchard — grafting apple trees? Yes, and there were beehives. He helped to take beeswax for the abbey candles, and carry it up to the Wax Gate. *Was* that where they made candles? It sounded right. Then someone from the kitchen sent him down the lane to the mill: no bicycle, of course, so he made his novice roll down the slope on a flour barrel. He fished in the pools, and swam in the stream — *six* baths, that year — and set a snare for a rabbit . . . when he started, Ralph had had some hazy idea of pointing out that things in the country didn't change all that much, or boys either — but he soon lost sight of this excuse; the whole thing turned into a game and he wrote on blindly, with inward laughter.

Once before, he had written something like that, and the English master had blue-pencilled a warning in the margin: *Stop before you go too far*. Well, he hadn't stopped, and he had certainly gone too far. What was that beastly word the master had written at the end? — fractious? No, facetious; that was what the examiner would say. He would get no marks at all, and they would tell Uncle Alfred what he had done . . . Now, a mile away over the hedgerows, he could see the abbeytower, black against the west, above the roofs of the town. With mounting gloom he watched it come nearer. The holiday was over.

His gloom lasted another hour; then something quite unexpected happened. Called from tea to the telephone, father said, "That'll be Aunt Lizard. I wrote to say we were here." Getting up, he looked across at Ralph, took him by the ear and said in a very different tone — half laughing, conspiratorial, with no trace of his earlier sharpness, "Here, you'd better talk to Liz. Come along. And for God's sake — *tell her you're enjoying yourself*." What did that mean? He had no time to find out. On the telephone, listening and answering, he was aware that father was watching him with that odd half-smile. Aunt Lizard did sound a little worried. He saw no reason for that either. Forgetting the past two hours, but still too subdued for enthusiasm, he described their doings in a rather lofty tone; oh yes, all quite amusing, he heard himself implying: nothing out of the ordinary, of course — a few rides, the odd film, a spot of poker in the evenings. Father removed him and took the 'phone; and at once, it seemed, he and Aunt Lizard began a long heated discussion, with Aunt Liz for once doing most of the talking. Father leaned back, smiling broadly now, yet looking somehow guilty, on the defensive. Afterwards, though he made no comment, Ralph was left with a distinct impression that Aunt Liz had actually been ticking father off; and it was something to do with himself, yet *he* wasn't being blamed. What could it be about? Because they hadn't stayed at the spring house — because she thought he would be disappointed? Her questions, he realized, had tended that way. Well, she needn't have worried. He was thankful they hadn't stayed there. A complete frost, that would have been. Coming back later from the cinema, stepping out of the black windy street into the long bright room, sniffing the hotel smells, coffee, cigarettes, brandy, he thought that in a way, in the past week, he had grown out of the spring house. He wouldn't much care if he never saw it again.

He saw it again, however, within a few hours. Next morning, as they dressed, father took something from a pocket. "Here, Ralph — what do we do with this?" Ralph looked at the object in surprise. It was the key to the house; father had brought it away: "You left me to lock up, remember?"

"Oh — yes." Taking it on one finger, Ralph explained, "It ought to go back, really. We keep it there. Tacker goes in to air the place on Sundays."

"I see. H'm. Suppose you slip out on the bus, then, and put it back?" Ralph exclaimed without thinking, "Oh, yes!" Father paused, glanced at him and said gently, "You like it there, don't you." Not as a question, not critically; but again with a shade of guilt and regret.

Ralph caught the Beaumarsh bus directly after breakfast; father would pick him up there in an hour or two, for the drive to school. At the garden gate he stopped and looked around coldly, with curiosity. Yes: he still felt aloof, a stranger. The charm was gone. It had vanished at that moment in the spinney, as though a child's house of sticks and grass had crumpled up and fallen. How cramped the cottage really was, how tame and colourless their life here, compared with the past week in father's company.

Fishing in his pocket for the key, he found the matchbox. He had forgotten all about that bumble bee; he shook it out on to the window-sill by his bunk. It still looked stiff and lifeless. *Was* it dead? It might be hibernating, like a dormouse. He poked it experimentally, and fancied one leg moved a little, then another. Well, it would be all right here. If it did revive, he would let it out when the warm weather came. He tipped a pool of runny honey out of the pot on to a piece of paper, and laid it beside the bee.

Outside he could see Joe and Ted pruning at the top of Old Park, Mr. Riley ploughing, Harry and Tacker clearing ditches. He wandered over and stood watching these two. The job looked cold and dull; dull as ditchwater, he thought. Tacker was lively enough, though. Had he heard about Fred Buckler? Gone back to the navy, Fred had, the day after the *Scharnhorst* and *Gneisenau* made their trip through the Channel. He'd come to work looking miserable as sin, but he wouldn't talk about it, except for one thing, very sarcastic: "Why didn't they call in at Brighton pier for a cup o' tea?" On the Monday they heard he'd cleared off down to Portsmouth.

Thinking of Fred's great age, the grizzled stubble on his weatherbeaten face, Ralph cried, "But they'd never take him, would they? He must be sixty!"

"Oh, they took him all right. For work in harbour and that. Been at sea more than thirty years, Fred has — and if it wasn't for my rheumatism I'd be after him."

Ralph wandered on. Sally, Jill and Tess were doing something in Little Stint. From here, it looked like a hopping race combined with a whistling match. They were planting blackcurrant cuttings at top speed, then heeling them in to the quick beat of the *Hut-Sut Song*. As they reached the road, the car stopped at the gate. Father came towards them, carrying a folded paper, smiling at Tess: "I saw they printed your letter?"

"Oh yes. Oh dear. And you saw I'd mucked it, as Ralph would say."

"No? Oh — you mean, the part about the relaxation of the warrior?"

"All those dances, of course I *meant*. I never thought, till I saw it in print. Oh well. My father laughed quite a lot."

"Never mind. I told you, editors like a gentle joke."

Mystified, Ralph took the paper and ran his eye down the letter page. He found Tess's name and read her letter carefully. She suggested a six-day week, with a staggered rest day, "since the best weather does often come at the weekend": but not a mere half-day, because that meant getting up early, as usual. He read one sentence again: "Has the farm labourer no claim to that recreation which is so zealously provided for members of the services?" He could see nothing funny in that, but would not for worlds have admitted as much. He said hastily to father, "Back in a minute. Just going to lock up."

He had already turned the key when he thought again of that bumble bee. Wouldn't it be safer in the matchbox? Supposing a mouse got in and ate it? He went in and ran up to the window. There, for the second time that year, he saw a corpse restored to life. He could hardly believe that this was the same bee. It seemed twice the size. The black fur, so drab and lifeless, now looked glossy; the three stripes no longer sand-coloured, but bright as dandelion petals. The wings, still half-folded, shimmered softly. Then he began to laugh: for the bee had found the honey. Standing over the golden pool, long proboscis delicately planted, it was pumping up nourishment, recharging its batteries with all speed. He touched it with a fingertip; the wings flexed, but the pumping did not stop for a second. Its whole furry body seemed to hum and vibrate with zest. The bumble bee was in clover. It must think it had died, and woken in paradise. He watched with the same pleasure he had felt when he saw the harvest mice. Here was something else to look after; only this time he had found it for himself, carried it here for shelter, fed it, brought it back to life. Like everything else here, it was *his*.

A blast of the car horn reached him at length. He would have to go; but not for long. In two weeks he would be back. The bee would be safe from frost in here, and well fed; he gave it another large ration of honey. Now that it was awake, surely a mouse wouldn't touch it? Touching it himself once more, he wondered if it might be a queen, if it would make a nest in the hedge bank, like one he had seen last year. Locking the door, running along the field path, whistling as loudly as the trio in Little Stint, he thought again what a nuisance it was to keep going away, leaving everything he cared about. One day he would come back and stay for good.

CHAPTER THIRTEEN

"A Day for the King"

Skimming silently downhill towards a millpond, Ralph saw a sleek black creature — Labrador retriever? — run out of a clump of reeds, pause, turn its head and rear up to watch his approach with interest, then dart back into the reeds. The moment it was out of sight he knew what he had seen: an otter. He pedalled hard, and drew up at the spot where it had disappeared, but the otter was gone. Not a reed moved, not a bubble or furrow on the pond betrayed its flight. He sat back in his saddle and waited, looking at the water rippling in the dawn breeze, soft pale green of hawthorns and willows, varnished gold of celandines and kingcups, the dark singing speck of a lark circling higher and higher.

To see the otter was a happy omen, a good start to his day off — "a day for the king", he had told Aunt Lizard he was having. "To drink his health, it means really."

"And what will you drink it in?"

"Oh — duckponds and dewponds, I suppose."

"I beg you'll do no such thing."

So he had emptied the tea-pot into a bottle, adding milk and sugar. As he prepared some rations, she murmured sleepily from her bunk, "What a lot of bread-ing and butter-ing. Are you going to be out all day? Well, if you find Lesley, ask her to come and see us."

She would be busy painting, he knew. He himself had worked for the past two days, side by side with the boy Sally, picking up prunings and stacking them by the woodshed for next winter's fires. Mr. Riley had said he might have the sticks, for the labour of gleaning them. Sally, on piecework, was paid a penny a row, and worked at full speed, totting up visionary pennies as he went along. He was saving for a motor bicycle.

Jill and Tess had been "suckering" last year's budded stocks, and Ralph carefully examined the rows by the Sea Eagle label. Each stock showed a sprout of primrose colour, like a brimstone butterfly, where the dormant bud had been tied; the new peach buds. The girls were rubbing off the darker green sprouts of the plum stock. He could not be sure which was his own — the mark had disappeared — but he marked another for the spring house garden. By autumn, Jill said, the buds would be four feet high, a thicket of maiden peaches. How soon could he transplant his tree? Perhaps in 1944. He felt, as in childhood, that everything took far too long. Once, when he had complained of this, an old gardener told him: "Wait till you get to be sixty, you'll start planting acorns."

This morning he had come out before sunrise. He had planned so many things, one day would hardly be long enough; besides, Tess said one saw more animals at daybreak. Once she had seen a fox trotting along by a hedge; another morning, passing a field beside a larchwood, she had watched three great jack hares leaping and cavorting. Quite near here, too, she saw a kingfisher every morning, and again as she went home. She had described the place exactly, so that he could watch for it; a pollarded lime by a willow stump. He had promised not to look for the nest, in case the birds might desert. Tess hoped one day to see a row of young kingfishers on the willow.

Taking deep breaths of the cold air, still touched with frost, he watched the red rim of the sun come up over a round hill four miles away. He looked at his watch: half past six. In five hours, just about, he should be riding down the south side of that hill, past the racecourse, beside the cone wood. Father had arranged for him to ride twice a week in the holidays; hoping, no doubt, that horses would lure him away from mice. Well, they wouldn't. Today he would find that copse again, where the hurdler was, and look for wood mice. As he sat by the pond, while the sun turned from red to gold, and mist drifted over the water, he heard the first cuckoo. How long since he had heard that note? Eight months? Nine? Of course, you could never tell which was the last cuckoo. Like the swifts, you simply noticed that they were gone. It was queer, he thought, that every spring the cuckoo seemed to arrive at dawn. Perhaps this one had been flying all night, over "enemy occupied territory", over the Channel, impatient to reach England.

Four hours, then, before he was due at the stables. Which should he look for first: Lesley, the hurdler, the orchard? The orchard must be the nearest; it was the one he had seen in October from the train. He rode slowly back up the hill, and paused to study the country. It must be somewhere down there, between the Beaumarsh level crossing and that row of poplars to the west. The poplars, he had already discovered, grew beside a grassy lane, where a cattle tunnel went under the railway. The top road he called "the switchback"; he raced along it, spinning down small hills and up again, then turned into the green lane. Reaching the poplars, he hid the bicycle and again took his bearings. The railway line seemed the best route. The straight rails flashed in the sun, a wire hummed. No one was in sight. He climbed the stiff wire fence and ran along the bank, starred with coltsfoot and dandelions, and huge wild strawberry flowers, white as paper. A fast train took him by surprise with a sharp note on its hooter — was it slowing, would the driver stop and chase him? No, it went on. Across the line was a fruit farm with rows of orderly trees, close-pruned. He thought — suppose the orchard isn't wild any more? The owner, in this third spring of the war, would surely have taken it in hand: the apple trees would be pruned, the birds gone. He stood still. Was it worth going on? Yes, he must see for himself. He crossed a stile, plunged through a copse, and here it was; still a wild place, tucked away between stretches of woodland.

He wandered in among the trees. The long grass was grey with dew. Twisted boughs, hoary with lichen, knelt in hemlock and nettles, massed with tight pink apple buds, snowy plum and pear, sticky knots of cherry blossom. Birds sang. In three minutes he had found three nests, a chaffinch's, a thrush's, a bunch of roots and twigs — a greenfinch building. After that he lost count. He heard goldfinches, the trill of the greenfinch, ringing cries of great tits, the tiny rasp of a longtailed tit, the first chiff-chaff; and all the time, coming nearer, the cuckoo. Here and there he found wrinkled apples, hard as twists of leather, clinging to the boughs. An ancient scythe, eaten away with rust, hung in a pear fork. Sitting in a high tree, watching trains, munching a marmalade sandwich, he listened to a blackbird: seven rich notes, a pause, then a new phrase. He dropped to the ground again and circled, looking for a gate in the wild plum hedge. There was none. The orchard, lost and forgotten, blossomed in the sun. He felt he had staked a claim. No one else wanted it, only he and the birds.

After a long time he looked at his watch, and looked again; it must have gone mad! He held it to one ear, muffling the other to shut out the jingle of the great tit. It was ticking away, but no faster than usual. Hell — he would be late for his ride. Scrambling back through the copse, he thought, I'll come here often. At the stile he looked back. Beyond the oaks he could still see a mist of pale green, pink and white. Tomorrow, he thought, I'll find a lot more nests. There'll be cherries in June, and wild strawberries, and those red apples in autumn.

But he did not go back the next day. Though he thought of the place for years, calling it "the lost orchard", picturing its dewy wildness, the grey nettles, the April light, hearing the ring of the blackbird's song — somehow he never went there again.

The horses were waiting, nodding bright-eyed over their doors. Five children had already gathered on the cobbles between the rows of stalls. Ralph was just in time. An old stableman led out Rory; but, as Ralph went to mount, James Seaton came up: "Ralph, how would you like to try Conker today? *You* take Rory," he told a whey-faced little girl; and then, in a muttered aside to Ralph, "Fearfully nervous child. Shouldn't be riding at all. Wretched mother makes her . . ." Who could resist such flattery? Perched high on the chestnut hunter — seventeen hands at least, and far too lively for comfort — Ralph was still kindly disposed towards the nervous one, and far too busy to notice with what tact he had been jockeyed into taking his next step as a horseman. Out on the main road, it seemed his hour had come. Suddenly faced by an army convoy, armoured cars and grinding tanks, he felt Conker begin to bunch herself ominously, backing towards an abyss at the roadside; five feet of crumbling cliff over a river. But no: James Seaton was coming up on the nearside, shutting off the ditch, forging quietly ahead. Ralph took a grip on the mare and himself; he spoke to Conker, she followed, they were past the tanks and turning into a field path. Mr. Seaton signalled to Ralph, who dropped back; they waited together as children and ponies went through the gap. Pulling up after a canter, the riding master said, "Saw you yesterday, over at Beaumarsh. Out in a field, weren't you?"

"Oh yes, getting apple sticks. But I didn't see anyone riding?"

"Horse box," said Mr. Seaton; and presently, "That little grey, pulling a hoe — have they had him long, d'you know?"

"Silver? A couple of years, I think." Describing Silver and his tricks, Ralph sensed that Mr. Seaton was listening closely; but after a pause he went on to talk about other things, shortage of straw, oats, petrol, hands; how the army were taking another paddock: long ago, the covered riding school had gone. Listening, Ralph saw that horse breeders, like rose growers, were under siege, clinging to the remains of their stock. Mr. Seaton did not mention Silver again till they were back at the stables. There he disappeared into his house and came back with something to show Ralph: a snapshot. Ralph looked at half a dozen riders in fancy dress, ruffs and doublets, surrounding a beautiful young girl poised sidesaddle, in velvet habit, ruff, a hat with a plume. She was mounted on a handsome pony, silver-grey, with a long mane; head up, ears pricked, her mount was gazing straight at the camera. Ralph looked inquiringly at Mr. Seaton, who murmured, "Silver Jubilee procession. Good Queen Bess, and so on. Our horses." His tone suggested a funeral rather than a jubilee. Why did he sound like that? Ralph studied the photograph again, and then cried out, "You don't mean — that's not our Silver?" Shocked, he scanned the pony's proud face and alert bearing. Mr. Seaton nodded glumly.

"But — that girl couldn't ride him? He's vicious! Even the men are scared of him —" He stopped. It was unbelievable; but Mr. Seaton did not seem in doubt. "Hunted him, too," he said. "Went like a bird. Arab-Welsh."

"Oh, what happened? How could he get like he is?"

"Must have been '38, he left us." The riding master seemed to muse. "Changed hands again, I suppose. *And* again." He shook his head slowly. And that, Ralph saw, was all he knew; or perhaps all he would tell.

"But," Ralph said with grief, "you wouldn't *know* him."

No answer to that from James Seaton, who had known him at a glance; the farm pony who had been this shining creature, parading through the town, with the trumpets and banners, a queen's palfrey . . . Silver. Ralph thought of a dire phrase in *Black Beauty*: "Ruined, and Going Downhill".

"Tacker did say — he's turned sour because he hates the cart. He was never meant as a drudge, was he?" Another rueful shake of the head. Ralph thrust back the snapshot. Taking his bicycle, he tried to remember what he had meant to do next. Oh yes; the hurdler; wood mice; Lesley. He felt weary. The day had lost its impetus. There would never be time, he saw, for all that. Oh well; he might as well go somewhere. No sense in just trailing home. Besides, if he did, he might come across Silver. Just now, he could hardly bear to.

Lesley Fraser was a former pupil of Aunt Lizard's, the girl who had owned Ralph's paintbox, and was now in the timber corps. They had heard she was working in a wood called Tatten's Hanger, six or seven miles away on the other side of the downs. Ralph found the place in time to share a teabreak in a clearing, lying under a sallow willow tree, looking up at the sky through a screen of yellow catkins alive with bees. Yellow pollen scattered a scent like gorse. Pale sawdust, smelling of sap, poured from a little sawmill in a wooden shelter. The tea kettle boiled on a brushwood fire, and six girls stopped work to scald the dust from their throats. Like Jill and Tess, they wore corduroy breeches and jerseys, lipstick, leather gloves, coloured scarves over long curling hair. In the last war, Merren McKay had said, land girls chopped off their hair so as to look tough and practical, "just like men." Their successors, no less hard-working, were less anxious to claim these qualities: rather the reverse. Lesley looked like the rest, except that her black curly hair was short as a boy's. Her scarlet neckerchief and purple leather skullcap seemed oddly natural in that woodland setting — toadstool colours, that's why! Ralph thought, and saved this up to tell Aunt Lizard.

Work started again; the snarl of the mill blotted out the drone of bees. A gang of woodmen had cut down the hanger. Only the willow had been spared. The trunks had been carted away, roots taken out, and the men had gone ahead to another wood, leaving the girls to saw up the branches and burn the rubbish. Then the hillside would be wired in, rabbits killed and young trees planted. Two girls fed boughs into the humming blades of the sawmill; chunks of wood fell into sacks held by two others. They waved to Ralph to stand back. It was a bit like threshing, he thought; only one was covered with bark specks and sawdust, instead of chaff and corn dust.

Lesley and her partner, for a rest, went to take their turn with the bonfires. Helping them, he told himself — this would be just the job for Sally. He pointed to the sacks of logs and shrieked to Lesley, "Firewood?" She was going to shriek back, but the mill stopped again, and in the lull she whispered, laughing, "Shh! — camouflage." The cut wood went to pulping mills, to be made into cover for airfields and factories, and some to build Mosquito planes. Ralph thought of something father had said, as though enviously, in the hurdler's copse: "A long way from the war." But he was wrong. It was like that song in *Pook's Hill*, about guns and arrows coming out of the "secret weald", and shoes for the war horses. The sawmill screeched, and again Lesley was shouting, "Over there . . . Waterbar wood . . . *Parachutes*!"

Parachutes? A secret factory, or a silkworm farm? Once, at a lecture in London before the war, he had handled a parachute. He remembered the snowy folds, the feel of the silk; but in the next lull Lesley said, "Charcoal burners — they make parachute silk with charcoal now, did you know?" He might have retorted, No, how could I? Instead he asked, "How can they?" She signalled that she had no idea. The charcoal burners had said so, he could go and ask them. She waved, and went back to the sawmill.

Wheeling his bicycle along a ride, he caught whiffs of some new smell, like woodsmoke, but more acrid. The charcoal burners had set up a little town of kilns in the middle of the wood; square iron boxes, fenced round with piles of oak and ash boughs. Older women were working here, sawing long brands into even lengths. A caravan stood under the trees. Hovering by a kiln, watching men filling it with wood — thick pieces in the middle, thin boughs round the edge — Ralph thought he might be frowned on as a spy; but the men grinned at him, teeth showing white in faces blacked like poachers'. The piled wood was topped by a tent-shaped lid with two chimneys, and then banked up with earth. Scorched earth — *that* was what the queer smell was; Russia must smell like that from end to end.

A man in charge gave orders in an accent Ralph did not know. His face was brown, not black; Spanish, could he be? or Italian? He was soaking bits of charred wood in paraffin, poking them through a trapdoor under the kiln, setting light to them. Blue smoke drifted from the chimneys. The fire had to smoulder twenty-four hours, the man told him; it would spread slowly from the centre to the outer edges, the smoke turning thin and grey. The kilns had to be watched all the time, in case of a flare-up. Tomorrow, they would take off the lid and leave the kiln overnight to cool down. Over there, look, they were shovelling out charcoal now . . . Crumbling a scrap of the grey-black brittle stuff, Ralph wondered if Lesley had been pulling his leg. It looked all right for crayons, or even puppy biscuits; one couldn't see where silk came in. But the man agreed, yes, it might go for parachutes, or barrage balloons: had Ralph seen one of those? Oh, from London, was he? "Irish, I thought you were." Much surprised, Ralph admitted to relations in Ireland. His next question made the man laugh. "Spanish! No indeed, Welsh, from Merioneth." He travelled about the country in his caravan, training new charcoal burners.

A team of horses came down the ride, drawing a load of tree trunks thirty feet long. Ralph mounted his bicycle and let them tow him, holding on at the end, by the red flag. The brown trees, sweet-smelling, stripped of bark, felt cold and smooth as marble. Sixteen hooves thudded over turf, crunched through dead leaves and bracken, clopped on to the gritty road; twelve hooves rang on the road to the timberyard. One horse had cast a shoe; he was unhitched and led off the other way, towards the village smithy. Ralph followed; a blacksmith's shop, like a mill race, or a bridge, or a keeper's gibbet, was always a place to linger. This one, the woodman said, had been in the same family a hundred years, and the old smith himself — grandson of a blacksmith at the battle of Waterloo — had worked there half that time. They found him sharpening a harrow that someone needed urgently tomorrow. Wiping rusty hands on his leather apron, he chose a horseshoe from a string on the wall, lifted the horse's foot and began to take off the old shoe. Watching him work away with pincers, hammer and nails, while the great horse stood quietly, Ralph found himself deep in a childish fancy, pretending he was here on his own account, waiting for his own horse; for Silver. Not the

Silver of today, but the spirited beauty of the photograph, with his touch of Arab blood — the hunter that "went like a bird". Oh — he almost groaned aloud — if only . . . then he came to himself as the blacksmith, the shoeing finished, threw him a civil word.

"Sorry — I didn't —"

"Want a job, I said? Could do with an apprentice."

Ralph said with truth, "I wouldn't mind."

The smith grunted, putting away his bit of banter with his tools. "Then you're not like t'other lads. There's not a blacksmith's 'prentice now, not one, in the whole of Sussex." He turned to another job; and Ralph, ambling homeward past green meadows and blackthorn hedges, turned again to his fancy. Mounted on Silver, he trotted along the lanes, strode up hills, cantered on grassy verges. Approaching a flat road, bordered last summer by wide cornfields, he was brought up short by barbed wire and red-lettered notices. Of course, this road was shut; Tess had said so. It was to be part of an airfield. He would have to make a detour and find the switchback road. But his mind was not on the road. He was thinking eagerly, But I could! I could buy him, set him free, change him back to what he was: his real self. He's a saddle horse. Why should he go on as a carthorse? If you petted him, if you treated him as a friend, he'd forget all his silly tricks. He only bites and kicks because he's unhappy. How much would he cost? A boy at school had had to pay twenty guineas for a pony. That was before the war. Temper and all, Silver might be worth more now. Still,

I can earn money, he reminded himself; picking up prunings on piece rates, hoeing, harvesting. Or he might ask father to let him save up, instead of riding at the stables. Now that was an idea. Eight weeks' summer holidays, two rides a week, a guinea a ride — why! a few months from now, Silver could be his. The thought of ways and means was exhilarating. He pedalled faster, up and down the little hills, down the long southward lane, past gardens where people gossiped in the late sunlight, locking up their chicken coops and rabbit hutches. He chafed at the railway crossing; gates shut as usual. Silver would be out in the paddock. If he hurried, there would be time before dark to take him a crust or a fruit drop, as Jill and Tess did every morning; though not venturing yet to offer them directly. Gnashing his teeth and rolling his eyes, Silver always made it clear that he would bite any hand that tried to feed him, except for Mr. Doggett's. Ah, but in a year's time — ! The gates opened, he bumped through and dashed on; back to earth now, on his bicycle, with Silver waiting for him in the paddock.

But tonight he did not visit Silver. Within a few minutes he was literally back to earth, after pitching off his bicycle; a thing he had not done since his ninth birthday. That was Aunt Lizard's fault. He reached the gate in the lane, opened and shut it without dismounting, started along the road to the barn — and there she came running, as though she had kept watch for him, calling something, waving a letter. Or was it a telegram, bad news? No, she would never come racing out for that. He caught the word "scholarship", braked fiercely and lost his balance. She tore up: "Ralph, did you hear? You've won a scholarship!" Sprawling among the blackcurrant slips, one knee gashed by a spinning pedal, he answered calmly, "No, I haven't."

Breathless, half-lifting him to his feet, she flapped a telegram: "Izard Spring House Beaumarsh Ralph has won scholarship letter follows Alfred." He brushed himself down and said in a daze, "But I can't have. You see —" He stopped. How to explain? He tried, "I made a mucker, right at the end, the history essay —" But she cried gaily, "Well, then, you made up for it with the rest. Well done!" He could say no more, and limped home with his arm through hers. Indoors there were signs of festivity, the painted bird mats on the table, tall gold candles brought from Chelsea — old as the hills, would they ever burn? — a dish of primroses and windflowers from the spinney. Supper smelled like a feast: potato soup, Cornish pasties, baked apples. Gradually, as he mopped his knee, it all began to seem possible. Uncle Alfred might be right; and all these weeks, dreading the news, he might have been wrong. Could they have agreed to overlook his lapse? He had never dreamed of such a thing. But it was so; it must be. The evidence was there. Besides the telegram, which had come at one o'clock — "I rang the stables, you'd gone already" — there was a letter from Uncle Alfred; she had walked to the post office after tea to fetch it. He was too wrought up to read the details yet; but yes, he might believe it. He had a scholarship; his future was settled, he needn't think of the other school, or of taking a third exam next term. He began to relax. Still Aunt Lizard was more excited than he; but he liked that. Tilting his chair back, spooning up soup, he noticed two glasses on the table, sparkling in the candlelight, and smiled, as though at a child's whim, when she said, "Of course I must drink your health." She was bringing a bottle wrapped in a napkin. "Not the sacred sloe gin?" he asked.

"No, that's for victory, or your coming-of-age, whichever happens first." She showed him a small wine bottle, dark green, gold-topped. He leaned forward to read the label, and slammed down his chair with a rattle of plates and forks. "Champagne!" He was overwhelmed. "Is it *real*?"

She laughed, "I've been saving it." He took the mushroom cork, watched the pale stream frothing into the glasses, sniffed the bubbles and sprang up crying, "Wait! 'A day for the king', remember?" They drank to the king, she drank to Ralph, they both drank to the future. He sipped again critically, thought he preferred ginger ale, suppressed the notion and realized that a nightmare of guilt and worry had slipped away from him. Like an airman whose parachute opens at last, he felt himself marvellously lifted and sustained, floating high up, safe and quiet, swayed to and fro by soft currents of joy and relief.

They sat on at the table after supper, talking quietly and happily. The orchard he kept to himself, but he told her about the otter and Lesley and the charcoal burners. He would say nothing yet about Silver. At length, after a pause, she said idly, "What made you think you hadn't done well? Oh, and didn't you say something about a history essay?"

He stared at her, blinked, and the room seemed to spin a little. He thought: Let's not start on all that now.

"Because," she went on, "funnily enough — that's the very thing that decided it."

He gasped. The candle flames dipped like windflowers and righted themselves. Eyes fixed on her, he could only stammer, "— decided? *What* did you say?"

"It's all here, in Uncle Alfred's letter. You must read it tomorrow. They wrote and told him . . . yes, here it is: "Good history essay, they were quite impressed . . . showed some historical sense . . . high mark." And Uncle Alfred says, "Tell Ralph how pleased I am." I think that's something to be proud of, Ralph." She looked up, and her expression changed. The scholar had given up trying to appear modestly pleased and amazed. Under her gaze, he slipped off his chair and rolled about on the floor, uttering peals of unseemly laughter; as though, she thought, peering at him in surprise, Alfred's letter were just a huge joke. But of course she was to blame — the champagne — a mistake, perhaps, at his age, though she hadn't let him refill his glass. Now he had sprung up, seized the cat by his front paws and begun to dance him round the room, singing, "*From out of a wood did a cuckoo fly — Cuckoo! He came to a manger with joyful cry — Cuckoo! He hopped, he curtsied, round he flew, And loud his jubilation grew — Cuckoo, Cuckoo, Cuckoo!*"

The third *Cuckoo* brought him up short with a crash, against the cupboard. The door flew open, he seized a kipper by the tail and whirled it about. The cat, more offended than alarmed, fled to a window, found it shut and began to climb up the curtains. She rose briskly, indicating that all this had gone quite far enough, and swept the helpless reveller into bed.

CHAPTER FOURTEEN

Silver

Green corn stretched away into the distance, meeting the gleam of the sea beyond the harbour. White clouds billowed in the wind. Flowering hawthorns were bright as snow in sunlight, dull as chalk in shadow. The young corn was splashed with yellow charlock; *harlocks*, in Shakespeare, Aunt Lizard said. Running up and down the drills, Sally and Ralph pulled out bundles of it, chopped off thistles and docks — roguing, Sally called it — and discussed the chances of a "Baedeker raid" on the abbey. Exeter and Norwich had had them; the only excitement here, Ralph learned, had been an anti-aircraft gun that had misfired, lobbing dud shells into Hammers: a good excuse for Silver to bolt with the hoe.

He could see Tess now, weeding the briar seedlings in the frameyard and waiting for Silver. She never harnessed him herself. She had been tipped off at the start, by Mrs. Doggett, that women were not welcome in the stables. Mrs. Doggett thought this was some kind of ancient rule, to do with horsemen's trade secrets; a woman was bound to chatter and give things away. "Men!" Mrs. Doggett added deeply, and laughed to herself. The girls wondered if Mr. Doggett talked in his sleep.

Ralph kept an eye on the road; Silver would soon be out with the cart. The sight would have been painful but for his plans. With every hour that passed, the pony's release came nearer. Yesterday afternoon he had made two shillings. By noon today he would have another half-crown. At the end of the Whitsun break he could write to father with his proposal: "I've earned this much, next holidays I can earn that much, please will you help?" The next thing would be to get Aunt Lizard on his side, to borrow that snapshot from Mr. Seaton, and convince her that poor Silver would change back from toad to handsome prince, once the curse was lifted. She *must* agree. It would all depend on her. He could point out that they would need a pony in the family, with his young cousin Rowan, over in Ireland, learning to ride. And Silver had been a girl's pony. Then, he would have to find out the price. Of course there would be tack to buy, and rent for grazing — and someone would have to handle Silver, and make a fuss of him, while he was away at school: George Doggett, and Tacker, and Tess and Jill. If only he didn't cost too much, and if father saw the point! For weeks he had been thinking out the practical side of things. Now, working under the windy May sky, listening to the larks, and the harsh note of a crow over in Sallows, he allowed himself to dream of a day next summer. He would call the pony to the paddock gate, and Silver would come trotting, ears pricked, coat glossy. They would go down to the shore, or up on the downs, or through Wild Hill woods. Next Christmas they might even try jumping. He would take the hurdles from the garden and set them up in the paddock. He wouldn't want them again himself; having come second in the hurdle race on sports day, and tied third in the high jump, honour was satisfied.

At the nine o'clock break there were shouts and laughter from Sallows. Some of the men were hoeing sugar beet, with Jill and a talkative schoolboy of sixteen named Rupert. Jill strolled down to tell them that Rupert had left his bread and cheese by the hedge, in a paper bag, and a crow had carried off the cheese; but he said he didn't mind. He had always wondered where the crow in Aesop stole "a large piece of cheese," and it was amusing to find out. Ralph listened with interest; next term, at the new school, men like Rupert would be running things. He was going in for farming after the war, Jill recounted; but not like this, with hoes and horses and muck-spreading. "Machines, he'll have for everything, like a factory. As for spudding thistles, he says it's feudal."

"He's quite right, of course." Mr. Riley appeared behind them. "Tell him I'll give him a job any day. You," he told them, "are the last boys who'll ever go roguing. After the war, it'll all be done with sprays and weedkillers."

During Sunday tea at the spring house, Ralph repeated this; and a WAAF plotter called Heather, staying on leave with Tess, remarked, "I should hope so. I simply can't imagine a more deadly job."

Tess began, "The funny thing is, it's not —" and then broke off, looking puzzled. Ralph thought she felt as he had done with father, about the mice, and the house itself; some things one couldn't explain. She finished with a sigh, "Well, we can't all have stirring jobs on fighter stations. Or plot a stray plane one night, and find it was Rudolf Hess." This had happened last year to Heather.

Lesley said, "No, we can't. That's why I took to the woods, before I found myself in khaki, drilling on a barrack square." Once, she explained, her school had taken part in a vast Empire Day parade in Hyde Park; as a form captain, she had to cry, Eyes right! in the march-past, as they wheeled towards the saluting base. "I was petrified. I knew I'd lead the wrong way and get the whole thing snarled up."

"And did you?" Ralph asked from his seat on the doorstep. The house overflowed with women: it was their first real party.

"No, I fainted. Flat out on the parade ground, in that hymn about "reeking tube and iron shard". Oh, the disgrace, letting down the Empire. I couldn't face all that again."

Jill said, "Anyway, I don't see that it's deadly. I always wanted to work in the country. I was selling hats in Oxford Street, the war got me out."

"And now," said Tess, "you'll marry Arthur, and bring up six little knifehands?"

"Seven, we thought. And, talking of stirring jobs — what about that girl ratcatcher who came here?"

Heather shuddered.

"Perhaps," Aunt Lizard suggested, waving a kettle for Ralph to refill, "land work's a bit like bringing up children. Not all Christmas Eve, I mean, and daisy chains in the meadow, and" — she caught Ralph's eye as he came back — "champagne celebrations. But if you just do the pretty bits, it's . . ." she groped for a word, Ralph handed it to her with the kettle: "Phoney." The melancholy word recalled the first days of war. Suddenly, Tess was saying that, in the summer of 1939, she had been at a London drama school. "A producer came to see a thing we did, and he actually wrote to me afterwards — he was putting on a play. *In the West End*. He thought I might do all right for one tiny part." In the last week of August, in a seventh heaven, she was rehearsing. "Two whole lines, I had." It seemed too good to be true, and it was. War came, the play was abandoned. Even now, one could see, it hurt to think of. "Millions of us," she said. "Not like you, Jill — the other ones. One minute your life was going to start, next minute there was nothing. Just the damned heart-breaking bore of the war. Only," she added, regretting her impulse, "you can't talk about that *now*."

"So you never did any acting?"

"Only a film test. We'll get in touch, they said, but of course they never did. So that's that."

"But after the war?" asked Heather.

"What, an old thing about twenty-five? Anyway, now I'll be married, in sixty-two more days." Sixty-one days, Ralph thought, to the end of term. Tess, like himself, must be crossing them off.

"But," Aunt Lizard said mildly, "stage people do quite often marry?"

"Yes, and then," said Heather, "you can join E.N.S.A. and gladden the troops."

"Oh, well — with a house and everything? There won't be time. No, I'll just work shorter days on a farm."

"Time!" cried Aunt Lizard. "Oh! You've no idea, not one of you, what years you're going to live — if you do live — and how many things there'll be time for. You," she told Lesley, "should never have sold your paintbox, and I should never have let you. You must start again at once, in your dinner hour, drawing trees. I've seen it so often, just like *Alice* — you think you've turned your back on something, and there it is coming to meet you."

"And I may be going to Denham, by way of Little Stint? Well," Tess laughed, "I'll let you know, I promise, if I do."

She kept her promise. In September they had a letter: Tess, having left the land army, had a part in a film about it.

Khaki was a familiar sight just then. Army manoeuvres were going on; trucks and cars sped up and down the dusty farm roads, and men trooped in to the well at all hours. On Monday morning, weeding young runner beans round the house walls, Ralph hardly glanced up when a truck stopped at the gate and a soldier jumped out. Then the man pulled two boxes from the back, came up to Ralph and asked, "Got any use for this lot, chum?"

Ralph came to look. Not rubbish, he saw at once; they were strong chests with padlocks, like large school play-boxes — just right for tools, or for storing nuts and potatoes in the autumn. He offered tea and cigarettes in payment, but the man was in a hurry. He carried the lockers through the gate, dumped them by the hedge, backed his truck into the barley and drove off fast. Looking after him, Ralph noticed idly that the number plate was plastered with mud.

Ralph went back to the beans. He felt guilty about neglecting the garden, but Aunt Lizard said she liked doing it in the evenings. She had been here for the past two weeks, working at her Shakespeare flowers, and would stay on for the summer; she had special leave, because the paintings were for America. This morning she was down in Beaumarsh, fetching irises and crown imperial from someone's garden. Ralph was waiting once more for Mr. Doggett, Violet and the horse hoe. Now and then, as he worked, he caught a quacking sound in the medley of bird calls. At first it had sent him rushing into the spinney, looking for a duck's nest; now he knew it was only a starling in the eaves.

Captain and Violet appeared at last, but Silver was not with them. Tess came bicycling along to join the hoers. Ralph met her at the barn: "Where is he? Not coming out?"

"Silver? Oh no, he's off colour. Mr. Doggett's sent for the vet. He's been a bit queer, you know — Silver, I mean — since we got shelled last week in Hammers."

Ralph wanted to fly to the stable, but he checked himself. If he were not ready to start with Violet, Mr. Doggett would call in someone else. He might lose a morning's work; for Silver, that could mean another day in harness. I expect he's tired, he told himself. When he's mine, I shan't let him get tired. From Mr. Doggett he learned that the vet might come after dinner.

He had not yet told Aunt Lizard his plan; at noon, though tempted, he still said nothing. Windows pulled to, keeping out the draught, they ate in an aura of paint so strong that he thought it flavoured the macaroni cheese. He swallowed his helping rapidly. Cuckoo, unsettled by the smell, was twitching discontentedly up and down the garden. Aunt Lizard worked away, fork in her left hand, brush in her right. Fleur-de-lys and crown imperial freshened in a glass, in the cool of the ferret cage. She was painting something else; a full-blown mauve tulip. Ralph thought — I bet that's not in Shakespeare; but he could see why she wanted to paint it. The petals looked strange and fragile, frilled and curved like shells, with a silver sheen. There was no time to lose; they would drop at any moment, at the first breath of air. Watching her brush, he was half dreaming when she asked, "What are those things out there?"

"Oh, those!" He had forgotten the lockers. Cuckoo, poised on hind feet, was inspecting them. "They're a little surprise for you."

"All right then, I'm surprised. From Tacker?"

He told her about the soldier. Mixing a fainter wash of lavender, she said, "I suppose they *are* empty? No odd bullets, no hand grenades?"

"No such luck." He scraped the burnt skin from the dish. Yesterday, for their party, they had had the first strawberries; there were still a few left. Nibbling one, Aunt Lizard looked through the open door, towards a clump of late Bramleys flowering on the west side of Sallows. "Strawberries," she said, "and an orchard in blossom. That's supposed to be a mistake, you know, in *Emma*. You see, it's nothing of the sort. Or it wouldn't be," she added honestly, "but I think she mentions midsummer." Ralph nodded, not thinking of *Emma*, which he was not likely to read, but of the strawberries; they too seemed to taste of paint. Coating a scone with treacle, he wandered outdoors to eat it. He bit a small gooseberry. After the treacle, it was almost painful. Teeth on edge, spitting out green seeds, he approached the two lockers. Cuckoo was now sitting on the top one, peering inside; the lid was a little way open. Ralph tipped the cat off and pushed up the lid. A stick fell away — a prop? Ralph took one look, dropped the lid and ran, shouting to Aunt Lizard — "Come and see!"

Curled inside the locker, on a bed of woodwool, they saw a spaniel puppy. Ralph lifted it out, afraid for a moment it was dead; no, asleep. It woke, stretched, whimpered and began to lick his hands. Aunt Lizard exclaimed, "And it's been in there all the morning! I haven't heard a sound."

"Fancy that soldier forgetting it. Oh — d'you think he knew it was in there?" Then he remembered the stick, propping the lid open. Someone must have known; they had wanted it to have air. "He'll be back for it soon, I bet."

The puppy yawned, wriggled, chewed his finger. He cried, "Isn't it a little beauty?" and she said in a faintly worried tone, "It is indeed." It was very young, silken-coated, dark brown and white. "English springer, don't you think?" she asked. Clasping it under his chin, he repeated, "He'll be back like a shot, when he finds he's left it."

"I wonder. Did you take the number, by any chance?"

"Number? The truck? Oh," he remembered, "I did look, as a matter of fact, but it was all smarmed with mud. I say, what did *you* think I'd found? A hand grenade?"

"No," she returned rather waspishly, "I'm afraid, if you did, you'd keep it to yourself. And blow your silly young head off on the quiet."

They took the puppy indoors. It lapped awkwardly at a dish of water, curled on Ralph's bunk and blinked its eyes. He knelt beside it.

"It is sleepy, isn't it? Like Badger, when — oh!"

"Yes," she nodded. "Doped, don't you think?"

"But why?"

"To keep it quiet? Till he was out of the way? Somehow — I may be wrong — I don't think your friend will be back. I think he's 'won' this somewhere, and changed his mind, and left us holding the baby."

Cuckoo joined them. They watched the foundling worrying Ralph's finger. Aunt Lizard said, "If no one comes for it, we'll have to trace the owner."

"How can we?" The puppy yawned. Ralph yawned: "I know, 'your leader or triumvirate will tell you'." This was from "instructions in case of invasion", published in the local paper. The phrase had caught Ralph's fancy; somehow he could not imagine Tacker, or Mr. Doggett, calling anyone their triumvirate. "Boss" was the nearest they were likely to get. Thinking of Mr. Doggett, he remembered that the vet might be coming — might be in the stable now. He told Aunt Lizard, "I'll go and catch him. He'll know who keeps springers, won't he? We might find out if a soldier's bought one?"

Leaving her to finish the tulip, he took a short cut to the stable, and was just in time to give his message. The vet promised to make inquiries. He and Mr. Riley and George Doggett went off down the yard, talking together. He had forgotten to ask after Silver. Peering over the half-door, he could see the grey pony lying down in his stall. Ralph unbolted the door, slipped inside and tiptoed along. Silver lay with his head up. He seemed to be dozing, but when Ralph whispered his name he turned, trying to get up, changed his mind, opened his eyes wide and gazed at Ralph. His expression was so gentle that Ralph had moved near and put out his hand before he pulled himself up — What am I doing? It's Silver — he'll snap my hand off! But Silver showed no sign of snapping. He gave a great sigh and turned his head away. Poor fellow, he *was* tired. Ralph said half aloud, "You have a good rest. Don't worry any more. When you're mine, you'll never go in a cart again." He could not help it — he found himself actually stroking and patting the pony, feeling a shiver of response as he ran his hand down the broad neck, smoothing the mane, even fondling Silver's ears, just as he had imagined. He would have stayed longer, but he and Aunt Lizard were going to swim. At last he tore himself away.

The soldier did not return. That night the puppy slept on Ralph's bunk. Ralph would have to go back to school in the afternoon, and directly after breakfast Aunt Lizard sent him down to the stable with a message for Tacker: if no one claimed the puppy, would Tacker like it? He had said he was looking for a dog. Tacker was delighted. Ralph hovered in the yard, hoping to visit Silver, but Tacker drew him away. The pony was still seedy, he said; no use upsetting him.

"But he let me stroke him yesterday. He wasn't upset. Shall I wait for Mr. Doggett, then?"

No, advised Tacker, not this morning. "You cut along to Sallows and try a bit of hoeing."

He found only Harry and Sally in the field. Rupert must be back at school. After trying the spare hoes in turn, and watching the others for a minute, he started on his own. Mr. Riley came and looked at him, asked in damping tones, "Which way are you working?" and walked off. The other two, on piecework, had little to say. Thinking of Silver and the puppy, he could not settle to a steady pace. Time went slowly; his attention wandered, he saw why people spoke of "hoeing your own row". It was easy to stray into the next. Then the crow distracted him, fluttering about on the headland; hoping, no doubt, for another hunk of cheese. Towards the end of the morning he realized that Tess had come out and was working behind him. He called to her, but she did not look up. Then, in the distance, he saw a sight that cheered him. Mr. Doggett was walking slowly along the field path towards the paddock, leading Silver. Mr. Riley and the vet were at the pony's other side. They were turning him out to grass: he must be better today. The little procession disappeared behind the spinney, and he bent again to the hoe. He would go along before dinner and have a word with Silver.

A sharp sound sent the crow flapping over their heads. Another shell? No, only a gunshot. He turned to Tess, laughing; she was close behind now. She did not answer, but he had a glimpse of her face. It was actually streaked with tears. "I say — what's the matter?" He was shocked. She muttered something and went away. Watching her go, he had a vision of disaster — her engagement broken off — her young man dead, or called up? — which? She took her bicycle and rode off towards the harbour; she had a room there now. He had done three hours; it was nearly twelve by his watch. He took back his hoe, jumped the ditch and set off for the paddock.

On the far side of Old Park he came on Jake and Jim Honeywood at work by the hawthorn hedge, filling in a hole. Jim called out as he passed, "Good riddance, eh?"

He stopped. He had walked quite slowly, but he felt hot, and curiously uneasy. "What is?"

"'What is'?" mimicked Jim, and spat. "Good riddance of a bad lot, say I. That ugly murderin' old grey man-eater — before he savaged us."

One word stabbed him: *grey*. He ran to the hedge. The paddock was empty, no sign of Silver. The scent of hawthorn filled the air. Flies darted and shimmered like kingfishers. He pulled a dock leaf, swatted at them, and stood tearing the leaf into shreds, watching the men shovelling earth back into a pit that looked so small and narrow, for something nearly fourteen hands wide.

CHAPTER FIFTEEN

A New Lease

Toiling up the north side of the downs, Ralph found a sea of corn spilling over the top. For the first time within living memory, this round hill was not green but yellow. All the way down, he had ridden through valleys thick with corn. If the weather held, if no fire bombs came, there would be a great harvest. Racks of firebrooms, birch and hazel, stood in every field. But up here, Ralph thought, no one had piped "Hands to thistles." There were not enough hands. A flock of goldfinches dipped over his head, piping their own signal, alighting to take the first thistledown seed. The crop was full of prickles, it would be like stooking bags of hedgehogs.

He looked away to the south, to the curving inlets of the harbour; found Beaumarsh, looked away and began slowly coasting down the chalky lane. Never mind hedgehogs and goldfinches, he told himself; you *must* think how you're going to explain. *Consider what a great boy you are. Consider what a long way you've come today* . . . .No, it's no laughing matter. And it was not. For a week, he had been sliding into an impasse.

As usual, he was in trouble before he had any idea of it. It was only today, in the train to London, that he had begun to have misgivings. The whole thing had started when the second-form master fell ill and had to go home a week early. His classes had been doubled up with others, but there was one period each day when two prefects — the head boy and Ralph — were sent to supervise the dozen small boys in the second form. The head boy, captain of games and victor ludorum, thought team games or a cricket match would be the best way to keep them quiet. The headmaster demurred, but said they might do a play — preferably in French or Latin. The two seniors looked over Mademoiselle's offerings, *Bluebeard* and *Cinderella*, and groaned. Ralph's colleague had a better idea. Why shouldn't Ralph himself write something for them, in Latin? Ralph — always impressed by this boy, his prowess and popularity, his good-tempered authority, his striking name, Merlin Teunon — agreed to try. Teunon reminded him a bit of Rupert, Rupert in turn of Aesop; what about a couple of those fables? Choosing two with good crowd scenes, *The Shepherd Boy and the Wolf* ("Lupus, lupus! Venite celeriter!") and *King Log and King Stork*, he set to work with a dictionary. Frog Latin, Uncle Alfred called the result. The frogs were a problem at first: "How shall we make them croak in Latin?" "Crocus, crocus," said Teunon flippantly. All that, he implied, was Ralph's affair; as producer, he had his work cut out. A master, appealed to, suggested borrowing a Greek frogs' chorus, "Brekekekek, ko.ax, ko.ax," and this was rehearsed with enthusiasm: team games, after all, would have been quieter. Truncus Rex threw up his part as too tame and joined the chorus; a property log had to be found, a roll of matting from the gym. Costumes were hastily devised, cottonwool wigs for the sheep, a shaggy rug for the wolf, a gown and beak for the stork, paper masks for the frogs; the art room ran out of green paint. The plays were repeated in the hall on the last night of term, with cries of Producer and Author; Ralph's protest — "Aesop! *He* croaked a million years ago" — passing off as a funny curtain speech. That was the end of his prep school life, but not of his alliance with Teunon. Weeks before, in fact, they had begun to eye one another appraisingly; next term, small fry once more, they would be together at the same big school. The plays had plunged them into friendship. Between rehearsals, Ralph had found himself describing Beaumarsh, the cottage and his doings there. Teunon listened with all the respect and envy he had once expected from father. It appeared that, despite his grandeur, Teunon had troubles of his own. Both his parents were in war jobs, he and his younger brother would have to stay at school for most of the summer holidays. Ralph said at once, "Oh, but look — I know — can't you both come and stay with me?" Teunon jumped at the invitation: "Could we? D'you mean it? Honestly?" It was settled. On the last day of term Teunon was called to the telephone and came back in triumph. "That was my mother. She says it's all right, if your aunt writes to her." And then, "I say, though — couldn't we come with you tomorrow? On our bikes?"

Even then, Ralph did not see what he had done. Steeped in the climate of school, he was only just aware of the need for explaining things to Aunt Lizard. "Perhaps I'd better go down first. You see, there's my aunt. She'll go and stay with Merren, I expect — but she'll have to pack. Better give her a day. Saturday, then?" Fixing up Aunt Liz, he called this airily to himself. Setting off with his bicycle next morning, ration book and toothbrush in his pocket, the school silkworms in a box — mulberry leaves were scarce in this neighbourhood, but there was a tree at The Race — trunk to follow by rail, he cried gaily to the brothers, "See you tomorrow!"

In the first train he had his first doubts; he dismissed them lightly. At St. Pancras, Aunt Emmy was in a rush, she had to get back to the office. They threw the bicycle on to a taxi and dashed across London, just in time for a fast train. She tipped him lavishly for lunch at Guildford; he was to bicycle from there. Rocking out of Waterloo, he thought — Tomorrow the holidays really start. Twice as much fun with two other men. They would have a high time on their own. Aunt Lizard? Oh, she wouldn't fuss. He was nearly fourteen, Teunon *was* fourteen, Teunon Two just a bit younger. He recalled with amusement how, when they first came to Beaumarsh, he and Aunt Lizard had wondered how they would manage by themselves. Tacker, he saw, had solved that for them. They had never had a moment's worry about repairs, supplies, practical help of every sort. Sheer kindness, Aunt Lizard said, for he rarely let her pay him. Ralph thought, too, that Tacker liked having a little place to take an interest in. He had no family, and lodged with an active younger couple who needed no help from him. In the same way, now her evacuees were gone, Merren always seemed to have a warden or two about her cottage. She said they liked to get away from town and potter about, chopping wood, digging the garden, bagging rabbits. Aunt Lizard would be all right up there. She had written that she would be painting downland flowers, thyme, harebell, thistle. She might as well stay with Merren and have them on her doorstep.

But suddenly, as though the train had slapped into a tunnel, his mood changed. Optimism dwindled. He remembered an absurd old book of grandmother's, read at Nine Wells; *Holiday House*. Most of it he had forgotten, but one incident stood out. The boy and girl in the story, Harry and Laura, left at home while their parents were away, invited a crowd of friends to a party without asking permission. When the old housekeeper found out — Mrs. Crabtree, you couldn't forget her name — she had refused to give them a drop or a crumb for their guests; for a turn of the screw, she sent up their usual supper, two biscuits and two cups of milk. As a child, Ralph had squirmed with sympathy for Harry and Laura. Years since he thought of that! Why think of it *now*? But he saw why. He began to have a creeping sense that he might be in the same sort of fix. Supposing Aunt Lizard said flatly, "No, I can't go away just now. It's not convenient." Or even, "You boys staying here by yourselves? Certainly not!" — what on earth should he do? How could he ever face Teunon again? He set off through Surrey, in the hot cloudy afternoon, with a sinking heart.

For, almost at once, he had seen that that was not the real trouble. It was something worse. Aunt Lizard was no Mrs. Crabtree. She would be surprised when he sprang this on her. She might say, as before, "Why not ask first?" She would certainly consult Uncle Alfred. But she would never let him down; not, above all, with a future schoolfellow. The boot was on the other foot. Yes, that was it. He had ditched her, without warning, after all these years. They had been together since that strange time, long ago, when his mother had died in China. Aunt Lizard was staying with them at the time. He dimly recalled that there had been talk of "going home", because of the war — *that* war — but he hadn't understood it. Then one day mother was ill, and the next day she was dead, and soon after he and Aunt Lizard were in a ship, on the way to Ireland. She had been with him ever since, until he went to school. They talked the same language, shared their own silly jokes. He had a newspaper cutting in his pocket now, sent with her last letter; a fragment from *The Times*, something about a "bilberry comb", for picking bilberries quickly. You could make it with a dustpan and a mane comb from the harness shop. In the margin she had scribbled, "What about a deadly nightshade comb?"

But, he thought defensively, we shan't always go on as we are. Things will change anyway. I'm older now. She'll know I want my own friends. He recalled his feeling of panic, only a few months ago, in case she and father might marry. Now, it seemed rather a good idea; they would be company for each other. It no longer seemed a threat to himself, or even his own concern, really. Then there had been that mad scheme about having father to stay; he might have known that wouldn't work. At least — with older people, you could never tell; you couldn't be sure which way they might jump. Look at the flap he'd gone through, over that essay. And even with Aunt Lizard, he had to be careful sometimes. He had never managed, for instance, to make her see that some quite ordinary swop — a grenade or shell off an army range, a bullet out of a crashed plane — was perfectly safe to handle, if you knew how.

Here he was, far too soon, at Beaumarsh, passing The Oaks field; nearly there. He must hurry and tell her, and get it done with. He put down his head and pedalled blindly. By the gate in the lane he looked up, and across the fields he saw Mr. Doggett leading three horses, Captain, Violet and a stranger. At that he felt such a wave of misery that for a moment everything else was forgotten. At school, that memory had seemed to fade; now it came back more sharply than ever. Leaning on the gatepost, he could have wept for the rescue plan that had been too late, shovelled underground with Silver. But perhaps, he thought bitterly, that sort of happy ending couldn't happen in real life, only in a book like *Black Beauty*.

The door was locked, Aunt Lizard was out. He fetched the key, let himself in and sat down on his bunk. There, under the south window, were the slots for the third bunk. Tacker would know about it. He felt stiff and tired, without the usual pleasant sense of homecoming. If only she'd been here, he might have settled everything by now. He glanced round, and it struck him that the room looked somehow different. Everything was in order, fire laid, water in the churn — he took a long drink — his holiday clothes, old shorts and shirt, ready on a chair. Then what — ? He realized that Aunt Lizard's things were gone. Not just put away. All her painting gear — only the smell of paint hung about; the glasses and vases for her flowers; her garden coat and shoes, the trunk with her other clothes; and Cuckoo! — his plates were missing too, his blanket, even the dried cowslip ball Ralph had made for him to play with — it was gone from its nail. He sat down again, looking about in amazement, suppressing the idea that she had guessed his treachery, taken umbrage, taken herself off. He passed an anxious minute, full of doubts and queries: She can't have. Well, she has. Why? Where? — before he saw her note on the table. He snatched it, read it and breathed more freely. Whatever all this meant, the note was quite plain and ordinary: "Come to Tess's flat. Lizard."

Tess had been staying in an attic on the harbour since the road was closed for the new airfield, making her roundabout journey two miles longer. Ralph knew the house; and, as he approached, there was Aunt Lizard watching and waving, like Sister Ann, from an upper window. Tess had left; Aunt Lizard had been helping her to pack. The room was large and light, with a skylight in the sloping roof, and a great window looking seaward. Next door was a small kitchen, with a miniature electric stove from which she produced their supper. A print of *The Blind Girl* hung over the sink; Ralph went to look at the rainbow and the butterfly in the picture, and then, thoughtfully, at the shining taps. They ate at a table by the window. The evening was clear and calm. White clouds floated in the sky, swans floated on the water, in and out of the mooring posts. A bird was still piping from the marsh. *Teunon*, Ralph thought it said: *Teunon*. He turned and began with a rush, "Look! You know Merren's cottage —" then the words stuck in his throat. Instead of saying his piece, he found himself listening to a tale about Merren. One evening in June, walking up from Tatten's Corner, from the Portsmouth bus, she had run into a spy, with binoculars and a sinister black box, right on the edge of the new airfield. He had glared at her so fiercely that she expected a knife in the back, but she walked on bravely, and then hurried to the home guard post to report. The guards marched down and arrested the man on the spot.

Ralph whistled. "Really a spy?"

"No, just a bird man, staying at the manor. Quite famous and respectable — trying to record a nightjar. No wonder he was cross."

Ralph made her laugh with a story of Bob Doggett's; early in the war there had been a crazy rumour that Seaforth wasn't a Scottish name but German, Seifert, and that the nursery owner had had all his fruit trees planted in code, for a signal to Nazi planes. "You know that triangle, in the corner, at the top of Old Park? They said the trees made an arrow, *pointing at the aerodrome*!"

Silence fell. Aunt Lizard looked out of the window, humming under her breath. It flashed into Ralph's mind — *she's* got something to tell, too, and she's wondering how to begin! He glanced round, seeing the familiar things he had missed from the spring house. Cuckoo, lolling on a divan, looked very much at home. He asked, quickly as he thought it — "You're staying here, aren't you? You've taken it over from Tess?"

She nodded, and said as though in apology, "I did think it might be a good idea. For the summer, while I'm painting. Then, you see, you can have people to stay. Uncle Alfred," she added, regarding him candidly, "thought you would like that."

He discovered that relief was struggling with pique. Was she actually deserting him, after all this time? Did she simply want to pursue her own career? Or — had she guessed, was she letting him down lightly? Was Uncle Alfred behind the whole thing? He might never know. Did it matter? The sea bird called, the water lapped in the reeds, the bewitching summer smell of the marsh stole upward. Aunt Lizard said, "I've just signed a new lease for the spring house, for three years. It's to be yours, for the holidays, for you and your friends. I know you'll be sensible. I'll expect you here for supper every night. And of course I'll bake for you. Tacker will keep an eye on you, when I'm back in London."

"Tacker — oh!" he exclaimed. "Has he still got that puppy?"

She laughed again. "He has indeed. Do you remember, we thought it was doped? Well, I don't believe it was at all. It's the laziest puppy you ever saw." Thinking of the puppy, they both yawned. She asked, "Will you stay here tonight? Do. Go and have a hot bath, I'll make up a bed."

"No, no," he mocked, "you can keep all that. Water on tap, electricity — oh, how you've suffered!" He went on urgently, "I saw a 'phone downstairs. Could I ring someone at school? You see, there's a chap called Teunon. Well, as a matter of fact . . ." He began to tell her.

The red sun was touching the water when they parted. Ralph looked so wild with excitement that Lizard was on the point of saying — *Oh, be careful. Don't expect so much*. But he would have been deaf to any warning. She had not said it.

He was thankful, after all, that the Teunons had not come with him. Tomorrow the place would be somewhere for schemes and adventures, harvesting and swimming, a holiday house; tonight it belonged only to him. He wandered about in the long twilight, and sat down at last in the doorway. The runner beans had flourished and run riot. They covered the grey walls like a vine, with green swags and garlands, scarlet flowers. Slowly the colours faded, until there was only the deep night sky, dark leaves and grass, the glimmer of cornfields under the moon. A line of poetry ran in his head: *Round the lone house in the midst of the corn.* The house, the garden and spinney were an island.

Over there, beyond the eastern arm of the harbour, people said there was a deer park under the sea, drowned four hundred years ago. Seaweed grew where the deer had grazed, and fish swam to and fro. One day that might happen here. The spring house might vanish under the plough, or under the sea: but not yet.

In the upper air, swifts and larks had caught the last gleam of daylight. Now they were grounded and silent. He could hear the pinprick squeak of a bat, the heavy swish of wheat flowing up to the last almond trees and along the hedge to his gate. Leaves fluttered on the Spanish chestnut. In Chequers the barley rustled, pale as champagne, full of whispers. He would never sleep tonight; he would not even try. Grasshoppers trilled like nightingales. The moon, nearly full, rode higher. The travelling light came round from the east window, laid a bright path to his feet and withdrew it again, while he sat on quietly at the door of his house.